Planting and Painting the Landscape

Also by T. D. Motley

The Art of Farming: Sketches of Life in the Country

Planting and Painting the Landscape

A SEQUEL TO THE ART OF FARMING

A NOVEL

WRITTEN AND ILLUSTRATED BY

T D MOTLEY

Published by

Stoney Creek Publishing Group

StoneyCreekPublishing.com

ISBN: 978-1-965766-89-7
ISBN (paperback): 978-1-965766-87-3
ISBN (ebook): 978-1-965766-88-0
Library of Congress Control Number: 2026907245

Cover illustration by T.D. Motley
Union Pacific Firefly Party, 2003
Vicki Foster Collection
38X48", acrylic on canvas
Reprinted with permission

Printed in the United States

For Becca, Sharon and Wyndi
This book, too, would not have happened without you.

Treat the earth well: it was not given to you by your parents, it was loaned to you by your children. We do not inherit the Earth from our Ancestors, we borrow it from our Children.

—Crazy Horse

Contents

Sol, the Miniature Donkey

Introduction

Annie and I sat together in the veranda's creaky old porch swing the other morning. Unexpected rain fell quietly and then was gone as suddenly as it had arrived. We held hands in the dark, like we did in college. In tandem, our bare feet effortlessly guided the swing's arc gently to and fro. It was early. Dawn was just hinting at her arrival with a faint light that appeared far off in the east somewhere over Nocona.

The farm was silent with no two-legged or four-legged residents stirring just yet other than the couple on the porch and a Great Horned Owl in a nearby tree. We felt the creature was hooting soft murmurs of gratitude for the rain that echoed our own. Barnes County had been experiencing a long stretch of dry weather. Nature was gently bathing us in that unique rain- meets-earth fragrance called *petrichor*. It's a term introduced to us by a dear artist friend, Sunny. She uses the word to describe her own sense of well-being when painting trees. The recollection of that earthy smell prompts her every brushstroke. Sunny's trees glisten and glow as if just after a morning shower.

~

The outskirts of Elysia, named by founders with Athenian aspirations, are changing as fast as Texas weather. On Wednesdays now when I make the weekly shopping run to town, I include a few minutes of additional sightseeing farther afield to the west just to entertain my canine carpoolers. The panting gang of passengers still includes one cat who thinks he's a dog too, of course. All my four-legged companions have many more roadside diversions these days, more causes to hang happy heads out of windows, dog tongues and ears flapping in the wind, with tails wagging like upbeat tempo metronomes. The thirty minute drive along the highway between our somewhat-still-quaint little hamlet and the newly named Barnes County College is hemmed in on both sides now by signs of progress, all the way to campus. For example, administrators way above my former faculty pay grade changed the name from "Community College" to just "College." I fear a clarity of purpose has been lost in the translation. Then again, Sam Bartlett's degrees are in painting and art history, not administration.

There's even news buzzing around the college these days (just gossip, I hope) that the buildings on campus may be renamed, or at least subnamed with corporate logos. I guess that means "underwritten?" A couple of the younger board of trustees members and a few vice presidents have formed a study group toward making such a recommendation. The purpose of said renaming is to cash in on an up-and-coming trend for publicly owned properties, something called "branding." The names of popular products may replace the names of people. I guess because the honored Barnes County civic leaders, philanthropists, educators, and athletes, whose names are etched above campus portals, no longer generate enough revenue from the fading memory of their once-historic contributions. Progress sometimes adopts a "don't look back" approach.

It seems the populace is eager for change at all levels. Maybe that's to be expected as we lurch midway into the first decade of the twenty-first century. I just hope that folks stay neighborly.

There's so much progress going on now in Barnes County that some of our top elected and appointed officials show up, beaming with enthusiasm, for even low-key local public ceremonies just to tout the region's upward trajectory. They feel a need, a kind of "calling," I guess, to roll up their dress-shirt sleeves and articulate for us how new investment and new vision have given new life to so much "undeveloped" land in this apparently sadly neglected backwater part of the state.

Just beyond the college acreage now, standing shoulder to shoulder, new houses on cleared land almost touch each other on streets named after trees that used to live there. Every couple of blocks, new storage facilities secure excess personal stuff; one features "Temp Controlled Units." The farm implement store's display lot looks a bit awkward with its backhoes, box blades, and bush-hogs abutting the colorful swimming pool slides, giant inflatable seahorses, and shiny all-weather kitchen appliances next door at the new Patio Living Center.

"Undeveloped" land up here usually means farmland. Me and my family before me have always considered our houses and barns and fields and pastures and ponds and paddocks and chicken coops and birthing sheds as land that we continue to develop with vision and commitment. It's an organic historic process, a simultaneously arduous and fulfilling life choice of diligent development called farming.

The Romans invented cement, but Cato the Elder and Augustus Caesar understood that the foundation of their culture was dirt. Agriculture provided the sustainable floor upon which to raise their architectural wonders and crops with which to feed the populace.

Somehow, Elysia's town square itself has survived pretty much intact, even thrived a bit. I've heard the word "gentrification" bantered about, but city council members have done their best to at least keep the construction of ubiquitous franchise enterprises outside the city limits. And there seems to be a kind of broader social embrace of nostalgia by new county residents that has benefitted downtown. Heritage Square has become a sort of secular sanctuary, a shaded refuge set apart from the not-too-distant noise of commercial development.

Most folks in Elysia and environs finally have accepted the intrusion of the seemingly perpetual red light that was installed out on the highway to facilitate access to the then-new supermarket. Locals are likely to just make a square-shaped route of a couple of blocks on either side of the thing to avoid it. Rural residents have long seen the reasoning behind stop signs at intersections of farm-to-market and county roads. They've been around since World War I. Stop signs keep farmers' combine harvesters from getting tangled up in wrestling matches with Dollar General semis.

But smalltown drivers get self-conscious, sometimes feeling downright silly sitting at the only red light in town like a hostage, waiting for the contraption to turn green with no sight of another vehicle in any direction. Elysia's oldest citizen and World War II hero, Jeremiah Brown, calls the infernal device an "A-bomb-ination."

The Ronning Family Bakery has a whole new generation of appreciative sweet-toothed pastry customers. The Ronning twins, brother and sister, have returned to Elysia with their respective spouses and broods in tow and happily continue the business their great-grandparents started. Beneath the storefront's new spiffy, blue-striped awning, they've placed several sets of French bistro tables and chairs along the sidewalk for neighborly outdoor talks over coffee and apple fritters.

Old Vet John's newly certified veterinarian son, Russell has joined his dad in the business. Russell's training also emphasized large animal care and treatment, but the office has many more small pet customers now as well, so father and son are on the lookout to bring in a dog and cat specialist partner. Since childhood, Russell has rescued many wild creatures who got injured or became infirm. At home, he and Dad John built large backyard cages and pens for the boy's undomesticated foundlings of varied sizes and species.

A few furry or feathered inmates lived out their entire rescued lives with Russell's kind wardship. Most were released back into nature's bosom by the same young hands that helped them heal. I recall one particularly commanding specimen that was lucky enough to cross the boy's path once, back in the deep woods. A large mature Great Horned Owl had come afoul of some carelessly discarded hog wire fencing and gotten tangled up. Trying to free itself, it had damaged its beak so that the upper maxilla twisted tragically askew, and the creature could no longer feed itself properly, could not tear its prey effectively. Russell nursed the great creature back to health. Though he consulted the closest zoo, he was told he was taking as good care of the owl as they would be able, so it was recommended that he keep the bird safe and fed at his place. Initially, he fed the big bird by hand but eventually trained the bird to be able to lift the small shreds of raw chicken on its own, sliding the morsels across a flat board shelf installed beside its perch. Russell named the old owl Methuselah.

Heritage Square still welcomes all, residents and visitors alike, to pretty downtown Elysia. Some folks just want to sit in the shade of 200-year-old native trees and admire the view of our grand Romanesque Revival county courthouse. The park's benches, picnic tables, and assorted fences, lattice, and arbors all have been given new coats of paint recently. The color has remained the same since the 1960s. It's always been a lovely dark green that simultaneously seals the wood and subtly serves a respectfully supporting role to the lush live foliage maintained by our town's groundskeepers.

Bartlett Farm has expanded, in a way, to the east. I'm leasing fifteen acres year-round now from my neighbors, half of the land for pasture and the other half for baling hay. José Cantú, our resident mechanical engineer, and Vern, soon headed into his senior year at the University of Texas at Arlington, installed new graduated fencing and a wide red metal gate between our shared property line for ease of moving livestock back and forth. Mutt and Jeff, the neighbor's giant Belgian draft horses, were entertained for days by all the new construction activity, their big heads nodding in conversation like urban humans chatting while watching skyscrapers being built.

Vern's majoring in mechanical engineering, though I always pegged him as a future veterinarian. It is a logical outcome, though, considering his teen years as incidental apprentice to José, who can build or repair anything. Vern and daughter Liz teamed up last summer to convert a small pond just above the herb gardens into a filtering source of clean, fresh water for the organic crops. The spring semester before, they individually researched the subject, then compared notes once a week by phone and email. They chose the best water-loving grasses and reeds to achieve a natural filtering solution.

In addition, daughter and hired hand designed a simple but effective dam/release system that allows a reliable transfer of water via soaker hoses to the raised bed herb gardens below. It's a brilliant but relatively simple gadget for the farm's irrigation needs. The project promoted unexpected dialog between shy Vern and talkative Liz because they shared a common design project that required discussion of problems and solutions. Annie gives me one of her all-knowing winks and a nod of her pretty head whenever she sees me taking note of prolonged conversations between those two.

For a full academic year Liz was enjoying teaching at a small college in northern Georgia, a temporary position she had filling in for a professor friend who had landed an overseas research grant to the Amazon. She especially enjoyed hiking in the lower Blue Ridge Mountain forests up there that were abundant in Red Maple and American Beech trees. The smooth, light-colored bark of beech trees and sycamores have always intrigued her. For the time being, Liz is an adjunct teacher at Barnes County College, teaching two horticulture classes. I know it's short term, but for now, Annie and I are delighted that she's back home in her old room.

Cataract-plagued Spin, our senior resident whirling dervish Blue Heeler, has been laid to rest next to old Murph, our handsome Bluetick Coonhound. They're buried alongside the main road that stretches between the barn and the round pen so they can keep up with comings and goings at the farm. Robin, our current farm teen supervisor, made a new grave marker for the two old running mates. She appropriately repainted the wooden sign to read "Boon Companions," plural, instead of the singular "Boon Companion" I had originally erected for Murph. Otherwise, anxiety-ridden Spin would feel "dissed," as Robin put it.

Blackie, the long-neglected regional rescue mutt, is now senior in charge. She is our main alarm system these days. The huge Pyrenees/Akbash cross, Caesar (named for the noble agrarian Emperor Augustus, not his uncle, the other one), has proven to be so effective a shepherd by himself that Sol, the miniature donkey, takes long and frequent breaks from the sheep to supervise other farm maintenance duties throughout the day. In Sol's little mind, such duties always include keeping an eye out for mercenary opportunities at my expense.

Regal Nike, named after the victorious winged goddess, is joined by old Blackie for chases across pasture and meadow, ensuring the farm stays mostly free of marauding interlopers like tortoises, raccoons, possums, and jackrabbits. The loud canine duo keeps the wild critters at bay, far away at the farm's perimeters, or sends them scampering back down into their dens and hidey-holes along the banks of Hackberry Creek. On hot mid-days, the pair will be found in the shade of the barn's wide covered side porch trying to catch a mountain breeze from the far northwest. Their articulated limbs lay flat out on the cool paving stones, looking much like seals' flippers.

Their shaded nap-space is just across the road from the graves of Spin and Murph. Having attended the burial of each of their dog-pack comrades, they seem to recognize the significance of the painted memorial marker identifying the shared site of both rituals. I imagine they often fall asleep peering at the landmark, remembering exciting animal adventures with their pawed pals. Tommy Cat naps near the dogs, stretched out on a repurposed wooden church pew we put out under the covered side-porch of the barn. The broad porch has a restorative, expansive view that includes the grove of Vitex and Desert Willow to the south, the handsome oak-plank round pen in between, and three acres of horse pasture to the north that borders the front drive all the way up to the entry gate.

Clare and Margaret have gone off to college and are boarding Pickle and Tofu at sites closer to their respective campuses. Blaze, the orange Quarter Horse, has become quite a capable cutting horse. Jake, our wrangler friend, bought the horse awhile back. He tells me that Blaze's unique bright orange coat has made a big hit with younger roping and cutting horse fans. They're on the road a good bit for the rodeo circuit, but Blaze is always boarded here when Jake is back home. Sol is still his buddy, so they frolic and graze together in the front horse pasture when Blaze visits for a horse reunion. All farm and ranch horses like to shed their working gear from time to time, kicking up their heels *au naturel*.

Statuesque and steadfast Samson, along with the yet unnamed old gray rescue-swayback, Dolly the mare, and Sol are the only permanent equine residents at the moment.

High-schooler Robin has taken over Clare's duties. She is particularly attentive to our poultry workers and monitors their egg-laying productivity like a mother hen. She eagerly lends a hand to any farm task that needs doing but has faithfully embraced the practice of sustainable responsibility for maintaining heritage breed chickens.

Annie sold her mid-century modern urban apartment unit, so this is her permanent home now, though she's still on the road a lot. Her books and articles on food and food history are widely read, so she spends as much of her time away from the farm these days for speaking engagements and book signings as she does for research and interviews. Our little thirty-acre farm is truly her full-time sanctuary now.

With some help and a lot of encouragement from Bartlett Farm, ag teacher Angus and staff now have as many Elysia high schoolers involved in gardening and crops as in livestock management. With a recently donated greenhouse and expanded campus area for new gardens, horticulture has become a popular choice for study. It's a sort of badge of honor at the high school to get employed at our farm. So, we have plenty of eager part-time helpers now just for Saturday farmers markets and harvesting for Friday deliveries to several Dallas-Fort Worth chefs.

My colleague, Suzie, still brings her art students from the Barnes County College for drawing field trips twice a year. At the students' requests, we've added some sketching time for drawing animals in addition to landscapes. Arranged with a phone call from Suzie, occasionally two or three will come out on their own to hike and draw or paint *plein air* for a few hours at a time.

The latest sunset paintings I've been doing get later and later. That is, I'm painting later dusk scenes or night-sky scenes, often with fireflies. I experimented a bit with painted fireflies years ago, but now they've become a primary theme in my work. I've researched night sky or low light painters such as Albert Pinkham Ryder and Winslow Homer. I'm fortunate that the Amon Carter Museum in Fort Worth and the Gilcrease Museum in Tulsa have splendid examples of Frederick Remington's night paintings. I've accumulated lots of practical knowledge just by parsing Remington's translucent overlays of infinitely varied greens, grays, and dark blues to imply nighttime. As I have graphically demonstrated to many a first-semester painting student, you can't illustrate a convincing night atmosphere, or even a successful dark shadow, by simply grabbing a tube of black paint. Night scenes, like day scenes, must use lots of colors to be convincing. The colors are just much darker, with shapes and figures pronounced against lighter monochromatic tones behind.

Some well-meaning colleagues have approached me of late, apparently concerned with my turning to representational landscapes after so many years' success with large color field abstracts. They haven't been shy, either, with their advice that I'm doing harm to my "modernist" reputation. One friend came right out and shared that he thought my recent work to be mere "nostalgic romanticism."

I'm surprised with such admonitions from friends who've known me a long time. They know I've taught students how to paint representational subjects, like landscapes, for decades. They've seen my own well-worn sketchbooks filled with such imagery, drawn in local and foreign climes. Now in retirement, I simply have more time to develop and adjust larger painted vistas and have found patrons who want the new representational work for their wide walls in commercial public spaces. Besides, I'm not painting to maintain a reputation. I paint because I love doing it.

I'm excited that the illustrators who inspired me in my youth, like N.C. Wyeth, Remington, and Tom Lea, have lessons to teach me these many decades later, especially about application of dark translucent layers to suggest evening or night atmospheres.

Thank heavens Elysia and surrounds still have relatively dark skies at night. No big auto dealership out on the highway yet, requiring constant full illumination across acres of new cars apparently in need of visual security even into the wee hours. The city council recently passed an ordinance maintaining "downcast" lighting within the city limits, a measure overwhelmingly supported by residents. We still want to see some stars at night over Elysia.

In the country, dark skies at night encourage better sleep for humans and domestic animals, and better hunting for wild ones.

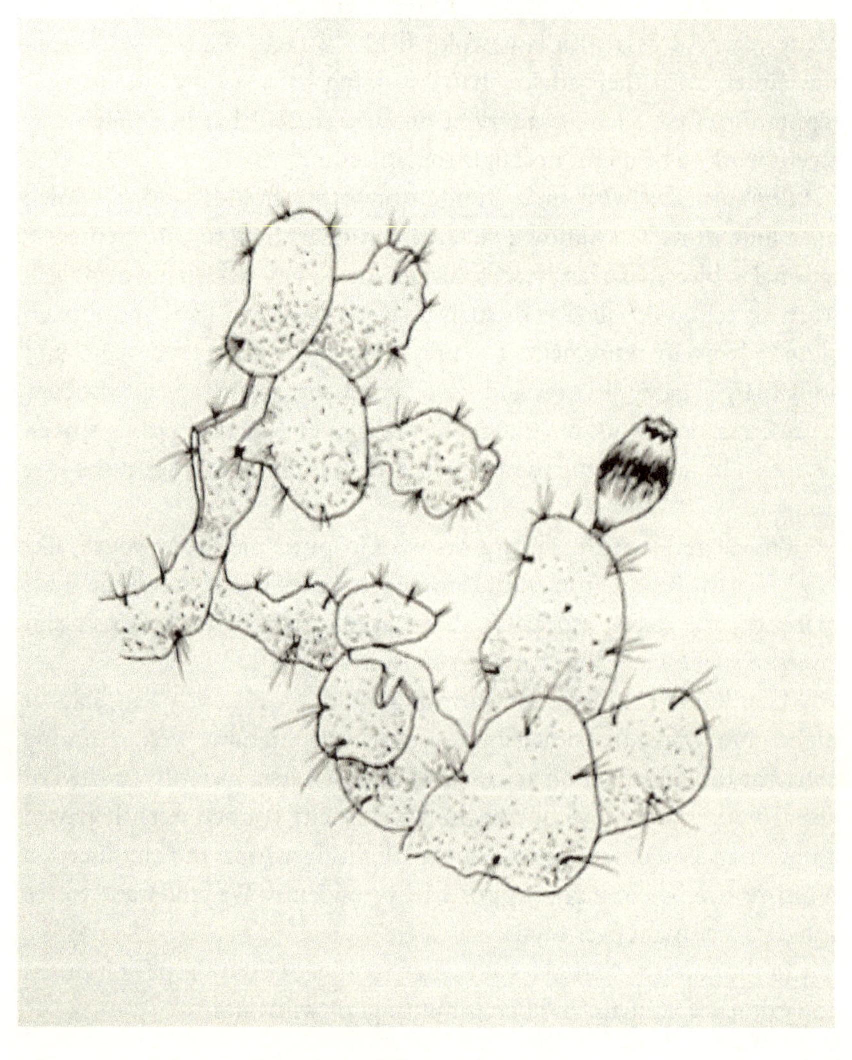

Prickly Pear Cactus

ONE

Slow Learners, Landscapes, and Ladybugs

When the Muse wakes you in the middle of the night, get up. There's creative work that needs doing, and the Muse doesn't want you to waste, ignore, or postpone inspiration. When I was a much younger adult, I sometimes was tempted to mumble an excuse to her, to childishly suggest that I'd get around to whatever inspired notion she'd awakened me with, but maybe later in the day.

Somewhere along my own life's long, slow learning curve, I realized how shallow and unthankful were such petty pleadings. For all my mature artist's life, I have risen when the Muse gracefully tugs at my sleeping mind, no matter the early hour; even an hour long before the arrival of "rosy-fingered dawn," as Homer splendidly describes sunrise in *The Odyssey*.

I've always advised my students to pay attention to their individual Muse. "Inspiration is calling your name," I tell them. What if the artist turns back over into slumberland too often? What if the Muse is denied too often? How incredibly horrid if once too often you mumble to the Muse, simply out of lazy, slovenly mind, "I'll get to it later. Promise. Just gonna catch a few more winks right now." Somewhere along the way, I asked myself "What if the Muse doesn't come back?"

I don't want the Muse to disappear, to not return, never to gently wake me from sleep once more to get up and make inspired art. The thought of her absence, of her disappointment in my perceived lack of commitment, is enough of a trigger-reminder that always shames me to rise and seize the day. Shame was society's primary motivator in Classical Greece.

In Book Five of *The Odyssey*, Homer finally shows us the king who was a farmer, the hero of the epic saga, slumped on a beach, weeping hopelessly like a baby. He's being held captive as the boy-toy of Calypso, a goddess who rules the island of Ogygia. Athena responds to his sad plight and his pathetic laments. She appeals to Zeus on his behalf. Zeus sends Hermes to deal with Calypso, and Athena becomes the inspirational Muse for Odysseus. It's about a third of the way into the saga before Odysseus first learns to ask for her help, and then he learns to burn fragrant herbs for her in thanksgiving for the gift of her divine assistance. He begins to practice these necessary and respectful rituals only about halfway through his epic journey. Odysseus was a fast talker, but a slow learner.

~

I was awakened this morning about three. Annie didn't stir, now long accustomed to my occasional Muse-driven late-night wake-up calls. Daughter Liz, back home between permanent jobs, snored gently, but just enough to be heard through her closed bedroom door. I don't tease her about the snoring. I knew that Nike, the beautiful goddess-named Bluetick Coonhound, would be sleeping on the floor by the side of Liz's bed. The soft sound of my daughter's light snoring always lulls Nike fast into dreamland. If Liz's door is already closed when Nike sneaks in, she winds up at the foot of our bed, but Annie and I are clearly second choice when Liz is in the house.

How the dog manages to be in and out of the house, seemingly at will, perplexes me. I certainly rarely notice the wily hound sliding her lean frame around me unseen, sneaking through the narrow space of an open door, for example. I suspect that Sol, our miniature donkey, has secretly been giving her infiltration lessons on the art of invisibility, of coming and going without detection. Sol is the smartest four-legged beast in our rural menagerie. He is a master of deception, is always on the reconnoiter for opportunity, and loves to recruit other animals to aid and abet his schemes. His small size allows him access to places where larger equines fear to trod lest they get trapped. At times he seems to disappear as suddenly as to appear. Perhaps he's a "shapeshifter" the Hopi have told stories about for ages.

If the little charmer had opposable thumbs, he would be the world's best pickpocket. Even Dickens' "Artful Dodger" would have envied our donkey's seemingly bottomless bag of schemes and deceptive tricks.

It had been a moonless night with a cooling breeze. Spring still ruled, but June would bring early previews of summer heat soon enough. City folks would describe it as "pitch black" outside, and request a flashlight, probably. But farmers with early chores and artists who paint night scenes know that Earth and sky are never truly "pitch black." Total darkness devoid of any light may exist in nooks and crannies of Carlsbad Caverns, but not in nocturnal exterior environs of Barnes County, in any season or weather.

Even without moonlight, the gray-toned gravel road leading down to the barn lit the way as vividly as any Texas high school football field on a Friday night. Like the women sleeping soundly in the house up the hill, the barn residents of canines, equines, and one cat stirred not a whit upon my entry into the grand hall from the side feed room door. Had I entered the main sliding double-doors, they might suspect it was time to rise and shine to see what adventures dawn had brought them.

I climbed the steep stairs up to my studio, the side walls of the stairwell lined with José Cantú had constructed the whole stair-well, top to bottom, with recovered 6-inch oak shiplap, securing the studio from barn dust below. He'd even found an eleven-foot-tall oak door for the stairwell access, recovered from a demolished turn-of-the-twentieth-century public library out in Motley County.

The barn below is forty by sixty feet, my studio above is twenty by sixty, with windows on three sides, and a gallery-lighted wall on the east side for display. Stretching across two large adjustable easels, my current landscape awaited my return. I adjusted the lighting, a mixture of cool and warm luminescence to simulate natural daylight, so that I could focus on the subject brought to my attention by the muse at three o'clock that morning.

I'd been wrestling with the wide painting for a couple of days. The foreground features a pumpkin patch in bloom with giant trumpet-size yellow-orange blossoms across the array of fat, edible serrated green leaves. The dimming, distant background depicts a rising hill of scattered woods, suggesting mostly blurred mesquites and Mexican Buckeyes, with a few post oaks.

The middle ground had been driving me crazy. It is what in the country we still call a "draw," a low recess in the terrain, often with a lean waterway or stream along its course. I wanted to visually punch this area of the composition, but not give it too much drama. I'd fallen asleep in the dark house, pondering the scene on canvas that waited for me in the dark studio just down the hill from our peaceful bed.

The Muse tugged me awake at three o'clock, a time she often chooses for some divine reason. The painting dilemma was still fresh in my sleep-mind, as I had been struggling with it, in and out of dreams, all night. Following hours of such arduous nocturnal brain battles, upon rising, I'm always reminded of Jacob wrestling with the angel. It's a kind of a commiseration memo for me.

As I walked in the cool darkness down to the barn, the Muse helped me lay out the procedure for solution of the problem. She helped project the required solution onto my mind's-eye canvas that would save the large painting.

I'd use cold bee's wax to create a layer of reduced visibility for the viewer across the whole width of the middle ground's receding "draw," like a wide trough falling away into the depths of the painting's central composition. The illusion would be one of early morning fog filling the narrow trough-like valley with a cool, atmospheric haze.

The lively colored foreground of pumpkin-patch leaves and flowers would receive vivid droplets of morning mist and dew, accentuating their tactile nearness to the viewer. Perhaps a shaft of horizontal light at dawn, after Jacob van Ruisdael's amazing sun spotlights falling on linear paths from heaven to Earth through dark seventeenth-century Dutch clouds, illuminating a particular object or scene.

What the Muse showed me as she tugged me from bed earlier was a compelling image that I could only imagine in a dream state. I needed a visual element in the background, above the deep draw, on the side of the wooded hill. I had already laid in a suggestion of a line of outcropped ancient stones protruding from the distant but distinctive cliff, overlapping each other. With half my thoughts still in the dream and the other half in the waking world, it was as if van Ruisdael had himself painted another thin ray of raking light across that remote rock ridge. The ray of light will fall across a linear array of implied Indigenous pictographs, symbols of birth and death handed down since neolithic times. The suggestive markings will provide a visual surprise for viewers to discover in the background, partially hidden by foliage overgrowth clinging to the cliff.

I've stayed on task at the painting right through sunrise. Time to turn out the studio lights and start the day. Robin is already downstairs filling feed buckets over the stalls' top rails and dog bowls in the hallway. She will soon walk up the hill to feed her favorite critters, the just waking heritage breed chickens, and gather the morning's egg production.

Looking out over the front horse pasture from my elevated studio aerie, I see in the distance that Vern's Dad's old pickup is already parked up near the herb gardens. Vern will be getting everything ready for us to begin building new raised bed frames later this morning. After one last lengthy perusal of my new landscape painting, and having carefully cleaned my brushes, I'll head downstairs to release the horses after they've finished chewing loudly and eagerly downing their breakfast of oats and cubes. They are frisky to get on with the day's adventures.

~

Driving up to the herb gardens today with a truck load of twelve-foot 2-by-8-inch cedar boards, I paused by the little grove of Desert Willow and Vitex trees that we planted a few years ago. My sidekick Annie thought we needed a "decorative feature," a kind of visual interlude along the curving road between the barn and the herb gardens up the hill.

Collaborating with Liz, our family forester and arborist, my sidekick with two green thumbs chose these drought-resistant and heat tolerant varieties for the spot and chose the exact location for each sapling's placement. Vern and I dug the holes.

The day that Annie and Liz planned the layout of the place at the top of the extended bend in the road, they were busy with a sketchpad that got handed back and forth, a tape-measure with one girl at either end, lots of pacing and retracing of steps, and considerable serious conversation of the many views they were considering for optimum impact. They arranged bright orange flags, marked either "V" or "DW" in big felt-tip letters, so that Vern and I wouldn't screw up the plan.

Deciding upon the final layout agreement, the girls tore out the plan from the sketchbook and delivered it then-and-there, straight to the feed-room door, proudly attaching the torn page with three carefully secured pushpins. This is the usual place where "marching orders for the day" are left for me. It's the one door on the farm that I must see at least twice a day.

Annie has an innate sense of design. Whether it's plating a meal, matching sweater to skirt, or arranging furniture, Annie has the eye. Her photographs are flawless and intriguing compositions that she just frames in the camera's viewfinder. I enter her photos in juried shows because she won't. Her work always gets accepted and occasionally wins awards. It's not that she's disinterested. It's just that her focus is her job, writing about food and its history.

It's the second week of May, and the trees have already burst out in an explosion of colors, blue (the Vitex) and red-violet (the Desert Willow). Vitex trees are additionally helpful as a source of free chaste berries, a good food supplement for older mares. Young horses don't need it.

In my artist's eye, I was seeing the Vitex trees in terms of paint-layers. That is, what transparent tones I'd paint over with an opaque light color, probably a Naples yellow, to give the illusion of overlapping branches beneath the vibrant blueish blossoms. This procedure, called scumbling, often is done in a dry-brush application of a lighter color applied on top of a series of dark transparent colors. Rembrandt was a master of this technique. The stunning effect is achieved as light passes through all the transparent layers down to the bottom opaque light layer. Since the light can't pass through the opaque layer, it is reflected, it bounces back to the top surface with a rich deep color of layers. My students often commented that Rembrandt's paintings seemed to glow from within, as if backlighted. And that's exactly the case.

I reached over to grab my sketchbook to make a couple of notes and do a quick cropped view drawing of the scene. Unless I have a passenger up front, likely to be Nike the pretty Bluetick Coonhound, there's always a sketchbook within arm's reach in that seat. In the upper periphery of my view through the open passenger side window, I caught a glimpse of a sudden movement of something out in the front horse pasture. Some critter had just moved to the other side of one of the wide-trunked 150-year-old pecan trees.

Peering harder toward the trees with tightly squinted eyes, I detected one swish of the tip of a little donkey's tail. It was Sol (full name Solomon), hiding from me. I grinned, considering again that Sol must have been an international spy in another lifetime. Oh well, I had lumber to deliver up the hill right now. I'd find out later what mischief he'd been up to during my absence away at the county sawmill. My first guess is usually that the little imp has tried to break into the feed room yet again, sniffing out loose lids on alfalfa cube or sweet feed bins. We keep the big barn doors open in the daytime for ventilation. The stalls and interior doors are all kept closed until evening feeding time. A first lesson for every farm helper is a warning about the dangers of leaving the feed room door unsecured. Horses, in my experience, will eat to the bottom of a bin if they get easy access and enough time. An unattended, open feed room for equines is a prescription for disaster, leading a horse to develop colic, a twisted or turned stomach, and to founder, called laminitis.

I made a rapid sketch of the Vitex tree closest to the driver's side window, and a couple of notes about the angle and nature of the dramatic raking light at that early morning hour. I pretended not to see Sol in the distance behind the old pecan. Why spoil his sense of achieved deception? He is an affectionate little criminal, after all, providing me with pretty much equal amounts of joy and irritation throughout the day. Life is a balancing act of perceptions.

The load of long cedar boards would become 4-by-12-foot frames for new raised beds. Vern was already at the top of the hill, having set up the portable power compound miter saw and stand. He'd attached a telescoping extension platform to match the saw's height and to support the weight and length of a full board while we miter the corners.

The tailgate was down on Vern's Dad's pickup, and I could just make out the furry form of Tommy Cat resting there, his tail slowly tracing "S" shapes in the air. As usual, Vern and the cat would be deep in audible conversation. Likely a descendant of the original Dr. Dolittle, Vern speaks fluently in all farm animal languages. Even my stubborn little donkey Sol pays attention when Vern is speaking. Vern doesn't talk down to the little guy, knowing that Sol is an adult, after all, who just happens to be short on inches.

Vern was home for the weekend, taking a break from his tiny studio apartment in Arlington, near the UTA campus. He's a junior already, approaching finals at the end of the month. As Annie predicted, he will surely graduate at the top of his class next year. Vern's Dad, G.T., would probably be smoking some ribs and brisket to celebrate his college boy's weekend visit home. As head of the Elysia Volunteer Fire Department, he is a master of fire and meat. I'd wager that Garland (his full name, but everybody calls him G.T.) is a direct descendant of that first human cook who combined meat and fire many thousands of years ago.

Vern's love of physics and mechanics helped him choose mechanical engineering over veterinary medicine, after all. That passion has only been enhanced during the years the boy has assisted José Cantú here at the farm, learning carpentry and machinery. Both men are quiet workers, and Vern learns quickly just by observing. Even after Vern starts building things as a career, I'm certain he won't lose his valuable ability to talk with animals.

After the boards are cut and the corners mitered, we preassemble the frames, squaring the corners, and predrilling starter holes for the Hex Head screws and washers that will secure the corners together. Cedar is dear, but bugs and mildew hate it, and it will outlast any other wood. Never use "treated" wood for any herbs, produce, or flowers you plan to eat.

Our procedure for preparing a site for raised beds stays the same. After mowing (scalping) the ground as close as possible, we define the perimeter of our rectangular box. We spray 20 percent vinegar over the entire designated space to kill weeds or grass. Rolling out enough four-foot-wide contractor's paper (also now called "painter's" paper), we lay the heavy cedar frame over the 4-by-12-foot space. A couple of bricks or large rocks may be needed to keep the paper from billowing if it's a windy day. A thin layer of dirt can be distributed over all safely if desired. Wait a week for the 20 percent vinegar to do its job. We usually add a layer of sand first, followed by layers of potting soil, followed by compost with manure mix, to fill the 8-inch depth of the box.

The contractor's paper will eventually decompose and become one with the soil. Each year we will add a new layer of compost with manure mix atop the bed, turning it in gently with a spading fork. Twenty percent vinegar is organic and leaches away from the soil in about a week.

I noticed Vern looked at the sun, calculating the time by the big egg-orb's position. I figured it was about one o'clock. Our lunch break was timed by the tasks completed thus far. We had cut and mitered all the boards, drilled all the holes and secured all the corners of enough milled timber for six new 4-by-12-foot raised bed frames. It was a good morning's work.

Liz had left early for the college, where she had a couple of student conferences. As an adjunct, she has no office, so would be meeting with her horticulture students over coffee at the campus cafeteria. The word horticulture comes from the Latin words "hortus," meaning garden, and "colere," meaning to cultivate. It sums up the things that matter to my complex daughter the most, cultivation of sustainable gardens and trees.

I was in the studio above the barn when I heard her horn toot twice as she drove out to the front gate. I paused to watch her perform a ritual she loved. Something about getting in and out of the vehicle to open and close the heavy metal gate pleased her. I understood. As an adult, she has come to see why Annie and I refer to the farm as "sanctuary" for our family and our guests. It is a meaningful word, rarely used aloud. Most often and most appropriately, the word will be spoken softly in response to a visitor's comment or observation about their sense of peace, or calm, or serenity when here. In essence, we have tried to establish, and to maintain, sanctuary here.

Somehow the farm's entry gate symbolizes the passage, or portal, separating the public space from the sanctuary space of the farm. The gate causes us to pause, to think for a moment about the transition from this place to that place. In this place, stewardship is practiced. In this place, the people, the animals and birds, the land itself, is all part of the organic sanctuary that sustains us.

Part of the farm's sanctuary-like ambience clings to our person as we pass out into the busyness of the world in Barnes County. The residual part of the world's cacophony and distress that follows us home, we try to leave outside the entry gate upon our safe return. The transition from public space to sanctuary needs recognition, or definition, that a *portal* exists between the two.

Perhaps the most effective resource I used when teaching about church design and purpose in Medieval Art History classes was Mircea Eliade's brilliant book, *The Sacred and The Profane: The Nature of Religion.* Eliade clarified the significance of the portal, the passageway between secular space and sanctuary. He wrote that "The threshold is the limit, the boundary, the frontier that distinguishes and opposes two worlds—and at the same time the paradoxical place where these worlds communicate..."

Liz secured the gate from the outside. I noticed that she paused a moment, half-in, half-out of the cab. She had one walking shoe on the ground, the other inside, illuminating the brake lights before putting the car in gear. The cellphone in my barn coat pocket stirred aloud. I watched her wave up to me from the open driver's side window. Her text read, "Lunch for you and Vern in the fridge," decorated with a little sideways smiley face made with a colon and an inverted parenthesis.

Liz and Annie had kindly prepared lunch for us farmhands very early that morning. My sidekick had preceded my daughter by about an hour in leaving, stopping off in Weatherford to pick up her old pal, Bonnie, on the way to DFW International Airport. They were headed to Houston to meet with publishers about their new cookbook on American regional rice dishes.

My mouth watered as I anticipated the coleslaw I was hoping they'd made for us. No one makes coleslaw like these two. Working in tandem, one woman shreds the cabbage on an old mandoline slicer Annie brought back from a trip to Reims, while the other juliennes Fuji apple slices from our one Fuji tree and sweet Nantes carrots from the garden. They trade off the chores in a seamless choreography of what needs doing next.

Their tangy dressing starts with yellow mustard and mayo, to which a squeeze of fresh lemon and a dram of raw apple cider vinegar with the "mother" is added. A tablespoon or so of light brown sugar balances out all that vibrant acidity. With mortar and pestle, dried rosemary leaves and fennel seeds get ground up and sprinkled over the slaw. Annie taught Liz how to release herbs and spices from an elevated height to insure the mix spreads more universally. With a gorgeous slaw-maker on either side of the wide mixing bowl, each holding their own grinder, like precise percussionists, Liz and Annie apply a soft shower of freshly ground Himalayan pink salt and crushed black pepper. I never tire of watching this orchestrated duet.

Robin walked over to the house from her barn chores while Vern and I walked downhill to meet her. We all washed up in the kitchen. I transferred items from the fridge to the kitchen island while Vern carried out tablecloth, napkins and silverware to prepare the old sturdy bois d'arc picnic table. Robin filled glasses with ice and tea as I uncovered the lunch: coleslaw, deviled eggs (made with Granny's piccalilli relish recipe), and chilled Pecos cantaloupe wedges. We all drizzled a bit of Louisiana Hot Sauce over the cold melon.

Robin, going into her senior year in the fall, has become quite the go-to authority on heritage breed chickens over at the high school. Especially around Vern, "a college man," Robin's enthusiasm for demonstrating her general farm knowledge elevated her volume, but especially she wanted to share her acumen with poultry. She liked Vern a lot.

Angus, her ag teacher, has recommended her for a scholarship at Texas A&M University in College Station. Robin's main source of college advice and counsel has been from daughter Liz, who's encouraging her to get her Bachelor of Science degree at Stephen F. Austin University in Nacogdoches. Liz did her graduate work there in forestry and had a best friend in the poultry science degree program, Katie, whose visited the farm a couple of times to see our heritage breed flock. Liz has put Robin in touch with Katie, so she has a firsthand account of the Stephen F. program.

Robin's family moved here from Pampa in the Texas Panhandle a few years ago. Not a lot of vertical foliage out that way, except for some cottonwoods and a few walnuts in the river bottoms. Liz has her convinced that East Texas is like Eden, verdant. As my tree-loving offspring puts it, "All hikes in the Piney Woods are shaded, any time of day."

Lunch with my two young friends was rejuvenating. We dined on the patio under dappled shade that Renoir and Monet would have painted. Annie's grandmother's faded, cherry-patterned tablecloth was familiar comfort for us all. During a lull in Robin's exuberant account of the history of heritage breed chickens, mild-mannered Vern actually got a word in edgewise, gently nudging the conversation in a new, un-feathered direction. Robin had paused to take a breath and a sip of iced tea.

"Rainfall forecast for this summer isn't promising," Vern interjected.

"No, it isn't." I responded. "But then it never is during that long stretch from May to October." We get most of our rain in Barnes County near the Red River during those months.

Robin opened her mouth to speak, her huge brown eyes as wide, but Vern continued his thoughts first.

"I've been thinking about the filtering pond above the herb beds."

Robin put her lips together and smiled politely, momentarily curbing her hunger for more chicken talk.

"If it's okay with you, Sam, I'd like to use the gravity water transfer system up there for my senior project this last year. " That was music to my ears, of course.

Robin's ears perked up, while making a mental note to put electrolytes back on her summer poultry watering schedule.

"That sounds great, Vern. You want to make it more fancy?"

He knew I was kidding him. The filtering pond project had been an interesting collaborative concept, what with Vern's singular-minded mechanical concerns and my daughter's desire for functional success along with aesthetic appearance. She grew up in the studio with me, so I'll take credit for some of that sensitivity.

Vern grinned, getting my meaning. "Well..." he began, "...I've emailed my basic idea to Liz, and she doesn't seem opposed or offended too much just yet anyway."

"What's her main concern?" I knew there would be one. And I figured it would be about the look of whatever contraption he was imagining in his mind's eye.

"Well, it's the look of the thing, of course." he said.

I should be a fortune-teller. I'm obviously a pretty good mind-reader. Guess I inherited it from Great Uncle Cecil, our family diviner who was paid to locate hidden water.

"Liz doesn't want the solar panel to stick up too high and distract from the pond grasses and reeds. I've got to be able to rotate it a bit, seasonally, so it needs a secure base with a pivoting column."

Radiant Robin looked over admiringly at Vern as if he must be the smartest man in the world. Nature is run on hormones.

My farmer's mind kicked in. "How much are we talking?"

"Oh nothing, Sam. I'm sure I can get a grant for it. That will be part of the project."

What a great, confident kid is sitting across the picnic table from me, I thought. Two great kids.

Vern proceeded to explain the mechanism to us. He wants to design a whole new setup with a valve-regulated feed, powered with a solar-generated pump. Plant-filtered pond water will be fed into the soaker hose distribution unit from a digital monitor taking a constant reading of the pond's water level. At least that's what I think he said.

My brain had already moved on to reminding me that I needed to connect Vern with an old friend, a Dutch engineer named Gerard Jansen, who works for an international firm in Rotterdam that designs and builds dikes, dams, and floodgates for sea-level shoreline communities around the world. Gerard has indicated he'd like to bring his young family to visit Texas this year. I'll take them down to Beaumont, Nederland, and Galveston. Our state's coastal lowlands will feel like home to them.

During the lull, as Vern and I simultaneously lifted our iced tea glasses for sips, Robin seized the opportunity to further impress, interjecting, "You'll never guess what I've learned about Australorps." She paused, waiting for a sign of interest.

"Well, Robin," I said, "I have a hunch you think we should order some. So, what should we know about them?"

"Yes, sir. I think we should. Order some. They come from Australia, and they lay 300 eggs a year each. They're big and they tolerate heat well if they have plenty of shade too...."

"I didn't know they could fly that far," interrupted Vern, with a big grin.

Mine and Robin's jaws dropped in amazement. We looked at each other, and then back at Vern, who has never been known for jocularity. We all laughed.

"Good one, Vern!" said Robin. They "high-fived," slapping their palms together in midair.

~

No time for an after-lunch nap, Vern and I had been back in the herb garden for a few hours. We noticed that the hummingbirds had retired earlier than usual from the gardens. The sun had been hidden most of the afternoon by dark clouds on the horizon from south to north. A low-hanging extended curtain hung just above the Earth, with ominous tails drifting down here and there like transparent drapery fluttering against the setting sun. Not funnels yet but threatening to be. The air and the space were tinted yellow-green, tornado atmosphere. Liz had promised one of her students that she would attend their music recital that evening, so she would get home late from the campus. I sent her a text, a parental reminder, to watch the sky cautiously tonight.

Vern and I had just finished securing the last new raised bed frame over its proper alignment in the herb garden. The sun was a bright thin arc, just the tip of its hot pate, sliding over the edge of the world, going down over the Monahans sand hills, probably. We had gotten a lot done, considering he only had this particular weekend to help for a while. Driving down to the entry gate, he waved goodbye to his admirer

Robin, who was just sliding the big barn doors open for the gathered equine dinner crowd.

The sensor had already turned on the outdoor light overhead just above the barn doors. Robin would text me shortly to let me know she was heading home now that she had sequestered all the critters away for the evening, starting with her favorites, the heritage breed chickens. Cell reception is always good up at the herb gardens, especially if you hold the phone up high and aim it toward Roswell, New Mexico.

I walked back down the hill and over to the house, scanning the dark horizon for signs of trouble all the way. Old friend George Clay would arrive early the next morning to spend a couple of days building stretcher bars for canvas paintings with me. Robin had already delivered and washed the day's egg production and put the cartons in the egg cooler on the back porch.

I planned to make a grilled cheese for supper with sourdough bread from the Ronning's bakery. Alongside, I'd enjoy some fat bread-and-butter slices from our canned pickles in the pantry made using Granny's pickling spices recipe, of course.

Having showered and completed the evening's ablutions, I headed into the bedroom. With a couple of pillows for back props, I leaned into the headboard, eager to dive back into an Easy Rawlins mystery. I reached over for the book. There next to it on the bedside table, was a newly framed photo. I picked it up for closer perusal. It was an old four-by-six-inch black-and-white photograph of a much younger Sam Bartlett—Sammy, in fact, probably as a second grader. Annie had left it for me early that morning while I was already in the studio above the barn.

I wonder where she found this old picture. Probably in a forgotten album in a box in the attic marked "Momma" on top. The boy in the picture had on a starched cotton plaid shirt with a big collar. As a boy, in addition to a fair array of freckles, my cheeks were rosy red in all seasons, even at the beach in Galveston summers. I took a lot of teasing as a kid for that. "Blushing Sammy" the older kids called me. I might have had anger rising in my boyhood cheeks, but I wasn't blushing.

Annie had positioned the photo next to a small frame that held a faded Polaroid of another fair-skinned, red-cheeked Bartlett boy, my little brother. It was tucked into the last post I received from Art. We were four years apart, so didn't spend a lot of time together as I grew through my teen years, working part-time jobs. Artie sent lots of letters to me from Vietnam while I was stationed at the Strategic Air Command base in North Dakota. We got to know each other, as adults, through those letters. In the photo, my brother is kind of mugging for the camera with a steel can of Pabst Blue Ribbon raised in the air as a hopeful toast. You can tell his face is sunburned even behind large sunglasses. Bartlett skin burns easy. He and a couple of buddies are posing together, leaning on the front end of an M561 Gama Goat, a sort of amphibious ATV. I still have the cleaned, but rusted, church key that came home with his other personal belongings in a small package sent by registered air mail. I keep it next to his letters.

Our paternal grandmother's English skin was like fresh white cream, right up to her dying day at 102. Her generation wore bonnets or hats and gloves, especially in bright summer sunlight, whether walking to church or working in the field. Skin cancer was unknown to the elder women in my family.

I have a memory-picture in my head. It's one of those graphic mental images that is distinct and immediately recalled. One of those memorable moments that stays in your head clearly, even more graphic than if a camera had been at hand to record the scene. My fellow veteran friend, George Clay, and Grandma Bartlett sat next to each other at a gallery opening in Fort Worth years ago. George and I each had pieces in an invitational group exhibit. They are laughing in my memory's snapshot. I recall overhearing a fun part of their lively conversation. Their discussion was on the subject of mules, of their efficacy on any farm or ranch, and their uniqueness as man-made equines.

Even though he has officially been a "senior citizen" for years, George's skin color and texture still has the appearance of freshly poured smooth fudge. It was Grandma's last year with us. Cousins had brought her to attend her grown grandson's art show. Her skin was still as smooth and light as fresh cream. At her funeral, we learned that she had once driven herself to Dallas alone to march in an anti-war protest. She marched in grief and frustration, along with other grandparents and parents and angry young adults. George said that during their gallery conversation, Grandma had leaned toward him, speaking in a near-whisper. She told him how sorry she was that her otherwise honorable hero, LBJ, had recklessly sent him to Vietnam without purpose.

George did not know at that time, nor did Grandma tell him, that she had lost her favorite grandson in the war. Art and Grandma were peas in a pod. Both were full of mischief, and they looked alike. They shared the same piercing blue eyes and had the same delightful dimples at the ends of their generous smiles.

~

Recently, Vietnam again came up as a difficult topic, during a serious conversation with Annie. It was a sweet spring night. You know, one of those cool, quiet nights that even if you live in town you want to open as many windows in the house as possible to get a cross-breeze of refreshing ventilation.

The black, moonless sky was clear from horizon to horizon and appeared to reach into infinity. So, I had lingered in the back yard. My head was leaned against the center slat of an old Adirondack chair, seeing just a curtain's edge of the Milky Way starting to rise up from the east. I was trying to secure that image in my painter's memory bank.

It was difficult to file away the present dark sky, with encroaching bits of Milky Way from the east. And my mind was distracted, due to the impeding memory of past nights of moonless black skies near Fort Davis. In July and August out there, the Milky Way eventually covers the entire sky, spreading like a wide fog, like an all-encompassing cosmic umbrella by 1:30 or 2 a.m.

I tried to draw my attention back to Barnes County sky reality by following the contour of my two-story barn's solid silhouette at the bottom of the eastern sky. The early Milky Way array seemed most vivid from behind that darker black barn-shaped outline at the bottom of the hill. My eyes were heavy, and they closed.

It was late—ten-thirty or later. Annie's always kept farmer's hours, so even as an adult is usually asleep by 8:30 p.m., even after just a half hour or so of reading in bed. I'd just crawled in beside her and closed my tired eyes. For a brief few moments, I was fast asleep.

I heard a baby crying. Two babies? Was it my baby crying? My eyelids were so heavy, so slow to open. The crying got louder. My eyes opened to see Annie perched up on her elbow, leaning over me. She was peering hard into the distance, and listening harder, head atilt. I cleared my throat to speak, but she put a finger to my lips, saying "Shhh. Listen." I did, and briefly I heard another burst of shrill crying from outside.

"Is it a child? Lost in the woods?' Annie wondered, trying to wake up.

We got up. At the end of the bed, in the dark, she almost tripped over Nike, the Bluetick Coonhound, who had once again snuck into the house silently to join us for slumber. Oddly, the hound paid no attention to the sorrowful crying human baby in the woods, nor to us stumbling over her lanky, bony body. The dog was at peace, in a prone yoga position, on Annie's favorite Persian carpet. Maybe the baby was crying at a frequency unheard by hounds, or Nike interpreted the sound to be human, thus out of her role as chaser of wild things.

We made our way out through the kitchen, hastily stepping into our Crocs on the back porch and descended onto the tree-lined patio. Emanating from the bois d'arc grove, we heard the sorrowful crying of a baby again. Annie pressed against me, clutching my arm with both of hers.

"Sam, what's happening? Is someone in the woods?"

The plaintive appeal rang out once more. We cautiously approached the darkened grove, Annie in her nightgown, me in T-shirt and boxers.

On the road, as we neared the woods, I took Annie's hand and said "Wait. Be still." We listened closer. A baby was crying from somewhere up in the trees. My brain had finally awakened enough for me to be cognizant again.

"It's a peacock." I said, relieved.

"A what?" Annie asked.

"Now I remember that sound...old Mrs. Majors in Irene," I offered, by way of an answer.

"Who...and what? What is it?"

"The richest widow in Irene. Mrs. Majors. When I was a boy. She had peacocks and peahens. Sometimes a courting couple would venture across the big pasture between her place in town and Granny's a mile or so away. It drove Granny crazy when it happened."

That's why the sound was disturbing to me, but somehow familiar, as it stirred me from pleasant memory or pleasant dream of the Milky Way. The broad swath of stars was overhead now. We held each other, eyes lifted into the heavens, dazzled by endless distant, ancient lights, and no longer troubled by the strange sounding wails of a wooing peacock in our trees. It was a big bird, caught in the throes of desire for a mate, perhaps prompted by the moon's position, a change in the weather, or simply the charm of the hen. Despite what our human ears are prone to hear, it was not a baby human making that noisy appeal.

Perhaps that night was a connection for us with ancestors from eons ago, maybe all the way back to Eden, the first perfect garden. In any case, Elysia, our closest semblance of urban civilization, was not yet casting commercial ambient light upon us, diminishing the night sky above. Not yet.

We stood together in the dark of night, having taken account of alarming sounds in the woods. Relieved that no child was in danger, abandoned or injured, we held each other closer and laughed at ourselves a bit.

The night was cool on our nearly naked bodies. Not quite Adam and Eve's experience, but we both commented on how refreshing the night breeze felt on our skin. Strolling back to the house, I proffered an idea.

"Annie. Let's go down to the tank and swim tonight."

Grinning up at me, she said "Skinny-dipping, you mean. On this 68-degree night."

"Yeah. Like when we went skinny-dipping at Turner Falls one night, and it was colder."

"What a sweet time for us, Sam. We had good hearts. We were going to change the world." she said.

"If you'll get us some towels from the house, I'll crank up the Rodeo."

Beautiful Annie ran across the backyard to the house. The screen door on the porch had barely slammed when she emerged again, thick beach-towels in hand.

She climbed in, happily kissing me on the cheek. Staying close, leaning across the console, she said, "I fell in love with you that very night at Turner Falls."

"Me too."

"I know." Annie paused, deep in thought. "But I was full of trepidation too. I loved you, but Mom made it clear that she would never approve me marrying an artist without money. And then when you joined up and left for the service, I became more and more worried about your soldier life. Four years seemed like an eternity, too much time to comprehend."

"What your mom really didn't like about me was the fact I had joined the Teamsters so I could make enough money to go to college by loading trucks."

"I remember."

The first time Annie introduced me to her mom, she had asked me how I was paying for tuition and room and board. I told her. She exhaled a weary sigh and rose from her cozy winged back chair. She turned her face from me, looked directly at her suddenly trembling daughter, and said simply, "Teamsters are gangsters, you silly girl." She left the living room without a backward glance.

During my long tour of duty, Annie and I only wrote a few letters. She immersed herself in a world of literature and history during those years. She was determined to become a writer and live far away from her parents. She did just that. Annie was now deep in memories. She whispered something about the sadness of the many years we stayed apart. Other lives. She finally spoke in a low voice, her thought-sentence becoming audible midway through.

"...but all returning soldiers were kind of 'suspect' back then. For college girls I mean, you know?"

I stopped the Rodeo and turned off the ignition. Annie was crying.

"I'm sorry those thoughts ever entered my mind, Sammy. I knew you were a good man. I knew you had to volunteer or be drafted. I knew you didn't want that war either. But I was swept up in the moment. I listened to all the fervor of noise around me, classmates, my parents, the TV, noises that provided no options for me but to proceed ahead in life without you."

"Annie. No regrets. We love each other now, just like that night at Turner Falls."

"Yes, but I'm sorry for the years we lost. I know we both needed time to live and grow up as adults ourselves. I know we both needed that, but part of me will always regret my having ended...us. God, I even stopped writing to you."

She was sobbing, slumped forward, her face pressed deep into her open palms. I placed my hand on her back, waiting.

She finally leaned back into the seat, exhausted, wiping the tears from her face with her bare hands. I waited to speak until she looked over at me, taking my hand atop the console between us.

"Annie. I missed you too back then. But I really wasn't very good at being an artist and a husband, at the same time, in my younger civilian years. Maybe the deities ordained that you and I would be better off together later in life, after a pause."

Annie smiled. "Maybe like Odysseus trying to sail home against the wind all those years."

"Yes, you beautiful girl. Like that."

We held hands as we walked down the path toward the large stock tank. On the west side of the farm, surrounded by prairie, void of nearby trees, the horizon was tall and wide. Ahead of us, the tank looked as black as the deep, legendary lochs I'd seen in Scotland. With occasional mowing around the immediate perimeter, and the hooves of coming and going thirsty livestock at the water's edge, the approach is more like the shore of a swimming lake than a grassy meadow.

Stars filled all the darkness by then and spilled down into the reflecting lake, now a huge, motionless mirror. Heaven and Earth were one continuous backdrop, one uninterrupted surface full of stars from top to bottom. We held hands and waded out into the sky that night.

~

Annie and I met in college. She was a freshman lit major, in her first semester at the University of Oklahoma in Norman. I was a junior advertising art major at NTSU (North Texas State University, now the University of North Texas) in Denton. I shared a big apartment with two roommates. The place had seen better days, but it was close to the art building. As a teen, I'd promised myself that if I ever got off the farm when I grew up, I'd live in the city and listen to jazz. At NTSU, half of that promise came through, big time.

The "One O'Clock Lab Band" was internationally famous. Jazz fans like me would sit on the floor in the halls of the practice rooms, and get ears full of expert tenor sax, clarinet, bass, piano, and trumpet students trying to emulate the greats—Miles Davis, Mose Allison, Chet Baker, and the like. Famous performers loved coming to North Texas. In the few years I was there, I got to see the Dave Brubeck Quartet, Woody Herman and His Thundering Herd, and The Bill Evans Trio, all masters of their craft.

Mentally, I still saw myself as an illustrator. Becoming a serious painter was not in my sights at all. I regarded "Modern Art" as stuff made by people who couldn't draw. Convictions seem so certain, so accurate, when we're young. I saw advertising as a way to get rich.

One of my room mates was dating a girl at OU. Her sorority was throwing a big campus party one weekend, so he talked me into going up to Norman with him. During semesters, my weekends were normally spent down in Dallas, loading trucks for Roadway Express as a part-time checker. I was an "extra," meaning that unlike the fulltime Teamsters, we college "extras" received no insurance, pension, or benefits from the company. Of course, none of us "extras" cared about any of that. As Teamsters, even part-time, we still earned three times the national minimum wage. As "extras," we could work eight hours on, eight hours off, so I could complete two eight-hour shifts in one day on the weekends, sleeping in the car between shifts. That kept me paying rent and eating during the week. But summers, at eight on, eight off, were when you could make enough to pay for college: tuition, fees, books, art supplies, clothes, gasoline, and dates. The car was a 1958 VW bug, by the way. A bit cramped, but it kept the rain off.

Annie's family had money, but she was more interested in becoming a writer than joining a sorority. She landed a job at the campus newspaper her first semester. Her hometown girlfriend loved sorority life and always invited Annie to attend parties. Annie was already a bit of a hippy, though that term wasn't used much yet. It was a changing time for many young people. Coffee houses shifted gears from featuring beat poetry to folk music. Suspended between being a beatnik or becoming a hippy, Annie never fully embraced either. She was simply a young, aspiring writer who loved journalism and literature. And she loved the prospect of leaving home.

The party was loud, as any weekend crowd of undergrads will be. Annie was stunning. She was sitting on one side of an orange and pink pastel-striped loveseat, wearing a short corduroy skirt with black leggings beneath. She was scribbling notes in a journal on her lap.

Glancing up, Annie immediately caught my fond gaze. I was embarrassed, so just smiled and looked away quickly. When I looked again, she put her pen down and smiled back. I took a few steps toward her, my squeaky leather Bass Weejun penny loafers feeling as if made of concrete, impeding my journey across the sorority house parlor to her. Strangely, I suddenly hoped I looked Ivy League enough for her. I felt clumsy, like a Teamster loading a forty-foot trailer with eighty-pound boxes of nails. I felt like one of my cowhand uncles shakily mishandling Granny's best bone china cups and saucers in her spotless parlor.

What could I possibly say to this stunning, smiling girl to make her love me? My brain wasn't working. I said "Hi." She held her giant green eyes on me all the way over. I stood in my shoes of concrete, as she looked up at me through large tortoise-shell glasses. "Hello," she responded. Somehow, I managed to ask if I could sit down, or join her, or is this seat taken...I can't remember what. I just remember her saying, "Of course." And somehow, we talked for an hour, her occasionally crossing and uncrossing her legs, me trying the same, lifting my concrete feet.

She loved reading *The Odyssey* and *Beowulf* in freshman lit. I had loved the same, before her. We agreed that heroes must have flaws and must be mortal, else how can we failed humans relate to them? We both admired Joan of Arc and agreed that Mark Twain had a huge crush on her. Annie had just discovered a new Irish poet, Seamus Heaney, and thought I'd like his work since he was also raised a child of farmers. In my freshman year, I'd discovered E.B. White's essays for *The New Yorker*, and suggested she start reading those, as they were sometimes about his urbane life in Manhattan and sometimes about his little chicken farm in Maine.

Annie had been the senior editor of her high school yearbook. I had been the art editor of mine. We agreed that newspapers were essential to free societies, and that comics were essential to newspapers. We had a lot in common. We walked on the quad that night, holding hands. We kissed. I promised to visit her on campus again, soon. I did.

Later that fall, her mom didn't like it that I was a Teamster and Vietnam took over all our lives.

~

My old artist pal, George Clay, had come up to the farm from Lufkin for a few days of camaraderie as we helped each other stretch canvas. Our purpose was partly to build sturdy stretcher bars for future paintings and partly for a few days to visit and catch up on things. You can get a lot of constructive conversation done with a friend working across from you on the other side of the same large canvas.

George, a well-known East Texas artist, and I have been friends for a long time. You know how sometimes in your life you meet a person and you just like each other from the very first go? That's how it was with George. We first met because of a drawing class in the early days of my college teaching career. He had been an Army mechanic in the latter days of Vietnam and had been home for a couple of years. His family and the Veterans Administration had helped him rebound a bit from post-traumatic stress disorder and a taste for drugs he'd acquired in Saigon. In his senior citizen years, George's ubiquitous exposure to agent orange during Nam is proving to be an unwanted prescription for serious trouble in the near future. Diabetes and the early symptoms of multiple sclerosis are impacting his stamina and flexibility already. George is a researcher, so he knows what's coming.

A handsome art student with perfect posture, George approached me at the end of the first-class lecture after most of the art students had left the studio.

"Professor, I'm George Clay," he said, as he offered a handshake.

"I'm pleased you've signed up for Drawing I with me, George."

As a couple of other students nearby waited to introduce themselves, George leaned in and said, almost in a whisper "I have a question for you."

"Of course," I answered. "What is it?"

"Well," he ventured "Are you a Vet?"

His brief question prompted immediate and sustained eye contact between us.

"Well, yes I am, George. I suspect I got home just a couple of years ahead of you."

"That's all I wanted to hear." he replied. "I'll see you next class."

We shook hands again with an understanding of each other that needed no more words.

~

Stretching canvas has always been therapeutic for me. Making art is not therapeutic. But stretching canvas is. Making art is problem solving. Making art is being creative, original, God-like. A good painting is like a poem. It exists. And though it may be bought and sold or traded, at times, it is not a commodity. A good, stretched canvas is a commodity, highly valued by artists.

I learned how to stretch canvas from a purist, Bob Newman, at the University of North Dakota in the mid-sixties. In those days, number-one-grade Ponderosa pine was available for making the stretcher bars. Excellent linen and canvas were abundant, thus economical. Painting large was possible, even for students like me, in the sixties.

Over the years, a junior or senior or grad student has given me a call just to thank me for teaching them how to make stretcher bars correctly. I tell them to thank Bob Newman. Expressing gratitude in social discourse makes for a healthy society.

I taught George how to build a proper stretched canvas, and of course he's taught others. There's an ongoing thread of craftsmanship in the sharing of this skill, an agreeable communal use of knowledge that manifests a useful product and an ambient sense of well-being that transcends the utilitarian nature of the thing. Emerson would say that participating in the making of the thing sends ripples of positive energy out into the universe. He'd say something like that.

George and I enjoy making stretcher bars and stretching canvas together. It's like cooking with a friend. A recent widower, George joined me for a few days at the farm. Annie has been concerned about George since his precious Rose passed. She was a beautiful woman, the love of his life, and an inspirational music teacher who kept a lot of tough urban kids out of trouble through musical instruments. Rose also kept George on the straight and narrow when she thought necessary. She was never mean about it. She just understood how he ticked. She understood his anger and was always first to recognize when his impulsive nature was about to get him into trouble. Rose knew how to soothe the troubled waters of George's post-Vietnam brain. She helped him to take a breath and pause a couple of moments before leaping into the lion's den.

Rose told us she was born and spent her first several years of childhood in the Philippines in WWII under occupation of the Japanese army. Her parents were physicians, so they stayed alive under house arrest for the duration. The little girl lived her small life in a small, enclosed yard with one swing, one little fish pond, two palm trees, and one yellow cat. The stucco walls around the yard seemed to her little eyes to reach into the heavens, they were so tall. Much of the year they were covered in lush bougainvillea of a bright coral tone that stayed her favorite color all her life. She was never allowed outside that yard. Visitors came and went through a heavy front gate made of thick *mangkono* or Philippine *ironwood* planks, secured with massive ornate brass hinges. Two armed soldiers stood on each side of the giant gate on the street entry at all times. Perhaps Rose learned patience at a very young age. She certainly learned that, from time to time, there were very definite limits imposed on individual freedoms in life. By the age of four, Rose had developed and practiced her own kind of Zen-like acceptance.

George and Rose met after their own respective children with other spouses were grown or nearly grown, not unlike me and Annie. They both had been single for a couple of years, and neither was looking for a new mate...Rose because she was patient and accepting of situations mostly out of her control. George because he liked his freedom and could flex his impulses to his liking. Rose had a beautiful and expansive smile that opened up to you amidst a sea of lovely freckles, like my own Liz. With handsome George in tow, the two of them could have made a fortune just posing for fashion magazine covers.

During one memorable long weekend's visit at the farm, Rose taught us how to make George's mom's seafood gumbo. She loved being in the garden with us, harvesting the several varieties of heirloom okra we grow. Annie loves to make dishes that demand patient tending, with periodic timely stirring, like gumbo and paella. She and Rose enjoyed soft-spoken kitchen conversations, mingled with long thoughtful pauses, as they cared for slow-cooking dishes together.

George and I share similar food histories growing up, me in the coastal lowlands of Southeast Texas and he in Louisiana, the states separated by the same rivers, bayous, canals and sandbars.

All the fresh waters of each state headed down to the Gulf of Mexico. The color of our skin is very different, but the color of our taste palate is the same.

So, Annie was pleased that George was visiting for a few days, though disappointed she would miss him as she's away to Nederland working on her "History of Texas Rice" book. That's my working title for it, anyway.

The ingredients for building good stretcher bars include ersatz 1-by-2-inch pine, half-inch quarter round, wood glue, 1-inch wire brads and 1-and-5/8-inch finishing nails. I say "ersatz" because industry uses measurement and weight numbers with creative artistic license. When I first started building stretcher bars under the instruction of Robert Newman at the University of North Dakota, a 1-by-2-inch pine board was exactly that size, and " a pound of bacon" was sold in sixteen-ounce packs, not ten or twelve ounces.

George had already cut many of the 8-foot 1-by-2-inch boards in half, to serve as the supporting center boards of what would become 4-by-8-foot stretched canvas. With his half of the 4-by-8-foot canvases we would stretch and gesso together, George planned to use for a series of vertical life-size portraits. Mine were destined to become horizontal landscapes, of course.

Our assembly-line consisted of several folding tables positioned on either side of the studio with a wide enough space down the middle for us to move freely. On one end of the arrangement, I carefully laid a bead of wood glue along the top-edge of each 2-inch-wide board, sliding the 8-foot 1-by-2 down the line to George, with an accompanying pre-cut eight feet of half-inch quarter round.

With a manual convertible staple/brad gun, George was carefully positioning the angle edge of the quarter round flush with top edge of the 1-by-2. At intervals of roughly three inches, George applied wire brads for the length of the assembly. The curved side of the quarter round must always face inward, so the canvas only touches the sharpest edge of the wood. Thus, the canvas itself is raised above the 1-by-2-inch board itself, stretched tightly across the curved quarter round only. In some ways, the brads and nails used for stretcher bars are necessary only to keep the wood surfaces together long enough for the wood glue to bond.

In a short time, the wood glue has dried enough for us to flip the assembled stretcher bar over atop a premeasured section of canvas. Leaving ourselves three to four inches of canvas beyond each side of the stretcher bar, we pull the cloth tight from opposite sides. Maintaining tension on the weave with one hand, the other hand secures the overlapping canvas to the back of the 1-by-2 board with a staple gun. For large paintings, the precision and time required for stretching canvas is a lot more fun with a trusted friend on the other side of the process.

We are stretching six 5-by-8-foot canvases so we'll have three each for paintings, horizontal for me, vertical for George. He's doing a series on family members and neighboring friends in Louisiana from his childhood visual memory. His uncles and cousins mostly that, like me, he grew up fishing and hunting with. His are mostly group portraits, three or four men or boys standing, talking, or working together. The figures in one of his paintings are depicted walking home after dove hunting with dinner draped over their shoulders. In another, similar figures carry strings of fish from a docked boat up a curved road toward an unpainted house in the distance.

George reminds me of Michelangelo. I mean that he's a really good painter, but he'd rather carve the figures in wood instead of painting them. George, like Michelangelo, simply prefers to express himself in a

3-D language. I think he paints the images of his uncles and friends almost like devotionals, usually of his oldest relatives. They capture the persona of the sitter. The sitters convey an evocative *presence* that deserves respect. The best of the best of these includes an element of *memento mori* (Latin for "Remember you must die").

A favorite such example is one of his Uncle Titus behind a *walking plow*, being pulled by an ancient swayback mule, silhouetted against a wooded hillside. If you look closely, you'll see a hazy cemetery in the background but presented at a position on the canvas so that the distant graveyard basically surrounds the head of Uncle Titus, though far off in the distance. That's George's subtle reference to *memento mori*. Holbein, and Shakespeare, for that matter, needed actual skulls to drive home the same message.

I imagine that Michelangelo had many sleepless nights fretting over the fact that he would never live enough lifetimes to be able to do the Sistine Chapel ceiling in 3-D, sculpted figures, which he would have preferred. I think he just wanted to get the thing painted as soon as he could. The fact that he was done with it in only four years speaks volumes. Frustration caused him to run away twice during the commission's completion. The Vatican's effective sixteenth-century Swiss Guard police hunted him down each time and each time put him back up on the scaffolding. He must have been miserable, despite his great passion for the church.

George loves his family and respects its unjust and painful history. But his large figure paintings allow him to paint, to record, much more testimony to that history than his one lifetime can ever achieve in life-size sculptural expression. Frankly, my old friend paints with a bit of expedience, a need to get on with it. He sculpts with the slow pace and attentive gestures of a hunter who pauses in the middle of a hunt to gently stroke the head and ears of his favorite hound.

It was late Sunday afternoon. George and I had finished stretching and stapling the last canvas together. We'd load up his three canvasses into his old Chevy van in the morning. He would leave for Lufkin very early, heading diagonally, southeast on U.S. Highway 287, trying to avoid Monday morning rush hour by staying south of Dallas.

We went downstairs to help Robin put alfalfa cubes and oats into all the horse buckets for their dinner meals and fill up the dog food bowls. She had helped out through the weekend so that George and I could focus on our canvas project for both days.

Daughter Liz was up at the house preparing dinner for everyone. Robin had called her folks earlier to make sure she could stay for dinner. Her phone rang. She took the cellphone from her barn-coat pocket and read the text message, translating the text without looking up.

"Liz says that if you two painters can spare me, I'm needed in the kitchen."

George and I nodded in the affirmative.

Robin had just opened her mouth to ask about the evening chicken-house duties: egg gathering, feed and water-check, tucking the girls in for the night, et al.

I spoke before she could utter a word.

"Go help Liz. George and I will take care of the chickens."

Robin smiled her own vibrantly wide and genuine smile and rushed out of the barn, blonde ponytail in the wind behind her. She loved hanging out with my still freckle-faced daughter, now herself a genuine college professor, albeit adjunct. Our bird-loving teen farmhand has gotten very serious and appreciative of her upcoming educational rite of passage from high school to college.

Later, we all held hands as I dutifully offered, by rote, the same perfunctory prayer my Grandad Bartlett had always recited at mealtimes. I do trust that these days, my own rote repetitions are devoid of his occasional heavy sighs of reluctance. Grandad did not share Grandma Alice's Wesleyan embrace of regimen. Saying grace at table is a family ritual that today gives me pause to remember them fondly and to share my affection for them.

During supper, George and I gave updated reports on the intended outcomes for the many canvasses we'd built. Robin asked a million practical questions of Liz about best practices during undergrad years to enhance opportunities for grad school stipends. Liz is enjoying her moment as mentor to our teen neighbor, make no mistake. She will take the responsibility earnestly.

After feasting on baby arugula, tat-soi spinach, and feta salad with pickled beet slices, oven-roasted carrots slaked with olive oil and balsamic vinegar, and panko-crusted salmon patties, the lovely evening wound down. We sent Robin home with hugs, despite her protests that she should stay and help us clean up. There were plenty of hands in the kitchen to do a good job, and she had school in the morning.

The kitchen clean, George bade goodnight and headed off down the hall to the guestroom. I sat at the kitchen table, making some notes about the coming week's projects. Liz sat down next to me, her big brown eyes intense and her posture implying serious business.

"Dad" she began, "I've got something you need to see."

I peered back at her huge brown eyes over the top of my reading glasses and asked "Yes?"

Liz produced an 11-by-14-inch portfolio, placing it on the table before me. "What's this?" I asked.

"Just open it. You'll like it." she grinned.

I obliged, releasing the elastic band and opening the flap. Inside was a smaller sketchbook and numerous drawings and watercolors of varied sizes. There were charcoals, ink and pencil drawings, and a couple of soft pastels.

I held the assembled art items slightly aloft with eyebrows raised in question.

"They're Robin's, Dad. Robin's drawings." I looked closer at the unexpected display before my eyes.

"Robin's been drawing?" I asked unnecessarily, the very evidence before me. "Why haven't I seen them?"

"Robin just showed them to me tonight, before dinner. She's been hesitant to show you. She's afraid they may not be good enough to bother you with."

"Holy cow," I said. "I never imagined."

"Well, she's been watching you draw and paint for a couple of years. She's helped you and Suzie get things set up for the visiting landscape drawing students twice a year. She's been learning here and trying it out at home."

"Enjoy." Liz kissed me on the top of my head and said goodnight.

Robin has always been a fast learner. Her drawings demonstrated good understanding of the art principles she was attempting to use. I would have helped her, if asked, to better understand how to apply this or that pencil or pen, but she had bravely marched ahead, on her own, trying out a wide variety of media.

While fondly considering the pages of the surprise teen portfolio laid out before me, I pondered for a moment that Bartlett Farm may be raising artists along with crops and livestock.

Before turning in myself that night, a newly formed comparison came to mind, most likely Muse-inspired. The wooden garden frames that I build provide the structure, the support, for the soil and the plants in that raised bed. The wooden stretcher bars provide the structural support for the canvas and the paints in that artwork. Both frame-like structures are carefully planned and built throughout the rural year at Bartlett Farm. The resultant products of these wooden constructs support the farm with income.

~

Recently, the farm was abuzz with the cheerful sound of joyful children laughing, and, if you listened carefully, the softer buzzing sound of ladybug wings. When I taught in Derbyshire, England, my students referred to ladybugs as "ladybirds." Makes no sense to me but live in the United Kingdom for a year and you soon learn that Texas English isn't English over there.

I'm having my morning coffee, finally getting around to answering emails and cards from parents and grandparents thanking us for our recent ladybug release event. Between sips of coffee, I'm relishing each complex forkful of a Ronning's Bakery blackberry streusel. The buttery delight is made with Bartlett Farm blackberries, of course.

Liz and Annie came up with the idea of a ladybug release a few years back. We chose this garden activity as an annual occasion to invite customers out to see the farm, up close and personal, for themselves. Though farms in central Texas often schedule similar events in mid- to late April, we plan ours for mid- to late May each year up here in the north.

We order enough live ladybug packets so that visitors can enjoy the thrill of releasing the little predators into our gardens and have a packet to take home for their own raised beds. All profit, beyond cost of the beautiful beetles themselves, from our guests' generous donations goes to the Elysia high school ag program. And, of course, it's those very teens who warmly welcome ladybug release visitors and show them around the farm. A couple of our teen docents experienced the magic of ladybug release as little kids themselves, not so long ago.

Starting in late afternoon, we offer garden tours and refreshments. Just before sunset, all the youngsters and their families position themselves throughout the gardens, ladybug packets in hand. To maximize effective coverage (and widespread expressions of oohs and aahs), our teen student tour guides direct the small groups to the most effective ladybug launch sites.

As the glowing orange sun-ball slides over the edge of the world, the anticipatory crowd eagerly chants in unison the launch countdown from "ten, nine, eight...," then finally and suddenly the hungry ladybugs are released into the soft evening air. Children's ears are especially entertained with the up-close buzzing sounds of ladybug wings flapping together at 85 times per second. In relation to their tiny size, ladybugs are loud little fliers. Their wings can flap independently of each other, allowing them to steer and turn like barn-storming pilots of old.

Wide-eyed, our young visitors watch and feel the beautiful tiny red-and-black insects wander over small bare arms, fly from little hands, circling in their myriad flight plans out and down into the waiting plants. At child's eye-level, the tiny insect aircraft squadrons fill the landscape all the way to the blazing horizon at end of day.

Devonshire Calf

TWO

The Fig King, Earthworms, and a Loose Appaloosa

I read a letter today that felt like it had come to me from a hundred years ago. It was on top of a short stack of mail that Liz had left for me after her trip to town yesterday. First, it was written in what I'm sure was an impressive, florid cursive at one time, like my Aunt Lorine always wrote, rest her soul. This lettering was a bit shaky but still carried the weight and confidence of experience.

The letter was written on a sheet of white paper with regimented pale blue horizontal lines, old timey notebook paper, folded in thirds. Tucked inside the middle fold was a perfectly flat and crisp new one-hundred-dollar bill.

I took another look at the legal-sized envelope that carried the letter. The fancy textured envelope was ecru, addressed in the same practiced but unsteady cursive to "Mr. Samuel Bartlett, Bartlett Farm, Elysia, Texas." No Zip code. I'm sure that Postmaster John and his associates found the quaint address of interest and kindly slid it into my post office box compartment with a smile. In the upper left sender's corner of the envelope, that smelled faintly of eucalyptus or some other commercial aromatherapy-type fragrance, was the return address. The first line began "Sunset Vistas Care" in a slightly embossed, mechanically printed mime of cursive.

The handwritten letter began "Dear Mr. Bartlett, my name is Malcolm Fortune. My n'eer- do-well son, Freddy, said he sold you my white swayback pony a while ago. Well, I can read between the lines whenever my lazy boy tells a story. I'm sure he never even thanked you for saving Douglas, that's the pony's name. Frederick says you paid two hundred dollars. I let him keep a hundred. I'm sending you my hundred, enclosed. Please spend it on some sweet feed for Douglas. He likes sweet things, especially apples. He's a good old pony and can pull a plow if you need him to.

Sincerely, M. Fortune."

I sat my coffee cup down on the kitchen counter and stepped off the back porch with a warm feeling in my chest. The screen door made a familiar, comforting sound as the spring latch pulled it shut behind me. The sun had just started to reveal the contours of the wrought-iron rooster-topped weathervane on the barn's roof.

Robin was already about halfway done making the rounds of her morning chores. School was out for the summer, and she was enjoying some reflective time while she worked. The barn doors were wide open, like a big cheerful grin.

"Morning, Sam," she said, not looking up from the bucket of cubes she was providing over the rail for Dolly, our stalwart mare.

When Robin started her senior year last fall, I told her she was old enough now to call me by my first name. The adjustment took a little while, as it has done for all my teen farmhands over the years. But she's okay with it now. After all, she's never addressed Annie as anything but "Annie." First names matter between friends. First names get to the point.

All the equines were hard at their breakfast, getting fortified for the day ahead. The swayback stood with his head jutted over the rail into the hallway when he heard my voice return Robin's greeting. He watched me closely, eyes wide, oat crumbs falling from the edges of his whiskered mouth. I had an apple in the pocket of my khaki barn coat. He probably noticed the bulge.

I caught Robin's eye as I walked past her in the wide hallway. I gestured with my head and a smile that she should follow me. The swayback was bobbing his head slowly, his standard morning greeting.

"Good morning, Douglas."

His ears shot forward toward the sound of his name suddenly being spoken out loud. He looked me directly in the eye, his long lashes unblinking, as if to say, "Yes, that's me. I'm Douglas." I scratched his chin. Robin, beside me, stroked his extended neck.

"You finally named him," Robin said, almost in a whisper.

"No. The old man who raised him finally told me his name. He's always been Douglas."

"Wow," my farmhand offered. "All this time, he's been waiting to hear you call him that."

Robin is a perceptive young adult.

"Well, I knew he'd figure out a way to tell me sometime. I just never figured it would be revealed to me in cursive."

Robin scrunched her brow a bit. "An email?" she asked.

"Nope. A genuine hand-written paper letter with a paper postage stamp."

"Wow," she repeated. "From where?" she asked.

"From another century," I answered, passing the shiny red apple to her. "Want to do the honors?" I asked.

Robin smiled her broad smile and raised the fruit, coupling the backside correctly in her palm, offering the treat to our now-named swayback, who gently but precisely extended his front incisors to begin proper deconstruction of the red treat.

"Hello, Douglas. I'm Robin."

For a week now, joy seems to abound daily at the farm. You'd think we just brought a new Bartlett baby home. In a way, I guess we have. Seems like everybody in Barnes County wants to welcome Douglas to the family, now that they know his name. Even Postmaster John stopped off recently from town to say "hi," and to say the swayback's name aloud. A neighbor told me that he overheard John telling a customer the other day the whole story about his role in the early days of Douglas' rescue. I'm telling you, I think this is how epic tales like *The Odyssey* got born.

Mind you, we'd all just seen John at the farm earlier this month. He brings his young grandsons to our ladybug release annually, so we normally have a visit to the farm from him once a year. This year, he's come out twice, in rapid succession, because of Douglas' identity being revealed.

My newest part-time teen helpers are instructed on the seriousness of this discovery by Robin. As if articulating the unearthing of a long-lost Celtic Rune relic, she does a formal introduction, ceremonially walking them down the wide hall to have an audience with the regal equine. Duke Douglas is attentive to each young varlet, probably expecting the gift of an apple every time. It's all very reminiscent of Beowulf in the Mead Hall, actually a hero's reward.

~

The figs are ripening right on schedule at Bartlett Farm. The first day of recognition always fills me with delight. Unexpectedly, my morning senses will be treated to a shaft of raking sunlight falling on fig tree limbs covered in the lovely bell-shaped fruits. Throughout spring, I'll frequently glance at the trees for signs hinting of bounty for this year's crop. I can already taste what the budding gems will become. The appearance of the actual definitive fruit-form contour itself is what the nineteenth-century English poet Gerard Manley Hopkins would have called "inscape."

This beautiful vision, revealed by nature's diagonally cast illumination, usually occurs in early June. The annual scene reminds me of dramatic morning light as depicted by Jacob van Ruisdael's painterly Dutch hand.

We grow two kinds of figs at Bartlett Farm here in northwest Texas —the Celeste and the "Texas Everbearing," which we've always called Brown Turkey. Celeste is the most cold hardy, but the Brown Turkey is my favorite for rich, hefty flavor, but not too sweet. If a severe winter is experienced, both tree varieties may skip a year of production. Like Texas Bluebonnets, sometimes they overwhelm, sometimes not so much.

When looking for fig trees to plant, pay attention to the designation "open eye" versus "closed eye" varieties. The fruit of open-eye fig trees sometimes fall victim to bugs and beetles.

Both Celeste and Brown Turkey are closed-eye figs.

It's a good idea to keep mulch at the base of fig trees due to their relatively shallow root system. Young fig trees in North Texas do better with several small doses of nitrogen a year. I like to apply slow-release granules in early spring, mid-May, and mid-July of 8-8-8 strength NPK (nitrogen/ phosphorous/potassium). Mature trees are fine with one annual application.

Small brown, sometimes purple Celeste figs came ashore in Florida with Spanish explorers in the sixteenth century. Celeste trees get large and are very productive, with our best harvesting from mid- to late-June. Being reliably very sweet, they were my Granny's favorite choice for making homemade fig preserves.

Sidekick Annie makes a lush puff-pastry dish of soft melted brie with fig-preserve filling, all inside a thin croissant-like crust. Spreading the warm goo on a homemade graham cracker is the best way to eat it, in my opinion.

Brown Turkey figs are medium to large size, with a milder sweetness. More savory, I always sense herbal or earthy flavors along with just a bit of sugar. Brown Turkeys are plump fruits with a short stem. They ripen into reddish brown, pink, or purple skin. The reddish pink pulp is hearty. We've known extended ripening periods from June right through August.

In deadly serious winters, hay or straw can be mounded two to three feet high on the trunks of mature trees. For young trees, we've devised wire cages to wrap around the thin trunks, and fill up the gap-space with hay, leaves, or clippings to provide insulation. Daughter Liz reports that fig rust, a common fungal disease, can be a problem in East and Southeast Texas due to more rainfall there. We don't have that problem in Barnes County.

Many years ago, during a sabbatical to Greece, I accidentally wandered into the main farmers' market in Athens. It's a bit overwhelming, with endless tasty distractions. The Varvakeios Agora, or the "Central Municipal Athens Market" is the largest food market in Athens, though *Laiki Agora* ("the market of the people") take place in different neighborhoods in designated places on specific days, usually to promote particular seasonal items. No big billboard signs announce these smaller markets. Neighbors just know and share the details by word of mouth. *Laiki* starts at dawn, once a week, and is closed at 3 pm.

Andreas, an artist friend, had a small studio in the Koukaki neighborhood of Athens. I visited often during my sabbatical, sipping Assyrtiko wine served with seasonal fruits. A group of local painters met there weekly. I'm convinced I was welcomed for return visits partly because I shared their communal passion for figs. One gorgeous blue-sky Saturday morning, this art gang took me to the main Athens market for one purpose, to introduce me to the King of Figs.

Tucked neatly in between a larger fruit-stand and a melon vendor's wide tables was a narrow stall that seemed to be about the width of a walk-in closet. Rising slowly from an old wooden folding chair, bracing himself on an ancient hickory cane, was the Fig King himself. The elder vendor's massive mustache broadened into a childlike smile at the sight of the young admiring artists gathered before him. Generous hugs all round ensued, including one for the visiting Texan. An old Greek who had served in the resistance as a teen, his English had Victorian British nuance.

With sparkling eyes and a face like leather, he looked me up and down, taking the measure of me. His bushy eyebrows pressed forward as he peered right into my soul. He asked, "Your family?" Greeks always want to know about your parents and siblings, I learned. It helps them grasp your perspective on the world.

"All farmers," I answered, smiling. I was "in," as all my Athenian painter friends knew I would be. Old Cosmo, as he was known, grew and sold one thing from his tiny farm, giant figs. He described them as ancient Smyrna figs, but I'm not sure if that's correct. In any event, they were the size between a tennis ball and a softball. He would slice the thing in half, stick a plastic spoon into the soft rich pink flesh, and hand the two halves to the customer on a piece of newsprint. It was ambrosia. The cool flesh was like pudding, served up in its own purple living bowl.

We became friends and had long talks, often about agriculture, but as often he wanted to hear stories about my WWII uncles. I got to know the grandson, an art student, who helped him set up his little stand in the morning and break it down in the afternoon. There was a small *kafeneia*, a cafe, around the corner, just a short walk from the King of Fig's famous establishment. On occasion, Cosmo would insist I join him at the cafe so he could treat me to an espresso-size cup of black Greek coffee, served with raw sugar and a twisted bit of lemon peel. The combination of sweet and bitter was right up my alley.

Greek coffee always reminded me of Grandad Bartlett's black coffee, sans the raw sugar and lemon-peel offered with every espresso-size cup in Athens. Using a dented metal percolator, Grandad boiled the coffee till it obtained a consistency just short of mud. As an occasional bonus, you might get a piece of eggshell in your cup, though most seemed to stay at the bottom of the pot. Even as a kid, I loved his thick, dark brew. If Grandma was heard approaching the kitchen, he would wink at me while surreptitiously pouring a dollop of cream in my cup, assurance to her that I was drinking "coffee-milk," regarded as an age-appropriate beverage for any child in those days.

When I left Athens at the end of my sabbatical year, I took Cosmo a little gift. I framed a small colored pencil drawing I'd made for him of a white saucer with one of his giant figs occupying most of the plate's surface area. I layered several glazes of increasingly darker violets and umbers atop a yellow orange base. I used soft waxy colored pencils I'd bought at the actual Derwent factory store in a gorgeous deep valley in Keswick, Cumbria, UK, the site of one of the first graphite mines in the early days of wooden pencils. With a blender-pencil of uncolored wax and much patience, a rich glazed surface can be achieved.

The Fig King loved my little drawing. Shortly after returning to the states, I received an airmail letter kindly signed by the whole Athenian painter's gang I'd hung out with. In it, they mentioned that Cosmo kept the drawing prominently displayed on his table at the market. The letter said that he proudly shows the fig-portrait to all customers, proclaiming it to be "Texas Art."

~

Figs are one of nature's candy-gifts. I've been hooked on them since my youngest days at Granny's place. My Granny truly had a green thumb when it came to fruit trees. Her little orchards basically surrounded their gingerbread-style house that looked taller than wide, much resembling a pop-up storybook house. She had three varieties of fig trees, Ozark Premier and Methley plum trees, a peach tree, a Bartlett pear, persimmons, and pomegranates. One fat pomegranate can keep a child busy and out of the house for most of a late fall day after school. My cousins and I used to try and keep count of just how many of the tiny sweet-and-sour red berries each of us was consuming apiece. All of us would usually lose count somewhere beyond a 150 juicy kernels.

~

Life brings you to some interesting and unexpected crossroads now and then. Those moments when you stumble upon unseen developments, possibilities, opportunities, even, that deserve further examination. It happened for us this summer. A weekend conference on soil sustainability came about after many months of advance planning at a big tree farm over near Cleburne. Numerous workshops and lectures were planned on topics as varied as "Erosion Solutions" to "Terraced Gardens" to "Scheduled Mulching."

Leslie, a friend near Joshua, has caught my attention the last year or so with her exploration of earthworm farming for profit. I'd attended a couple of lectures on the topic. Also, as a personal nod of gratitude for the amazing creatures, I usually paint a couple of pictures each year that feature earthworms. So, when Leslie called me to see if I'd be interested in attending the conference as a speaker, I jumped at the chance. I wanted to speak on the historic symbiosis of earthworms and farmers, and how such contortionist-excavators are as necessary below ground as pollinators are above ground. I've been struggling of late to achieve painted expressions of just that notion, without getting too heavy-handed or literal about it in the artwork. Organizing my thoughts and research for the lecture would surely benefit the art project as well.

For several months off and on, discussion at our farm often centered on the topic of earthworms and my upcoming lecture about them. An unexpected contrasting viewpoint was introduced by Liz, who gave us salient details of how disruptive earthworms can be to native forest seedlings.

After several dinner conversations on the subject, Annie offered an idea she'd been hatching.

"I think you should talk to Leslie about expanding your presentation." Leslie was one of the conference organizers and a big fan of Annie's writing. After taking a sip of tea, Annie continued thoughtfully with her proposition.

"I think you and Liz should both talk about earthworms at the conference. I'm sure it would draw a big crowd. Leslie could publicize it as something like *Dad and Daughter Duel*."

Thus, it came to pass that Liz and I were scheduled to speak at the same soil sustainability conference, both of us to talk about earthworms. Annie had taken a break from her latest writing project, so joined us for the weekend adventure. We left the farm in Robin's capable hands. Vern, our farm resident mechanical engineer, was attending a seminar on erosion and water quality at the same conference. Driving straight down from his studio apartment near the UTA campus in Arlington, he would arrive much earlier, so would greet us at the event.

It promised to be a perfect June day for a short Texas road trip of but a hundred and fifty miles or so between Elysia and Cleburne. Only eighty degrees was forecast for the high temp. We left before dawn, but even as we dropped down through Mineral Wells, the day was already sunny, with fluffy cumulus clouds suspended across a dense cobalt blue sky. Monet could have painted that sky, what with his love of modern cobalt blue paint for depicting water below and sky above.

The setting for the conference was bucolic. The various talks and workshops would be held in three huge canopy tents (what the Brits call *marquees*). These were arranged around a shaded area with picnic tables and a serving line for lunch featuring local produce, protein, and artisan pastries. It was a festive gathering of academics, non-profits, merchants, ecologists and farmers.

My lecture was titled "Earthworms, Garden Ventilators," and was scheduled from 11 a.m. until noon. Liz titled hers "Earth's Little

Lumberjacks," scheduled for 1:30 to 2:30 p,m. I noticed that Vern was late getting to mine, taking a seat in the back row of metal folding chairs. After lunch, I saw that he was already sitting right up front for Liz's presentation. Thoughtfully, he saved two seats for me and Annie, who was grinning at me again like the Cheshire Cat.

Both our talks were well attended, with much the same crowd. Annie was correct, and Leslie was pleased, that the *Dad and Daughter Duel* concept was an appealing draw. We each told compelling stories about earthworms, with totally opposite takes on the effective little creatures' impact on the Earth. Liz had the tougher sell. Gardeners love earthworms, and there's something admirable about the level of indefatigable dedication they bring to the task at hand. Harvesting produce for market, however, is just a bit different from harvesting timber for market. My audience was so full of a high level of gratitude for worms that they even oohed and aahed over the several examples of my annual earthworm paintings I showed them.

Liz painted a compelling picture of forest floors badly damaged by earthworms. As she implored the crowd to consider the plight of seedlings trying to survive in an ecological niche deprived of nutrition, I thought some folks were about to start weeping. I guess I would too, were I to be in the lumber business. The photos Liz used to illustrate the plight of trees at the hands of earthworms left no doubts in the minds of the audience that earthworms are not universal blessings. Liz concluded her talk with a forceful summary, a kind of warning, saying earnestly, "The forest floor is the foundational structure, the nursery, if you like, in which native seedlings germinate and grow. Earthworms agitate this fertile seedbed and make forests susceptible to invasion by non-native plant species, which often thrive in such micro-excavated soils."

Take no prisoners, little daughter! It was sheer genius to leave the audience with an image of immature plants in effect being badly harmed by the sheer presence of dastardly earthworms.

Liz asked me to join her up on the small dais to field questions. Annie and Leslie thought the Q & A would be more fun for the crowd if Dad and Daughter answered audience questions together. First question out of the hat, someone asked, "Who won? Dad or daughter?" Taking my hand, Liz grinned her lovely wide grin, still with a good spray of freckles across nose and cheeks. Simultaneously, I said, "She did" while Liz declared, "He did." We laughed at each other.

Seated on the front row facing us were Vern and Annie, laughing too. Annie was so happy she had tears in her beautiful green eyes.

In another, older, section of my brain compartments, I was suddenly taken back to a time when my freckle-faced child was nine years old. She'd won an award for an essay she had written about pollinators and their importance for food production. Like her dad, Liz had spent many days of her childhood in Granny's Hill County garden helping and paying attention to her aging great-grandmother's lessons about how pollen becomes produce via bees and butterflies. Granny was in the audience when Liz read the essay aloud at a national science fair for kids, so short she had to lift her head up by her tiptoes toward the microphone. At some point after, little Liz had taken my hand and was boldly marching us around the event, introducing her proud dad to the judges. In my awakened consciousness, on that simple public platform, somehow time had compressed kid Liz and adult Liz, and two speaking events, years apart, coincided all of it into one intersecting moment of family magic.

~

Though conceptually we're all about "no till" farming for corn, okra, and bush beans (we grow the fancy and tasty French Haricot Vert beans), we do a light tilling. It's more like *turning* the soil, as one would do with a spading fork. Come harvest time, especially with okra and corn, harvesting is a breeze if you've got easily navigated rows to follow on either side of the plant.

My Granny preferred her grandchildren's small hands for harvesting young, tender okra from deep within the many branches of the tall plant. Older grandkids were assigned to the higher branches. In fact, Granny annually used mature okra plants as benchmarks against which she'd measure each grandchild's annual height growth. As okra can grow as high as six to eight feet, there was little chance any of us grandkids would outgrow the plant. When picking okra, even the smallest child soon learns why long-sleeve shirts are mandatory. Picking cucumbers or okra can result in contact dermatitis on uncovered skin. We didn't know the term as children, but we sure knew sleepless nights from okra's itchy residue. The sticky stuff lingers even after a good soapy scrub. Okra is one of the most delicious and unique flavors from the garden, but it will make you pay a price for not wearing armor.

When mature okra is in bloom, it is one of nature's most spectacular floral displays. Okra's huge blossoms are as big as a grandkid's head. The giant petals are so white they look bleached, each with a deep red-violet center. Okra, cotton, and hibiscus are in the same *Malvaceae*, or the mallow family. Ergo, all produce similarly stunning flowers.

Okra is a generous giver. With the exception of making careless harvesters itch, okra's contributions to us humans are humbling. Every part of the okra plant is edible. The buds, leaves, flowers, pods, stems, and seeds are all edible. Granny would assure her helpful grandchildren, nieces, and nephews that okra was one of the original plants in the Garden of Eden.

Okra also has a sense of humor. That is, it likes to play hide and seek. If you only pick the numerous pods so close they poke you in the eye, you're missing lots more. The pods hide all along the length of branches, right up to the tall trunk. You just can't SEE all the pods, so feel along the branch deep into the plant's forest to locate the treasure you can't see inside. (Wear gloves, if you must).

Like kids, okra pods grow fast. Silver Queen and Cowhorn pods commonly reach seven to eight inches in length, but even those varieties are best picked at half that size to insure tenderness.

Any bigger than four to five inches, okra quickly gets tough and woody. Daily reconnoitering and picking are a must. In fact, it's a good idea to check morning and evening to ensure you're taking the pods at three or four inches long. Some that looked too short in the morning will have become plenty long by that evening.

I'm in the future okra patch early this morning, planting okra seeds in orderly rows spaced a bit wider apart than, say, for peppers. This late July planting will provide us with an abundant crop to sell in the fall market. Most Texas palates like batter-and-fried okra throughout the summer months, usually with fried chicken or fried fish. But in the cooler fall and colder winter, even the most dedicated fried food loyalist will cave in and enjoy a hot bowl of gumbo, stew, or soup replete with young, tender okra. In our kitchen, any time of year, Annie will oven-broil okra lightly brushed with olive oil, or I'll grill it over coals outside. Grilled okra pods alongside grilled Pecos cantaloupe wedges is a favorite summer combo at the farm.

We plant two varieties of heirloom okra. The Hill Country Red produces short, flavorful pods that can be fried or stewed whole if gathered young enough. The elegant-looking Stewart Zeebest gives us longer, yet ever-tender pods. Both are Texas heirlooms and, for us, have been consistent producers.

~

Sol and I were watching the sky together this afternoon. *Cirrus uncinus* clouds were streaking across the northern sky like a theater curtain gone awry, the pleats undecided whether to stand vertically or diagonally. It was an odd sight, the mostly eastward leaning striations seeming to rise up from the Red River bed itself, from horizon to horizon. Sol would occasionally look at me quizzically, then back toward the heavenly apparition.

I was idly rubbing his left ear with my right hand, at a relaxed waist-high level. My curled fingers gently stroked the full length of the soft inner side as my thumb glided along the furrier backside. He's very calm in such moments, his little barrel chest leaning against my leg. Then, his apparent state of serenity could be simply a posture, a ruse. He's not against pulling the wool over my eyes with a placid demeanor, trying to hide some tomfoolery he's been up to. I love the little guy, so don't really enjoy scolding him. Sometimes his shenanigans sorely test even my Methodist-instilled patience, but not today. He and I are simpatico at moments like this, standing side by side in awe of nature.

Most of our dramatic weather here in Barnes County attacks us from either due west or due north. DFW and environs are sometimes beneficiaries of a Gulf storm that rages so fast and furious as to spread its rainy fingers far enough across the state right up to the northeast tip, including DFW. We rarely receive the remnants of such magnanimous Gulf moisture this far out west.

But this static sky concoction of directionally confused winds is hard to figure out. That is, it just doesn't seem to be moving horizontally *toward* anyplace, just kind of wiggling in one position, in stasis. Will it decide to accelerate eastward only, blessing Arkansas, as it often does? Or will it grace us with a sudden assault? Was the heavenly show a harbinger of needed rainfall? Or would it wind up a being a tempest in a teacup (to borrow from Cicero), only to dissipate into sheer ether from having worn itself out?

Sol, my four-legged assistant, was helping me walk the fenceline along the south edge of the herb garden from the roadside, of course. Several months ago, neighboring farms experienced considerable damage to their vegetable gardens due to an unruly family of feral hogs. Most of these incidents occurred in bottomland areas usually bordering on a creek or gully. The large herb-garden is on high ground for good drainage, but you can never be too safe. So, we want to make sure there's no gaps or signs of hogs trying to force one. Another thing we'll be looking for is secure latches to keep nosy little donkeys from opening gates and thereby gaining access to territories off-limits to them. Sol feigns interest when I'm examining such hardware, pretending to be my four-legged handy-man helper. But I know he's mentally recording the location of any sprung hinges or worn catches that might be worth a return examination by him later. As I've said before, I'm convinced Sol had a career in espionage in another lifetime.

Sol has always been a fast learner, so he advances quickly through any course of study. Not only is he an accomplished shepherd, but he has become an indispensable wrangler in his own right. Whenever I need help getting a recalcitrant critter loaded up into a trailer or through a gate these days, Sol will load them up for me.

This useful skill of his was revealed quite unexpectedly one day. I suppose it shouldn't have come as such a surprise, owing to the speed at which he cottoned onto herding and corralling sheep. But last year, while coming home from a Wednesday shopping trip to town, I came upon a nice young gelding standing right next to the county road, grazing just as pretty as you please along the fence line about twenty yards from our front gate. He was a small dark umber Appaloosa with perfectly round white dots across his backside, and he was wearing a red halter.

How this handsome little horse had avoided getting run over by a vehicle, I will never know. I parked in our entry drive just far enough to get the truck's rear-end well off the road and told my canine passengers to chill for a bit. As I walked around the bed of the dually, I reached in to pick up a lead rope out of the back. I didn't want to spook him, so I spoke in a lowered kind of assuring tone, as a parent talks to their toddler who's wandered too near the fire pit or top of the stairs.

He jerked his head up as I approached as if to say, "Well, just who the heck do you think you are?" (Some youngsters are just full of themselves). I'd quietly halved the distance between us by now. He could see me clearly. I stopped and stood perfectly still. As I continued comforting the beautiful boy in a soft voice, I reached into the spare horse-ration pocket of my barn coat and drew out a fat heirloom Danvers carrot. These beauties average eight inches in length. As I held the treasure aloft directly in his line of sight, he began to recognize its distinctive shape. He paused, letting the big taproot's image register in his memory, then cautiously came right up to the carrot, took a sniff with those big, gorgeous nostrils, and began chomping, paying no attention to my other hand. Gently, I raised the lead rope and easily clasped it to the halter without a fuss.

Having finished his treat right down into my palm, with little or no tension on the lead rope, I walked beside him to the gate and opened it. I released him and watched until he'd sniffed his way out toward the middle of the front pasture. Then I moved the truck inside, closed the gate behind, and drove up to the barn where I could safely release the Hounds of the Bartletts. The dogs went in all directions for farm adventures, having spent much of the day's journey to town and back napping in the truck. They paid no mind to just another ubiquitous equine, efficiently grazing for grass out in the horse pasture. (As if he had to look for it).

As I prepared to close the rear door, Tommy Cat meowed at me, sitting up tall on his rear haunches at the edge of the seat. He's started doing this lately, hanging back, while the raucous hounds bound out like a sudden break in the dam. I lifted him up, holding his purring body against my ribs with one hand, stroking his chin with the other. I closed the truck door with a shove of my own haunches.

Tommy Cat and I mounted the stairs up to my studio office. I needed to make some calls and take notes to see if I could locate the owner of this awesome and unfamiliar little gelding. Why in blazes such a grand specimen of horseflesh was loose on the busy county road was beyond comprehension. From my second-story studio window, with cellphone in one hand and a cat in the other, I paused to watch the handsome young steed suddenly kick up his heels and simply run for unimpeded joy across the big pasture. I thought, "This fine fellow belongs in Hollywood, or better yet, a classic children's book." Tommy Cat purred in agreement.

~

The solution to the escaped horse quandary didn't take Sherlock Holmes to solve. It turns out that_a neighbor's kid, the Sunday Farmer Family of fireworks fame, had carelessly failed to secure the latch on their little paddock where they were housing the pretty Appaloosa. (Locals call them "The Sunday Farmer Fireworks Family" or just "The Fireworks Family.") The kid went in the house to play a video game. As the unsecured paddock gate slowly fell open of its own weight, the curious horse simply moseyed out of the paddock and strolled down their drive and out onto the county road.

The wife, Brenda is pleasant. She smiles a lot. The husband, Brad, and their teenage son, Brad Junior, are full of themselves. When talking with him, the father lifts his chin as if looking down his nose at you. He seems to be just about my height, five feet, eleven inches, so it seems odd when he takes that posture. Maybe he just likes to flare his nostrils, like the little Appaloosa, out of exuberance (or for emphasis?). Or maybe he's used to speaking from a position of perceived authority.

Dad Brad doesn't have a trailer..."yet," he says, so he has to depend on the kindness of others to move his stock when necessary. Brenda finally returned my voicemail and text about the loose horse. Brad was too busy. She got home to find the paddock gate wide open, the horse gone. That's when she checked her cellphone. She found Junior upstairs, taking a nap in his room with the TV going.

She apologized profusely as if she'd done something wrong. She was upset, and she was embarrassed, mortified, even. I could tell she was wiping her nose and drying her eyes while trying to express thanks for me saving the horse from harm. Besides possible injury to the animal, Brenda had no idea the costly legal problems that arise when a cow or horse is struck by a driver on a county road; legal problems for the animal's owner, that is. I planned to point that out to the family if I got a chance.

On the phone, I tried to be reassuring to Junior's self-effacing mother but would be direct with Brad about the costly family tragedy that had just been avoided simply by sheer luck and coincidental timing. If he'd listen. Without Brenda having to ask, I offered, "If you'll give me a little time, I'll load up your horse and bring him home."

"Thank you. Thank you. Thank you, Mr. Bartlett. I'm so sorry...," she began again.

"It's okay. Nobody got hurt. What's his name, by the way?"

Still rattled, she blubbered, "Who?"

"The runaway," I answered.

"Oh, I am so sorry...of course you mean the pet...gosh...." She paused to gather her thoughts.

"Firewheel, Mr. Bartlett. Brad named him Firewheel. I don't know what it means," she said.

"Indian Blanket," I replied. "It's a wildflower."

"Really? I thought it was a town, or a resort, maybe?" Brenda was calming down. I could hear her breathing more slowly now over the phone.

"I'll text you later when we're on our way. Okay?"

"Yes. Yes, of course. I'll open the pen for you."

I didn't say it, but I figured that paddock gate was still open from earlier in the day, so she needn't bother. I'd suggest a better self-latching catch later, if I got a chance to talk with Brad the Elder, as I doubt he would pay much attention to any advice Brenda might pass on. I looked at the late afternoon sun off to the southwest, hoping to time my horse delivery so that Brad could at least pretend to assist in unloading his own ward, Firewheel. He might even make Junior participate, God willing.

Here's where the tale gets back to Sol, my shortest equine. I hung up the phone, to use a phrase from the previous generation of electrical communication technology. Robin had arrived just in time after school to get started on the farm chores so I could focus on getting Firewheel back home. Of course, Brad (or Junior) was probably thinking of the colorful pyrotechnic "firewheel fountain" as a catchy name for the creature, as the family had set several of those off when they first moved in nearby. Livestock, dogs, and horses for miles around had been disturbed and gone missing. We almost lost Caesar as a result. That's when locals quickly began referring to the new neighbors as simply "The Fireworks Family."

Brenda had offered profuse apologies all around our small corner of Barnes County, but never a peep from husband Brad. I saw no purpose in surmising that the motive of her men for naming the horse Firewheel was an associative reference to fireworks. She would have just felt more miserable about that unfortunate night when they loudly introduced themselves, without warning, to their farming neighbors with a bang, as they say.

I walked out into the pasture to give Firewheel a clear sightline to me. At a distance, he raised his handsome horse head in my direction. I raised a big carrot. As he approached, I could only admire his superb conformation. This youngster is a points-winner for sure, given a chance. We went through the same protocol as out on the county road. He sniffed, big eyelids drooping dreamily, and took a bite as I gently clipped on the lead rope. I schmoozed him in a calm voice as we walked toward the barn together.

Robin had already attached the single horse trailer to the truck, left the door open for me, and gone back in the barn hallway to continue working on the stalls. The rear of the trailer hung low enough for any horse to step easily up inside, no ramp needed. As we approached the open trailer, Firewheel stopped suddenly and proceeded to slowly back up. I slid my hand near the top of the rope, just under his mandible, and said softly "whoa...." stretching out the ending of the word. He stopped, looking cautiously at the gaping open rear end of the trailer. Firewheel was considering that it was darker inside the trailer than outside in the sunlight.

I prayed we weren't headed into a battle of wills, as the young horse outnumbered me by two legs. I was becoming very fond of this four-legged youngster and wanted all our dealings to have positive outcomes for both of us. The old proverb "Patience is its own reward" was truly applicable in this case, as things ensued. I just stood in a relaxed *contrapposto* pose, the weight of my body supported by one leg. I stayed quietly at his side, letting him stare at the trailer, then glance over at me at his leisure, then back to the trailer.

Wise Solomon was in my periphery vision, sizing up our little predicament, apparently cognizant of the little Appaloosa's apprehension. Sol looked up at Firewheel and back at the open trailer. He cocked his head to one side quizzically as he often does, and stepped gingerly up into the trailer, turning around to look at Firewheel from inside. The horse walked ahead and stepped right up into the trailer, leading me in beside him. Sol exited silently, leaving me to attach the lead rope with enough slack for Firewheel to enjoy the alfalfa hay Robin had already placed in the feed bin. The horse chewed contentedly as I stepped down and closed the trailer door, without a hitch, so to speak.

As further pre-loading precaution, I'd stuck an apple in my other barn coat pocket just in case I needed it for the Fireworks Family's runaway. Sol stood before me as tall as he could stretch, little hooves firmly planted in pea gravel, as if waiting for a "thank uou" from his caretaker. I leaned toward his big eyeballs and said, "Good boy, Solomon," while extending the apple to his salivating muzzle. He blinked those alluring long eyelashes of his while relishing the big, sweet Fuji in my palm. Maybe it's just because of Sol's size, but I often find myself talking to him as if he's part of my canine gang.

In my periphery, I saw Robin leaning on a barn scoop shovel. She'd been watching the "load up" of Firewheel into the trailer from her vantage point at the barn entry. Scratching Sol's apple-juice-soaked chin, I looked over at our smiling farmhand.

"Did you see all that?" I asked her.

"Yep. Sol could have helped Moses lead his people out of Egypt!"

Robin turned back into the wide hallway to resume her stall

cleaning duties. I straightened up, knuckles on hips, admiring the little ass as he trotted off to find his pals out in the pasture. Sol is truly a gregarious fellow, charming all four-legged and two-legged critters on the farm.

It was a short ride around to the neighbor's place, Firewheel's home. I passed the old cemetery between our two properties before turning into their road. Lined on both sides of the drive were evenly spaced long-lived hackberries. I liked the orderly planting of such disorderly, often disdained trees. The common hackberry is native to the northern High Plains of Texas. "Trash trees," many urban landscapers call them, discounting the reliably hardy habitat they provide for countless birds, butterflies, bugs, and lizards. These beauties at the Fireworks Family place were planted at the turn of the last century over a hundred years ago.

Approaching the paddock ahead, I could see Brenda standing with her back to the open gate as if holding it still. She needn't worry; the weight pulled the wrong way. Instead of the default position pulling the gate closed, it fell in the other direction. Beside her stood Junior, arms crossed and brooding. His mom had probably forced him to come outside, hopefully to generate some interest in the return of the boy's own assumed ward, Firewheel. I pulled around the centrally located paddock and back onto the drive so the rear of the trailer would face the open gate. I got out of the truck and walked back to shake hands with Brenda and son. From the short trailer's side-window, Firewheel's handsome head watched me pass by, his mouth still chewing the tasty alfalfa hay.

Brenda took my hand in both of hers, thanking me with ebullient gratitude. Her son waited to uncross his arms until I turned to him and held out my hand. I took Junior to be thirteen, fourteen, maybe fifteen, even? It's hard to tell with some boys in those growth-spurt years.

There was a long, slightly awkward pause as we three stood in a little group. After decades of teaching young people, I'd learned to be patiently silent with them in certain circumstances. Junior had been taught to use a firm handshake but released it as soon as he could and put his hands in his jean's pockets. He looked over at his mother. She put her hands on her hips, her forehead and eyebrows glowering at him. Junior finally turned to me and said, "Thank you..."

After a brief pause, the boy added "...Mr. Bartlett."

"You're welcome, Junior." And quickly, to end the uncomfortable moment, I asked, "You want to unload Firewheel and lead him back into the paddock?"

"Sure." said the boy, following just behind me to the rear of the trailer. His mom watched, hands clasped before her. I showed Junior how to open the trailer door and to ease it back around to the receiving catch on the outside wall. We stood together briefly, looking in at Firewheel.

"Okay," I began. "Just untie the lead-rope from the feed bin and walk him out. It's an easy step down for him, and you."

I stood away, beside his mom, hoping there'd be no ensuing fracas with the horse or with the boy. It was an easy exit for both critters. Junior guided Firewheel into the paddock, his mother securing the gate behind boy and horse.

"Why don't you walk around with him a bit, " I suggested. "Horses like to be walked with a lead now and then."

Junior began walking beside, but a little ahead, of Firewheel's ears with too much slack in the lead rope.

"Walk more beside him, between his nose and shoulder," I advised.

The boy adjusted his stance. Leading a horse is a pleasant and confidence-building exercise for any youngster. The human, I mean.

Brenda and I talked, as we watched the two walk around the paddock together. I showed her on my cellphone a better type of latch and catch system for the paddock gate, and suggested she take Junior with her to Pete's feed store in Elysia so he could show her good options.

Brad was working late I guess, so I ventured ahead with some cautionary warnings about possible disasters with loose livestock on public roads. I explained to Brenda that injury to the animal is horrible enough, but injury or death to vehicle passengers due to such a collision could cost her and Brad everything.

"Don't worry, " she said with conviction. "It won't happen again."

Junior came out to say goodbye, closing the paddock gate securely behind him. The three of us chatted awhile about what a great horse they had. I mentioned that usually a couple of times a month, neighbors' kids bring their horses to our big round pen for a day of training and practice together. Robin or Liz and I supervise the teen and equine gathering. Maybe Junior would like to join us?

"How would I get him there?" the boy asked, now interested. Brenda said to me, "We wouldn't want to bother you with that." I could hear silent thoughts in the air about the unlikely possibility that they'd be getting a trailer anytime soon.

"Well, you could just ride Firewheel over."

"Really?" mother and son asked in unison.

"Sure. There's a good path through the cemetery over to our place. You'd come through our back gate and take the road around the gardens and on down to the round pen. No public roads, " I added with a grin.

We chatted some more about what a fine animal they had. I suggested that Firewheel could certainly win some prizes if Junior wanted to train him.

"It would take some time and patience," I offered, addressing the boy.

"If he can take himself away from that video game of his," Brenda replied. Junior lowered his head, embarrassed.

"What's your favorite?" I asked.

"It's an old one," he answered. "Earthworm Jim."

"Oh, I know that one. The hero can stretch and contort himself like an earthworm, right?"

"Yeah. He kills lot of evil beings. He's a good guy."

"Right" I said. "You know, every semester I'd have a couple of students who planned to become game designers. They always kept me informed on the latest."

"What did you teach?" the boy asked.

"Art."

Brenda spoke for her son. "Bradley Junior wants to be an artist."

Brown Turkey Fig

THREE

Deliveries and Drawings

Friday is our delivery day to DFW and downtown McKinney chefs. We start early, having washed, packaged and stacked the heirloom herbs and produce in one of several long commercial coolers late into Thursday night. Our heavy-duty hand trucks convert to upright or flatbed positions easily, so moving the big coolers in and out of restaurant kitchens is readily accomplished, even with just one set of hands. The August and September harvests this year have been bountiful with special items the chefs have been planning for, including dishes that are already on their menus. We have enough seasons under our belt now with the same chefs who know they can count on us. If something looks iffy with a crop, I give them plenty of notice ahead of time for us to discuss substitutions. I've worked very hard over the years to build trust, sending "heads up" announcements of what's been seeded and when items will be available during all four seasons.

I usually do the deliveries alone, but depending on the season's orders, I'll have a companion- assistant join me. Not often, but if she's home, Annie rides shot gun and schmoozes the chefs while I deliver the goods. It never hurts to have a popular, good-looking food author accompany you into restaurant kitchens.

As much as possible, I try to arrange my Friday delivery route in a kind of teardrop-shaped pattern. That is, the most stops should occur along the widest outside curve of the teardrop, with the departure and return trip to the farm along the narrowest phase of the teardrop. This is a trick I learned long ago from printing salesmen who were on the road all day servicing existing clients and recruiting new ones for City Printing Company. I worked there part time, on Dragon Street in Dallas, while I was in college at NTSU. I learned everything about contemporary offset lithography there: four-color printing, layout, half-tone dots, the works...all while I hand-set letter type in a composing stick for letterpress printing, like Ben Franklin's helper, the Devil's advocate, in my college "commercial printing" class. I wouldn't call it "false advertising" exactly, just badly outdated technology in the classroom.

Sometimes life brings you full circle. As a kid, I never imagined the seasonal hard work I contributed to the family farm would ever arrive at an intersection with art. Yet that is where I am today. Growing and selling my own organic, heirloom herbs and produce, discussing taste and appearance of original dishes and recipes made by creative chefs and artisans, all the while brain-storming with them and advising them in their very kitchens, the labs of their own kind of alchemy, was a future life experience I could not have foreseen as a weary, bored kid hoeing tenacious Johnson grass clumps up by the stubborn roots down yet another row of cotton. Swarms of gnats on your eyes, ears mouth and nostrils, seeking the shade of my junior-size straw hat. (See my old notes about the sun, cloud shadows, et al, while working in the crop fields.)

The lowest September temp in Dallas was 36 degrees in 1942. September is definitely cooler this year. Winter always arrives earlier in Oklahoma than Texas, but we're close enough to the Red River for that Ouachita Mountain range fridge to open its door on us here before those counties to the south get hit with chilled air.

This morning I made myself a bowl of oatmeal. I only do that in the winter. This may be the earliest in the year I've ever eaten oatmeal. I tell a lie. Grandma Barnes ate a little bowl of oatmeal every morning, rain or shine, cold day or hot. Plus a stewed prune and a thin lemon wedge squeezed over the prune. Grandma passed away at 102. She played the mandolin for us at her hundredth birthday party, singing "Methodist Pie." That year she fell and broke her hip. Being bedridden so much depressed her to death.

I like my oatmeal very creamy, so I boil the oats in extra water, stirring constantly while it bubbles, as in a witch's cauldron. I often think of Macbeth's witches' phrase "Double, double, toil and trouble..." during any diligent stir of thickening oatmeal. Instead of eye of newt, however, I always add some butter, brown sugar, and a bit of cinnamon into the last couple of stirs before covering the pot and letting it stand several minutes. I like it with a piece of toasted sourdough bread. The tartness and texture of the sourdough toast contrasts nicely with the milky pudding-like quality of the oatmeal.

Many favorite dishes demand constant, vigilant, stirring. Oatmeal is one. Grandma Bartlett, for example, never made "mashed potatoes." She only made labor-intensive "creamed" potatoes, as she called the dish. Paella is another. Roux for seafood gumbo cannot be rushed. Polenta is a poetic thing to watch liquify with religious dedication. I like polenta in any form, fried or grilled in sliced rounds, but especially served as a kind of cornmeal stew, with tiny, diced bits of sauteed sausage and onion stirred into the mélange in the last few rotations. I first had creamed polenta served this way at a little trattoria near Cerveteri, home of the famed Etruscan necropolis, with accessible walk-in tombs.

Etruscan tomb carvings and castings found on sarcophagi and funerary urns at Pompeii and Vulci illustrated early "last supper" themes. The depicted banquets featured the dead person dining with a god or goddess. Etruscan families would enter the tombs to have a feast with their dead ancestors.

My mother's family followed much the same tradition, meeting at the Salem Cemetery in Hill County on the first Saturday of June. Called simply "The Cemetery Gathering," descendants of the founding families of Irene (originally called Salem, to give you an idea of the founders' sense of piety) held an annual reunion to trim up the landscaping, place flags on the graves of soldiers, and to share stories and tables-full of fried chicken, potato salad, green bean casserole, deviled eggs, banana pudding, and dozens of pies.

The late September gardens have been very generous this year. Annie loves eggplant, so we grow different heirloom varieties each year. There's an up-and-coming young chef in Mckinney, a big fan of Annie's publications, who is equally mad for eggplant. This fall, we're growing a plump roundish striped eggplant just for her. *Listada ge gandia* is so pretty it shines like a Christmas tree ball.

The basils are prolific, as if wanting to give us a grand finale before the temps drop to forty and kill it off for this season. Friday we'll be delivering Red Rubin, Purple Ruffle, and lime basil. I convinced a popular mixologist in Fort Worth's southside to try crushing lime basil for her *mojitos.* It's taken off like wildfire, so now she's experimenting with all the basils.

The majestic Pineapple Sage has gotten a second wind, which it always does in the early fall. With the Texas sun and heat, much of the plant has turned woody and lost much of its foliage by late July. But come mid-September, the dense green leaves return, and a new bloom of the deliciously sweet long red flowers will keep chefs happy for at least two more weeks.

Chocolate mint is putting out its most emphatic growth spurt of the season. Leaf-filled vines go in all directions, trailing over all the wooden bed frames. Keep it trimmed back to the bed frame. If it escapes, it will take over your garden. Liz has been practicing Annie's seven-layer chocolate-mint cake recipe for a couple of years, so now Annie has a backup when too many requests are made. Annie purees the chocolate mint into the cake batter itself and of course is generous with it for the icing. It's everybody's favorite fall cake. It's heavenly, served with a hot cup of rich Sulawesi dark roast coffee or with a glass of hefty Shiraz.

~

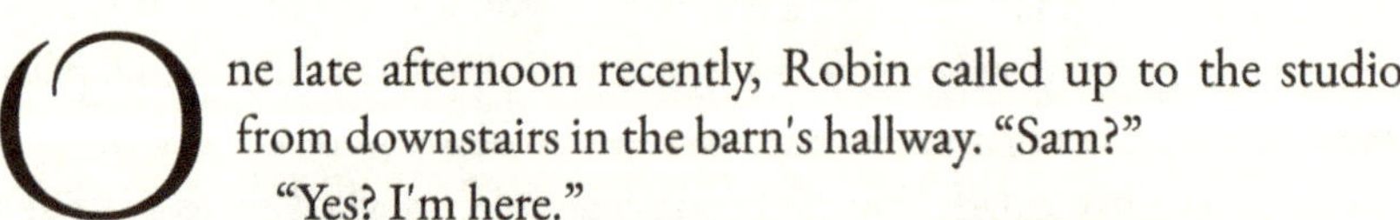

One late afternoon recently, Robin called up to the studio from downstairs in the barn's hallway. "Sam?"

"Yes? I'm here."

"Need to show you something up at the chicken house," our poultry warden said.

I was in the process of laying early contours of the largest shapes for a new landscape composition. The wide canvas was suspended across two big easels, side by side. I dropped the vine charcoal stick I was drawing with into the wide pencil tray and headed downstairs.

"What's Sol been up to now?" I teased. Robin adores Sol. She treats him as if he's simply a misunderstood toddler.

"Sol's been up to nothing. He's a very good boy."

"Okay," I offered, "Let's see what you've found."

To save time, we jumped into the old Rodeo, drove up around the herb gardens to the chicken palaces, and parked in the dirt median between the two big coops. Robin led me around to the back of the west side building and pointed out two excavated holes, one at each corner.

"Dang it," I said. "Please tell me it's not another raccoon."

"No, sir. I think it's either rats or snakes," Robin said, her arms crossed in consternation.

"Yeah. I saw the carcass of that eleven-footer you pulled out last week."

"Full of heritage chicken eggs too. But I recovered most of them uncrushed, Sam."

"Yeah, you did good. Okay, before we fill the holes again, call Pete at the feedstore and tell him we're coming to pick up a few large bags of cedar mulch. We'll mix a bunch of cinnamon and cloves into it. That should run off the snakes for a while."

"What about the hens pecking around that stuff?" Robin wisely asked, knowing cedar's toxic properties for chickens.

"We'll just apply it along the outside of the foundation, here at the back. The hens won't get near it."

Robin made the call while I examined the holes outside more closely and then checked inside to see if there were any interlopers lurking coiled up in a box or stretched out thin along a stud (a favorite hiding trick for snakes).

Down the hill, I stopped at the barn. "You have your sketchbook with you?"

"Of course." Robin answered.

"Get it. You drive, and I'll look at your new sketches."

Robin ran into the barn to retrieve the sketchbook from her book bag in the tack-room. I climbed into the passenger seat. Some time had passed from when my teen farmhand had first bravely asked daughter Liz if she thought the drawings worthy of my attention. Now Robin is eager for every opportunity to get a critique of her work. She is committed and diligently draws something every day, even if only for ten minutes or so.

As I study her new drawings, I sometimes flip back to compare earlier ones in the sketchbook. Robin tries to keep her eyes on the road but often glances over to see which page I'm on.

"Just drive, okay?" I suggest.

Like most of our teen helpers, Robin loves driving the manual floor-shift Rodeo. She loves the cool triangle-shaped front door vent windows that direct fresh air right into the driver's face...and the occasional bug.

Her drawings improve exponentially with each new assignment or critique.

"You drew a lot as a kid, right?"

Robin's response was typical of serious art majors. "It's the earliest thing I remember enjoying to do. Mom called it 'coloring', but I knew it was drawing," she said.

"I love art, but I'm serious about poultry. I want to learn more about geese, ducks, and game birds too," Robin added.

I knew she was thinking about college again, this being the start of her senior year in high school. She hadn't decided yet on Stephen F. Austin in Nacogdoches or A&M in College Station for pursuit of a poultry science degree.

"You can do both in college, Robin."

"How can I do that?'

"Well, you'll be asked to define a 'minor' field of study after a year or so, wherever you wind up. You can minor in art. Or just take a basic drawing and a basic design course, for your electives."

"That's gonna' be a tough sell for Momma." Robin frowned in thought about the prospect of suggesting art as a minor to her folks. Her mom, Gayle, is a no-nonsense achiever, a CPA with her own tax-consulting business. Robin's father is a popular mechanic who bales hay on the side at their nearby small acreage farm. He's a jovial guy who comes over now and then to fish with his daughter in our stocked tank for bluegill and small-mouthed bass. Robin has grown up knowing that her mom will tolerate only As on report cards. Gayle reminds me a lot of my paternal Grandma Bartlett, who was the same way about grades.

"There's no money in art, mom says," continued Robin. "No offense, Sam."

"None taken. Your mom's a smart woman, just looking out for you. She knows statistics and compares averages. But you can be a rich poultry expert and make art too."

Food for thought. As we pulled up in front of the feedstore, Robin put the Rodeo in reverse and turned off the ignition. I handed her the sketchbook.

"Work on your varied line weight some. Just draw a bunch of vertical, horizontal, and curving lines, increasing and decreasing pressure along the same line so it goes from thick to thin and back. A thicker part of the line will appear closer to the viewer, and then farther away as it becomes thinner. " Pause. "Make sense?"

"Yes, sir. Kind of like what Paul Klee said about 'taking a line for a walk,' right?"

"Excellent! Are you sure you're not an art major?"

"Time will tell, I guess.," replied the reflective high school senior, staring straight ahead into her imagined future.

"Okay. Let's scare some snakes and/or rats away from the eggs."

While an after-school helper loaded up the back of the Rodeo with several bags of cedar mulch, we watched Pete scratch his head over an instruction sheet that lay beside a new catch-and-release small mammal trap. To set the trapdoor catch looked like a task requiring three hands. I reached over and held the trigger-fingered trapdoor open so he could focus on the release spring. All the while, Pete gave us his opinion on the proper mix for snake repellent recipe. With enough hands on the job, Pete is a multi-tasker.

Liz was home when we returned to the farm, so she came out to join us in snake defense duties. She drove the little garden tractor, with a ten-cubic-foot dump cart in tow, up to the targeted chicken house. A large container of cloves and another of cinnamon bounced around inside the cart bed. With a spading fork and a hand-shovel, we three pitched in to mix these spices into a cartful of cedar mulch. The resultant concoction filled the air with pleasant aromas that hinted of Christmas, to human olfactory senses only, we hoped.

After filling the recently acquired varmint holes with heavier pea gravel to discourage further excavation, we spread the repellent mix along the edge of the building just beneath the overhang. No rain was forecast for days, so the deterrent should be active for a while, fingers crossed. Liz shook up a cedar oil spray which we applied, soaking all the boards along the outside base of the structure. We waved goodbye to Robin, headed home to her supper, a blazing sunset behind us.

Liz and I gathered the evening's supply of eggs, mostly out from under feathery bottoms of sleepy heritage breed hens. The yellow egg of the sun left a single thin arc of light across the horizon, sliding off the Earth somewhere out near the eerie Monahans sandhills.

Liz drove the eggs and garden tractor back up to the lawn-tool and mower shed behind the house. She'll prepare some comfort food for supper. For my freckle-faced daughter, that usually means grilled cheese on sourdough bread and a couple of the dill pickles we can ourselves. That sounds comforting to me too. Annie has been off on a book-signing tour of southern cities. In the evening, she'd sent us both a photo of herself and Birdie, proprietor of a favorite little seafood cafe just beyond Mobile. In the snapshot, the two fun friends are seated at a small table with a shiny red-and-white checkered tablecloth. grinning back at the camera. Before them is a plate of saltines, the ubiquitous little bottle of red hot sauce, and two bowls of steaming gumbo, heaped with freshly harvested okra, shrimp, and coastal rice. Birdie lovingly stirs possibly the best gumbo roux in existence.

I walked down the hill to put all the four-legged barn residents to bed for the night. They all stood erect, heads and faces staring intently at the closed barn doors. Samson, the grand bay stood above the anxious throng, his devoted little pal Sol beside him. Douglas, the rescued sway-back, totally chill and contented now that he's found his tribe. Dolly the mare, fat in foal, is wondering if her girth will clear the stall door when she gets inside. The dogs are alternately weaving around like streams of water or suddenly plopped down on haunches to raise a paw up to scratch an itchy ear. I make my way to the front of the hungry horde and barely get one door slid open fully when the dam breaks and the river of critters jostle each other in mass, flooding the hall of the barn.

I stand aside, my toes curled up tight in my boots, praying my feet don't get crushed. All the horses and one short donkey rush into their stalls, heads immediately plunged into buckets of alfalfa cubes and oats. The dogs and one cat "sit" upon command before each individual's bowl, obediently waiting for me to pour out the rations. No bedlam is allowed at feeding time. They wait in turn, sitting with tails occasionally sweeping the floor behind them. It's a civil canine community here at Bartlett Farm.

Walking back up to the house, I pass the old pecan trees in the front pasture, silhouetted giants against the darkening night sky. It won't be long, and we'll be gathering pecans from beneath these majestic beings for stuffing Christmas stockings and for baking seasonal aromatic pecan pies. José Cantú's mother makes her pecan pies with Mexican coffee liqueur. She has José bring us one the day before Thanksgiving every year. I am very thankful for that pie.

A chorus of frogs and crickets accompanies me on these late evening walks from barn to house.

The screened-in back-porch is illuminated by three windows casting rectangles of light from inside the kitchen out over the top of a rescued rattan sofa on the porch. From the backyard's winding flagstone path, I can see Liz at the stove, spatula poised in one hand, reading an open book in the other. Liz and Annie are multi-taskers, as they often remind me.

My art colleague, Suzie, recently brought her drawing students, sophomores mostly, for their fall semester landscape drawing trip to the farm. It was a smaller group than usual, about a dozen. All of them fit in one long passenger van, with a 5-by-8-foot open trailer behind, stacked high with donkeys (wooden drawing benches) secured with multiple bungee cords across a blue tarp cover.

I waited for the art gang about halfway up the road to the herb gardens, as Suzie and I had agreed that we would arrange the students under the old pecan trees. Our landscape view would be the front horse pasture with the oak-rail round pen in the middle ground, and the cedar-board barn in the background, just beyond the curve of our farm road. They climbed off the van, some instantly pitching in to unload the donkeys from the attached trailer, others watching the process, but not sure how to help. A few just stood in the pea-gravel road, staring gape-mouthed in all directions, trying to take in a landscape devoid of tall urban buildings or trappings.

With only a dozen or so art students to wrangle, Suzie decided to keep the group in one human herd. We'd all draw together, with roughly the same view ahead. As a number of her students have kept requesting, we spend some time drawing animals, in addition to landscape. I suggested to Suzie that we do both. That is, we'd draw a landscape view, with one or more animals somewhere in that view—middle ground, for sure, and foreground for the brave artists in the group. Drawing live animals is pretty much like drawing the human figure in that you get better at it with repetition over time. Grazing farm animals move pretty slowly, certainly slow enough to record some good gesture lines for volume and contour lines for shape. With beginning students, the urge is often to go straight for surface details, and that always ends poorly, proportion-wise. The best procedure is to draw basic shapes first, details last.

Suzie asked for their attention, introduced me, and instructed the class on the day's protocol and purpose. Sol stood beside me, sizing up the young crowd, no doubt waiting to hear Suzie say his name. Finally, his patience almost gone, he heard her introduce my little four-footed companion and explained that though he may be grazing for grass in and around the students' wooden "donkeys" (and occasionally looking at their drawings with inscrutable interest), Sol posed no threat and had never in her experience harmed a student. I noticed several students draw apples from pockets, positioning them nearby on the ready to appease the little wild beast should he draw close to them.

Drawing outside in nature can be of great assistance toward helping students get in touch with their ancestral selves, even their primordial selves, when humans were prey as well as hunters. It's humbling, and a bit scary, to draw outside in nature, sharing the space with unpredictable bugs, birds, reptiles, wild mammals, weather, and this time of year occasional falling pecans. Such moments charge a young artist's creativity with an unusual tension, apprehension, and a distinct focus not experienced inside the studio. A survival memory kicks in, eyes open wide, and students become intensely acute observers of nature as subject. This newly revived primitive awareness becomes even sharper as a nearby pack of coyotes howls loudly in the midst of a kill. It induces a "moment of mindfulness," for sure.

Suzie, the digital savvy art teacher, advises the students to keep their 4-by-5-inch laminated card printed with the six time-proven principles of *atmospheric perspective*. These include choosing a view "with overlapping forms" (the barn positioned behind the round pen) and noting that "parallel lines converge in the distance," as in the sides of our curving farm road seeming to narrow toward each other as the road falls away into the distance. Students who forgot their instruction cards take photos of their neighbors' cards with their phones. Art students sink or swim together. Most all of them remember to bring their portable "viewfinder" (a cut mat with a 5-by-7-inch opening). The viewfinder allows the student to "frame" a landscape into observable compositions, searching for just the right combination of shapes and lines to maximize the illusion of depth with a convincing sense of foreground, middle ground, and background.

Discovering and cropping an appropriate view for oneself is a crucial part of the individual "owning" the scene, owning the drawing. The choice of view sets the artist in the right direction, clarifies the subject, and becomes the blueprint for all the following lines and blended values (lights and darks) that will mimic nature's poetic *instress* and *inscape.*

Observing one student's rendering, deciding which two or three things for him to work on, I glanced up to see Robin's Dad's old pickup driving up the road. She parked the truck near the school van behind us so as not to block our landscape view. I was happy to see her walking toward us, her 18-by-24-inch drawing board and pad under one arm, and her toolkit of pencils and charcoal in the other. She was excited and grinned ear to ear. This was to be a big day for her, getting to practice drawing surrounded by genuine college art majors. I could tell that she was "over the moon" about it.

She scanned admiringly the serious art students astride their donkeys, drawing away with purpose.

"So, you got pardoned enough to join us today, huh?" I asked.

"Yes, sir. The warden let me forego classes today, so I can draw a landscape. Can you believe it?"

Robin's high school principal is a caring person; she just doesn't care about art.

Robin looked around till she spotted Suzie, who was seated at a student's donkey-bench, suggesting some adjustments to be made. She looked up at Robin and pointed with emphasis at the sole empty donkey among the remuda. Taped to the vertical board of the bench was a sign drawn in heavy felt tip marker. It read "Reserved for Robin." Suzie looked over at me and winked. I nodded back, approving her thoughtful gesture for my teen farmhand.

~

Sol had grown bored with greeting all the young visitors and critiquing their drawings by tilting his classical donkey head this way and that. He'd moseyed along to a position between the assembled artists and the round pen, grazing on rye grass. Occasionally, he raised his long head to look back at the artist crowd. Maybe he was deciding that the young artists needed a handsome equine such as his grand self to enhance their pictures. Several students recalled Suzie's morning instructions, including her advice that they use their cellphone cameras to record any animal that might wander into their view momentarily. The image could be useful to add to the drawing later, to add interest to the subject, and to enhance the illusion of depth.

A master of rearranging scenery in the wild was the brilliant American landscape painter Thomas Moran, whose work is well represented at the Gilcrease Museum in Tulsa and the Amon Carter Museum of American Art in Fort Worth. Like an accomplished stage designer, Moran understood that sometimes props needed to be added or subtracted from a particular view to improve the narrative depicted.

Prolific photographer and friend William Henry Jackson accompanied Moran to record visual characteristics of particular views or particular objects that the painter could employ later in the studio. Unusual stone outcroppings or tortuously twisted limbs of a Sassafras tree could easily be transferred from photo or sketches into, say, the foreground of a painted view that had no such natural thing *in situ* at the location named.

Moran's paintings sold the American public on Teddy Roosevelt's mission to create Yellowstone National Park. Huge colorful prints and posters were made of the paintings that were distributed and paraded through the halls of Congress and public buildings around the country. It was perhaps Teddy Roosevelt's most successful military campaign. Moran's ability to capture the spectacular colors of the light and the sheer breathtaking grandeur of the mountains, valleys, sky, and waters of the American West inspired travelers and tourists to venture west to encounter nature's majesty in person, to stand in awe of the landscapes that poets, writers, and adventurers were singing about and swooning over.

The Transcendentalists, Roosevelt included, had found their illustrator, the artist who could depict nature's magical atmosphere, a moment in time found nowhere else than Yellowstone. There was a social conscience emerging, even before "global warming" was known about, before "species extinction" was considered probable, like a clarion call for a newly discovered public cause, the preservation of natural beauty.

It was nearing lunchtime. The sun's glow was softened by fluffy clouds moving slowly toward the southeast. Students pulled jacket collars higher over their exposed necks. Some had wisely brought scarves, as the afternoon chill rolling down over the Panhandle was arriving a bit early.

The cinematic qualities of the clouds in motion over our barn reminded me of Guercino's 1622 *tour de force* ceiling painting of Aurora, the Goddess of Dawn, in the entrance hall of the Casino Ludovisi in Rome. In the jaw-dropping scene, Aurora soars across the bright sky, her chariot buoyed by such translucent fluffs of moisture, first revealing bits of sunlight, then obscuring the same. Guercino, incidentally, was a nickname, meaning "one who squints," a perfect moniker for an artist.

Aurora's chariot is pulled by two big draft horses, Clydesdales probably, though their breed was not revealed in the classic account or by Guercino's notes for his famous fresco. The ancient writers did name the equines, however—Lampus and Phaethon—so that gives us a starting point on bloodline pedigree. Needless to say, Guercino would not have likely chosen Douglas, our resident swayback, to pull Aurora's golden hackney. But he's a noble steed to us.

Douglas had joined Sol in the students' viewfinders, prompting lots of discussion amongst the young artists, comparing the two distinctly different grazing equines before them. Samson was out of view on the north side of the pasture with Dolly, who's in foal. Otherwise, the students would be delighted at the sight of our little donkey grazing quietly beneath gentle Samson's tall chest. He's kind of like Sol's own portable parasol on hotter, sunnier days.

It was time for some human grazing, as well. I asked Robin to lead Douglas and Sol over into the round pen, lest the two of them decided to try and make drawings themselves, all the while without opposable thumbs. They could have knocked over lots of empty wooden donkeys like falling dominoes, given the chance. A couple of the college boys rose to help pretty Robin achieve the difficult task of leading the two equines to a hay bale inside the round pen.

Annie was home from her two-week book signing tour through the South. In our case, absence truly does make the heart grow fonder. I can join her on some of her junkets for a couple of days here and there, but it's difficult to arrange temporary farm caretakers for extended periods. Besides, more and more, Annie enjoys being home for long enough stretches to get back into the rhythm of the farm.

When scheduling their field trip, Suzie was thrilled that we offered to make lunch for her art students. Our respective calendars all lined up for once. Early the morning of their visit, we set up two of our long market tables, end to end, covered with Annie's grandmother's faded print tablecloths and a couple of vases full of colorful zinnias. We'd have our meal on the flagstone-paved back patio on the south side of the house, out of the wind. Besides, the sun had come out from under Guercino clouds, so the air was warmed around us.

Robin and I left our drawing spots a little early so we could help Annie back at the kitchen. The drawing students stayed behind, having a critique of their morning's work with Professor Suzie.

It's amazing how instructive it is for individual students to see their own landscape drawing surrounded by many other landscapes, all depicting more or less the same view. Comparing effective use (or not) of directional lines, blended values, or proportion of objects, becomes glaringly evident when seen *en masse*.

For lunch, Annie roasted portobello mushrooms, Nantes carrots, fingerling potatoes, Red Burgundy onion halves, and whole striped Russian Red garlic cloves. Her garden *mélange* is swathed in olive oil before roasting and drizzled with aged fig-flavored balsamic vinegar just before serving. A giant salad bowl of leafy lettuce and greens cushioned rainbow-colored cherry tomatoes stood by, looking like an opulent eighteenth-century Rachel Ruysch still life painting.

Grilled smoked sausages from the butchers at Greer's Grocery were in a long pan on the stove, and a basket of warm Vienna rolls from the Ronning's Bakery filled the kitchen with yeasty aroma.

It was fun to see a line of art students up and down the back steps, making their way to the countertop serving station in the kitchen. Plates, cloth napkins, and utensils greeted the diners, along with a large empty pickle jar for donations to Elysia's small but needed food pantry. At Suzie's suggestion, Annie had taped an 8-by-10 photo on the big jar, showing local high school student volunteers working at the pantry. Our visiting college art students were very generous. One of the students noticed that Robin was in the photo, sorting bags of lemons into carts.

As students filed out to the patio in ones and twos, the seats slowly filled. I attended and advised the growing crowd to dig in while their plates were warm. After all were seated, Suzie rose to say kind words about us and Bartlett Farm. She included Robin as part of the family, introducing her as our resident poultry expert. I could tell she was having the time of her life hanging out with this college crowd.

Lively chatter ensued. Suzie's "pets" listened attentively to whatever she wanted to say. Several students near Annie knew she was an author and asked her practical questions about the writing process. Those at my table variously asked about the animals and about my studio. I assured them that Suzie had allowed time for those interested to visit upstairs.

Robin got up and took a small entourage off to see the chickens. They'd never seen so many different types and colors of hens before. I'm sure they got more than they bargained for, poultry knowledge-wise.

Soon, the class was headed back down the hill to work on the second half of their landscape assignment. They'd be practicing added and subtracted marks with soft compressed charcoal applied broadside and a liberal use of pink pearl erasers to pull out highlights, plus further defining edges and textures. Annie and I followed the throng last, hand in hand.

"Nice kids." she said, leaning her head against my shoulder as we walked toward the pecan grove. "How's Robin doing?"

"Progressing nicely. We've done a couple of sessions together, so she's been able to watch me closely, drawing side by side. She's certainly held her own with this group of art majors today."

Annie looked at me as if I hadn't heard a word she was saying. Squeezing my hand tightly, she added, "I meant how's *Robin* doing? Is Gayle softening to the idea she may have an 'artist' daughter on her hands?"

"That's a tough one," I answered. "I think Robin's decided to lay low regarding the prospects of claiming art as a minor once she gets to college. It sounds like her mom has said 'no' to that idea. My hunch is that Robin will feel more comfortable making a choice once her feet are on campus, away from home."

Robin had confided in Liz and Annie some time ago that her mom saw little purpose in doing art other than it being a harmless hobby. The main counselor and the principal at the high school agreed with Gayle, touting the same message that math and science rule the world.

In their minds, art was for kids who don't do well with either. Since Robin was great at both, it made sense for her to pursue an ag degree at A&M, with a minor in math or physics. It's a bit of a tightrope for us, meaning me and Annie. For that matter, Robin's adoring dad is on the same tightrope with us, as he just wants her to follow her own dreams...and go fishing with him now and then. She will excel at being a poultry science major and can make As in art at the same time. But we aren't her mom.

Annie watched the class of earnest students draw for a while, then motioned to me she was headed back up to the house. I followed Suzie's lead as to which students needed comments next.

One student achieved gorgeous, blended surfaces applied in accurate directional strokes that conveyed volume but was less diligent in rendering precise contours that mimicked the organic turns and twists of tree limbs that hung down into the foreground. On another student's work, I took the pink pearl eraser and wiggled the angled edge of it back and forth while dragging it downward through heavily layered soft charcoal that represented a tree's trunk.

"Wow," he said. "That's beautiful, man."

"Well, it's a fairly effective way to suggest tree bark, at least."

"Yeah. I get it. Thanks, man," the student replied, then returned to his drawing. He proceeded to use my wiggling technique with the eraser on every tree trunk in view, even on the smaller ones in the far background. I said nothing, knowing that during Suzie's final critique, he would soon realize how flat and pattern-like his drawing looks compared to other students' examples. Because he used the same marks on the trunks of all the trees, his drawing lost any sense of depth. He left the viewer with light/dark marks across the format's surface that are all the same size, as in a wall-paper pattern. At day's end, I'd advise him and all the students not to go home and make adjustments or corrections on today's finished drawing. Keep it as a recorded lesson, as a student in golf would keep a coach's video of their swing. We can't learn from a drawing we've erased or covered over or discarded. We can't improve if we're unwilling to keep an ugly drawing for comparison with a later, improved one.

Suzie's late afternoon critique was masterful. I'm very proud of her, having watched her get better and better about staying on purpose, about honing the craft of drawing herself and honing the craft of teaching others how to do it. I was smart to hire her right out of grad school years ago. Drawing is her forte. Her students benefit from her soft-spoken manner too. That is, Suzie doesn't have to do all the talking.

A good teacher asks good questions that elicit responses from the student that reveal exactly what the student best understands about a concept or technique, or not. I'm very proud of Robin too. Our farmhand held her own, performing well while surrounded by seasoned college art students. I'm sure she has a visual edge over the others, drawing scenes here at the farm where she works every day. She knows the lay of the land here pretty well.

Araucana Rooster

FOUR

Equine Lordosis and a Moonlit Hayride

Our young vet, Russell, now comes out to the farm regularly, completing the livestock checkups his dad used to do. John works almost entirely now out of the old office in Elysia. He examines more papers than he does horses these days. Russell, famous in these parts for his longtime habit of rescuing injured wild things, loves to come out here to be around large stock. Perhaps because we rescued Douglas, the neglected swayback, Russell's taken a particular interest in him. I think he may be studying the horse for a paper on Equine Lordosis, excessive curvature of the back.

I've learned a lot about lordosis from young Doc Russell—"Doc," as all the teen farmhands call him. He's been fascinated about genetic traits in species ever since high school. Russell calls equine lordosis a "social disease" in that society tends to find the look of a swayback horse objectionable. In fact, almost all horses with lordosis live out their lives successfully carrying riders on their backs or pulling passengers in carts. Douglas is an old hand at plowing, for example.

In one of his first farm visits as Elysia's new official "large animal" vet, Russell spent a long time studying our swayback rescue horse. As if attending a medical classroom lecture, Doc and Douglas had gathered quite an audience around the stall. Annie and Liz were having morning coffee on the patio up at the house when they saw the vet's truck pull through the front gate. Liz called Robin on the cell, inviting her to take a pause in her poultry protocol at the chicken coop and join the crowd. The women walked down the road to the barn together, arm in arm, laughing like The Three Musketeers.

I shouted an invitation up to José, who was working on installing some new gallery light fixtures in the studio above. So, the five of us were lined up along the front of the stall, elbows resting on the top rail. Make that six of us; Sol was alternately squeezing in between this one and that one of us to get bonus scratches on his head or withers. Sol liked Douglas but always seemed disappointed he couldn't walk under the swayback's low-hanging belly, as he so easily does with tall Samson.

After a thorough checkup and treatment, Doc slowly dragged an oblong stiff bristle brush down the full arc of Douglas' curving back, from withers to rump. The motion reminded me of a skier gliding down a steep ramp. The horse had been facing his audience, but Doc turned him so we had a full side-view.

"Questions?" Doc asked. He was delighted to share some insight about Douglas's condition.

Robin, our resident teen ornithologist, jumped in first. "What is it? What happened to him?"

"Probably his parents," Doc began." "*Equine Lordosis*, or swayback, is caused by a failure of the ligament support structures all along the length of the back. The gene that leads to the odd-looking condition is recessive. So, for it to occur, both parents must pass on the gene to allow the trait to make an appearance."

Liz asked, "Is it always genetic, or can environment play a role?" She was thinking of trees, I bet.

"Mostly genetics, Liz. But I understand it can be caused by other factors sometimes. Like riding a young horse too young too much before its back muscles have developed. But just as in humans, sometimes it develops from old age. Older broodmares can develop lordosis just from too much foaling, for example."

"So is Douglas' swayback genetic, or is he just very old?" Liz pressed on.

"If the gene has been passed on, the trait can show up early, even in a very young horse." Doc rubbed our rescued equine's lower neck while studying the full length of his curved, sunken back.

"Does it hurt him? Is he in pain with it?" I asked.

"Horses can live a long time with lordosis and the condition isn't normally painful. And Sam, I don't think Douglas is as old as you've been thinking. Other than the swayback, maybe his overall appearance was just environmental, just the result of several years' worth of neglect."

"Gosh," Robin blurted, seeing Douglas in a new light. "Poor thing...how old do you think?"

"My best guess is nine or ten, only. He has lots of years left now that he's here." Standing back, admiring Douglas, the Doc added, "I mean, look at him. He's a very healthy horse with a funny-looking back, that's all."

"He cleans up real well too," José said, with an appreciative grin toward Douglas.

~

Younger vet Russell comes out once a month to participate in our monthly neighborhood horse training day. Several local horse owners, mostly youngsters, bring their mounts out to take advantage of the oversized round pen at our place. A couple of our teen farmhands, and even daughter Liz when still an undergrad, were interested in driving—that is, driving a horse pulling a cart or buggy. Anticipating continued interest in the sport, I built the round pen large enough to accommodate two carts driving at the same time, one near the rail, on the outer circle, and one on the inner circle. An old-timer told me it would be good training for the youngsters to drive their respective steeds past each other now and then.

As things turned out, carts and harness equipment were out of reach for most of our teen farmhands and their folks, so the use of the round pen has been pretty much buggy-less over the years. But the size of the pen has allowed us to do fun things with multiple riders at once. It's not as big as the Dickies Arena in Fort Worth, but it's big enough to keep several horses and riders active simultaneously and perform maneuvers together.

Russell showed up one day with some dated harness rig and reins gear and an old surcingle that fit Douglas perfectly. He said that someone had left the tack as partial payment for services rendered by his dad many years ago, and he figured that Douglas would get more use out of it rather than just hanging on a peg in his dad's barn. The swayback and the junior vet have become great pals. I still wonder if Russell isn't doing some lordosis research, with Douglas as his primary lab subject. Robin and I helped Russell get old Doug hooked up, pulling the long reins back through the surcingle. The gray speckled rescue horse, as his former owner assured me, had done a good bit of plowing with a single blade back in the day, so was very familiar with a human walking behind him, giving instructions with clicking tongue and single word commands.

The first day we tried out the rig, Robin and Russell were having so much fun driving him cartless around the pen, and back and forth, that finally Douglas looked over at me during a halt-pause with an entreating expression, as if to say, "I think that's enough for today, Boss."

Now on "training day," we'll have horses on routine maneuvers inside and outside the big round pen, along with folks of all sizes and ages guiding the reins, pretending to plow a row or drive a cart in the pasture, walking happily behind patient, reliable Douglas.

We are also now joined once a month with the neighbor's boy. That's right "Brad, the Brat" as the other teens sometime call him, of the infamous Fireworks Family. As I first invited him to do, he rides his handsome Appaloosa, Firewheel, over, taking the cemetery path through to our side gate_I gave him the lock combination—and then down our road to the front pasture and round pen.

The first couple of visits, Brad rode Firewheel bareback, which was fine, but some of the training for his horse required a saddle. I talked with Pete at the feedstore, and he came up with a well-used small saddle ideal for the young man and young gelding. Brad paid for the saddle by working at the store after school for a few weeks. His mom was ecstatic. Brad walked over to the store after his last class, and his mom Brenda picked him up after work.

At the end of one day's training session, as Brad and Firewheel rode up past the pecan trees, Brad turned and waved an unusually friendly goodbye. Robin stood beside me. We waved back.

"Sam..." she began "...that boy draws all the time."

"Really?" I asked. "I seem to recall his mom said he liked art."

"More than that. He is religious about it. Makes up his own comic book characters. They're good too. I've seen them."

"And?" I waited.

"He's reluctant to show you. He says they're just comics, 'not serious.' I think he wants to learn to draw like we draw, landscapes and such, from life."

What am I, an ogre? Hearing Robin tell me about Brad's drawings is *deja vu,* like when Liz first told me about Robin's shyness about showing me her own drawings. Am I that unapproachable?

I must be getting cranky or something in my old age...or at least giving off that vibe to youngsters?

"Okay. What's your suggestion? Since he's hesitant to show me his comic book drawings. Which, incidentally, are not serious, by nature."

"Sure," Robin agreed. "But he's a kid."

"Out of the mouths of babes," I thought silently.

Robin said that if I was okay with it, she'd invite him to join us for her next private drawing lesson. It was to be a review of "atmospheric perspective" principles anyway, which she thought he could handle, and would be a good starting point for him to jump in. It would certainly be a challenge for him to learn about the concept and process of transferring 3-D space to a 2-D space. It would be good experience for him to sketch the same landscape view along with us. And he won't have to ask his dad for money since we have all the supplies to get him started. Robin's got a good heart to care about Brad the Brat.

I walked back up the hill toward the house. Robin would finish getting rations laid out for the horses in the barn stalls. I told her to get on home after that. I'd let the four-legged gang in just after sundown and fill the dog food bowls then. That's one way to make sure that Nike the hound will stay in the barn long enough for me to close her in, preventing a night of howling and prowling through the woods. She'll "sit" like the other canines to wait for her supper.

Near the rear entry gate of the patio, I lifted and tied up the bin bags from 55-gallon barrels marked "Trash" and "Recycle," while Annie finished up with the pots and pans. I walked into the kitchen just as she approached the door, egg baskets in arms.

She held the baskets aloft, with her generous smile aimed at me, while asking, "Help me gather eggs?" My answer was a kiss. As we stepped off the porch into an evening sprayed in orange, pinks, yellows, and reds from another grand sunset over Elysia, our walk-and-talk continued.

"I saw Robin's truck down at the barn, so I assumed she would leave for home after that. The chickens will just have to do without their favorite female for one night."

I took a basket from her. Annie took my arm with her free hand as we walked out to the chicken palaces together.

"Robin's drawing was as good as any of those college kids," she observed.

"Yes. She's really getting the hang of subtractive drawing with soft charcoal. She's not afraid of applying too much value anymore. Robin's lucky to have a great teacher like Suzie invite her to join the class."

"Hmm," Annie said, squeezing my arm. "Suzie had a great teacher too, Sam."

We split up, each taking one of the big coops in hand. As Annie turned to secure the chicken yard gate behind her, she reached into her barn coat pocket and pulled out a small bike headlamp. Adjusting the straps to aim the lamp straight ahead, she looked up to notice I was watching the procedure.

She blushed a bit, turning on the lamp to shine it on me, standing at the other chicken-yard gate. It wasn't dark outside yet, but it would be dark in the coop. And there's always the chance a long snake is already inside, shopping for eggs. They're not venomous, just big, and twice as scary in the dark.

"Don't tease me, Sammy. I can't help it if I'm 'chicken' where snakes are concerned."

We both laughed. "You look more like a coalminer than a chicken," I replied.

The soothing sounds of hens clucking softly in the evening in preparation for bed should be an option on those "white noise" machines folks are using these days. Before climbing up to individual favorite roosting spots, jostling siblings for position, each hen will eat a last bit of grain, drink some water, and turn in. As the nights turn colder, they'll press closer together on the roost, then finally wind up huddled in twos and threes inside each nesting box. Heating lamps help on frigid nights, but it's concentrated heat, very localized.

We parted at the patio gate. Annie would take the eggs in, wash them, place in cartons, and then stack the cartons in the egg cooler out on the back porch. I headed down to my four-legged assembly, a couple of horse heads pressed directly against the barn door planks, waiting impatiently. Maybe they were trying get the doors to open telepathically, using equine ESP. Horses have a strong will, when they put their minds to it. In Sol's case, his data input always goes first to a fat mental file in his head labeled "Nefarious Schemes."

As I squeezed past him to open the barn doors, I gave Sol's withers a good scratch, right at the intersection of the dark cross-mark, or dorsal stripe, across his back. He brayed loudly, in gratitude for the gesture.

When I first got Solomon, he was delivered to the farm in an odd-looking long trailer with a very low roof designed for carrying miniature animals of all sorts to petting zoos and the like. The cute little guy stepped off the low trailer and looked around the place like he owned it. Sol shed no tears as the old trailer, now empty of passengers, rattled its way back out to the county road.

He looked like an explorer, ready for adventure. He stepped lively toward the barn. I guess I was already charmed by the little fellow and was following him too close for comfort. He threw back one of those skinny hind legs kicking me in the knee with a little hoof that felt like a metal arrow-point. I'm sure he heard me fall to my knees, one a badly wounded knee, by the way. He never looked back but just stood his ground, staring straight ahead with his rear-end facing me. His jackrabbit-like long ears twitched back and forth like radar, listening acutely to my moaning. I guess he was waiting to see if I'd learned my lesson. I had done that for sure. For a full week, my right knee sported a goose-egg the size of an ancient Athenian Smyrna fig.

~

For months, Annie and Liz pestered me to do a hayride at the farm this year. Robin joined in as an enthusiastic member of the women's hayride trio, so the event was put on the calendar long ahead. We pulled the eighteen-foot flatbed trailer full of guests around the farm with the Kubota. Vern made us some rails to support hay bales around the edges for about twenty folks to sit on, while still having room to stretch their legs forward. He offered to help if we'd do it on a Saturday, so we accommodated. I'm sure his doting mom washed and folded a week's worth of laundry that weekend so that he could head back to grad school in Arlington on Sunday like a new man.

We scheduled the hayride for the third week in October, on a Saturday with a full moon and no rain expected. Octobers can be tricky for outdoor events. Historically, in Barnes County, October and May are our rainiest months. But this year Mother Nature blessed us with a star-filled sky and a giant round moon. Out in the pasture, you could almost read a book that night just by moonlight lumens.

The party started just after sundown. Horses, donkey, and dogs were in stalls having supper. It was a pleasantly cool night, so the occasional equine head would project over the stall's windowsill, observing briefly the comings and goings of human actions outside, but otherwise disinterested. My pair of shepherd guardians, Caesar and Sol, had earlier brought the flock up into the sheepfold near the barn. It was kind of an English *folly*, reminiscent of stone sheepfolds I'd seen in the Peaks District of Derbyshire when I taught there. We built the round structure with a solid wooden gate to be just over six feet high. Though open to the sky, the thick stone wall discouraged coyotes and provided a cozy enclosure for our ovine residents.

Everyone parked along the curving edge of the horse pasture, directed by Robin and Brad the Brat, who was helping out. His mom, Brenda, came also, lending a hand to Liz and Annie up in the kitchen. The friendly crowd included a number of folks who'd never been to the farm and got to know each other as they introduced themselves and chatted their way up to the house. They enjoyed bowls of veggie stew or chili at tables set up on the patio. A string of lights on the patio's perimeter looked cheerful, but the moon provided plenty of visibility anyway.

Annie makes a delicious veggie stew, a *posole verde* dish, really, with roasted poblanos and tomatillos joining the requisite hominy and some shredded cabbage, topped with lime and avocado slices. Handfulls of chopped lime basil are added to the pot liquor. Small bowls of cilantro are offered on the side for purists. Everything for the evening's warm feast came from our gardens, of course, except for the rich avocados from Michoacan and the stone-ground nixtamal, which is partially cooked corn that has been soaked in lime.

After the crowd fortified themselves with fall victuals and libations, the "all aboard" was announced, and the hayride passengers made their way from the patio out to the waiting wagon. Liz and Robin had draped orange, yellow, and black bunting around all the side-rails of the trailer, adding a seasonal touch. Soon the cheerful crowd began loading onto the farm transport. Individual camp blankets were stacked in a pile at the rear of the trailer for any riders who hadn't bundled up enough. Hayrides always encourage hugs and cuddles, if only for shared body heat.

The trusty weather-worn and dented Kubota purred gently in idle, all twenty-eight old horses waiting for my command to sally forth into the night. With a gentle jerk forward, a communal yelp of surprise came from seated bodies suddenly pressed together by the sheer g-force of the powerful little orange tractor. The group looked a bit like falling dominoes for a second. Everybody had a good laugh and settled in for the night ride.

Looking over my shoulder, I scanned the close-quartered revelers to make sure all were seated. I admonished them to "keep hands and arms and legs inside the wagon at all times, please."

More shared jovial laughter ensued, and our company's autumn campaign began. As I turned my head forward toward the road passing slowly beneath our long carriage, an unexpected image passed across my inner eye. In my brief security scan of the passengers, had I seen, out of the corner of my eye, Vern and Liz leaning into each other at the back of the trailer, holding hands?

"Just a mirage." I told myself. Sometimes our view is skewed. Sometimes nature plays with our visual capabilities. Like the rippling heat-waves rising to the sun off a late summer's tilled field in Hill County, or an early morning Beaumont fog, slowly undulating a translucent gauze that makes us see things in the mist that aren't there.

I shook off the distracting mirage, refocused my purpose, and returned to my duties as host and driver. The night was so bright I didn't need the tractor lights turned on. The gravel road looked white, with eerie shadows cast on both sides from overhanging foliage or fence line. We drove up the hill slowly, past the old cemetery. It was a Washington Irving tableau, a deadly diorama that eyes could not avoid. The bright moonlight filtered through 200-year-old oak and pecan trees, falling here, then there, onto carved tombs and headstones and footpaths. It was like a funereal patchwork quilt. Shadows danced here and there, becoming apparitions within the compelling scene.

All the passengers behind me had fallen silent. No one spoke a whisper. Arms held closer; some had goosebumps. Gradually, I allowed the tractor to come to a halt and turned off the motor. A soft breeze that had started out in the Panhandle found its way to the farm that night. The old trees' arms creaked, rubbing against each other. Without warning, an errant branch would break loose and fall in stages through other more sturdy living limbs. Broad leaves would break loose and be carried diagonally across the terrible stage set before us.

Behind me, Robin's voice gently broke the silence, with a shaky alarm.

"Sam..."

All eyes turned toward our poultry professor, including mine. She was standing in the middle of the trailer, her hand held in mid-air, pointing toward the road ahead. She spoke slowly, with fear in her voice.

"There's....there's something in the road ahead."

Riders craned their necks for better views, some stood up, some put heads in laps and closed their eyes. A figure was approaching our hayride assembly, revealing itself from out of the darkness ahead.

Someone screamed. I turned on the tractor lights, illuminating a horrific apparition. Standing before us in the road was a zombie with convincing shreds of torn cloth and perhaps skin, hanging from the torso. Our gang was in tears of fright and delight as the terrifying thing dragged itself alongside the wagon. Relieved communal laughter filled the chilly night air.

"BOO!" said the young zombie, clutching the side-rails with both hands and grinning from bloody ear to ear.

"It's Brad the Brat!" one of the teens shouted, seeing through the disguise. The boy's moniker had become a kind of badge of honor for him. It carried the weight of history.

Some got off the trailer to examine Brad's outfit at close range. It was an Oscar-worthy creation designed and sewn by Liz and Annie. For days, they had chuckled and howled, trying various looks, selecting just the correctly offensive fabric or color to achieve zombiehood.

Poor Bradley was often called into the sewing room for a fitting adjustment, a teen mannequin sometimes accidentally pin-pricked by his over-enthusiastic tailors. The joy shared by my two favorite females in the world over the weeks of planning and preparation for their desired hayride was considerable and contagious.

The young zombie's makeup was flawlessly frightening too. Liz had borrowed a headpiece from the college theater wardrobe department. Used in their performance of "A Christmas Carol," Scrooge's fake pate consisted of a bleached white skullcap with straggly, irregular strands of hair hanging off the sides here and there. The bald head glowed in the bright moonlight.

Makeup for Brad the Zombie's face was an eerie montage of dark streaks and light patches that included seemingly sunken cheeks, dark circles around the eyes, and a couple of apparently open wounds on cheeks and jowl. The wounds were Brad's idea, no doubt inspired by some of his favorite video games.

Revelers surrounded the boy in the road, alternately taking selfies with him, their cell-phone cameras lighting up bits of the scary dark night like so many digital fireflies. Photos taken and fear subsided, the assembly loaded up once more onto the hayride trailer. Brad was squeezed in between appreciative neighbors on hay bales. They alternately amused each other and the recently discovered actor amongst them with comments like "Don't bite me, Zombie boy!" or "Something on this wagon smells dead."

We continued our hayride, like a mobile version of Albert Pinkham

Ryder's spooky night painting, *The Race Track (Death on a Pale Horse).* I drove up over the hill, pausing so the crowd could enjoy a rare night view of the deep valley to the north. Far below, the county road curved its serpentine way in parallel with Caterpillar Creek, now full of October rains, its gentle, moist movement enhanced by the moon's reflected ribbons of light. Alongside, a large freshly plowed field looked sculpted, especially with rows at the edges that snaked along the same contours of the road and creek. A distant farmhouse looked cozy, leaking small rectangles of warm light from occupied rooms inside.

As we rode down beside our own farm's little creek, with dappled bits of moonlight falling all around us through the old gnarly post oaks, a family of resident owls were talking to each other from the branches' dark recesses. I turned off the motor so we could listen to the gentle hoot-hooting of their conversation. The creek added a soft, rhythmic gurgling to the sylvan gathering.

The ride up over the dam road was thrilling to my hayride passengers. I paused mid-way at the top, the narrowest section of the road, so we could watch the bright round moon mirror itself in the lake. Such a vivid image stays printed on the brain somehow. Empirically, my brain knows the scene is just a reflection of the Earth's own moon, what the Romans called Luna. But my memory will record the view as strangely magical, as if the huge white orb is an emanation originating in the lake itself, an image of its own accord, if you will. A second moon, perhaps? Jealous of her sister?

After a moon-inspired silent interlude of reflection, a few of the dumbstruck passengers disembarked the carriage momentarily to peer down into the little dark ravine below. The dam's culvert full of overflow water cascaded down into Hackberry Creek with an audible rush and roar. Peering uneasily over the edge, a couple of cautious voices murmured about the wisdom of bringing the hayride wagon across this narrow gap, near such a menacing drop-off on one side. I broke the silence by advising aloud that all hayriders would be safer riding with me at the wheel rather than wandering ahead into the dark on unsure feet. The doubters quickly climbed back aboard.

Riding across the moon-lit expanse of the wide front pasture, passengers sighed aloud, raising their eyes toward a monumental moon set in a heaven filled with stars in all directions. I pulled the softly chugging little tractor to a stop alongside the orderly row of vehicles. There, 4-H teen parking lot attendants, armed with flashlights, had diligently directed arriving visitors to the farm's official parking area. Horse heads occasionally poked out of open stall windows, watching the human comings and goings with mild equine curiosity.

Returning to their own cars in groups of twos and threes, arm in arm, the muted guests shook hands and shared hugs. Once more, nature left us in hushed awe, with humble smiles and sparkling eyes.

~

Alone, driving back up the hill to the covered tractor shed, I was troubled by a nagging image.

Surely, I had misread what I thought I saw. Trying to put the thought away again, I renewed my focus on the road, on the clutch, on anything, to get my mind off the idea of my freckle-faced daughter in a courtship with Vern. For heaven's sake, he's practically her little brother. What is she thinking? Why, he must be three years younger than her! I forced myself to put all such thoughts on a back burner, at least until I could run them by Annie later. After all, maybe it was just a mirage, a trick-of-the-eye due to the sights and sounds of a magical night.

~

As Thanksgiving approaches, one of the Devons has just dropped her first calf. What a cutie. Very agile from the get-go, the little curly-headed, all-red calf bounds around as if she already owns the world. Not a fear, of course. Momma is never far away, providing unconditional love, which certainly seems to have bolstered the bravado of the newest member of our little herd. The reality is that baby calves, at any sign of threat or danger, are never shy or embarrassed to cower beneath their protective mother's massive presence.

The sight of this tiny crimson creature, tucked in between her hefty mom and heftier aunt at the hay ring, with her own little head shoved into the round bale just like the big girls, is quite a sight. Having a calf to care for is a standard rite of passage for human farm kids. The daily chores of responsibility for calves and cows teaches youngsters important lessons about consistency, compassion, and patience. Calves project innocence and need through their pretty faces and movie-star eyes. Their gentle nature and love of playful running and jumping are perfectly understood and applauded by human youngsters.

Some of our cutest critters on the farm have been near-Thanksgiving babies. That's fine with us, and such events are truly reminders of how much we have to be thankful for. The entertainment value alone of these livestock infants is worth the cost of their feed. Watching the joy of the little red calf as she suddenly bounds off in no particular direction, tail curled up and waving in the air over her back, so full of herself, well, it's better than any action movie or series.

Sol was a near-Thanksgiving baby. All of twenty-six inches high, the little newborn bravely bundled himself into a pre-leap arch and confidently jumped the one-foot distance from his mini-trailer down to the ground. He was full of himself and walked right over to me to introduce himself and to enjoy a bit of grain I held out in my palm. Already in a perfect-fit red halter, to which I clipped a short lead rope, Sol walked with me down the long, winding road to the barn as if we had done it a thousand times. His demeanor of confident authority, the way he nodded his little head this way and that as if approving all he surveyed, prompted me to name him Solomon that very day.

We were instant pals from his first arrival at the farm, just one day before Thanksgiving. Family and friends joined us for the holiday that year, as we felt satisfied enough with our initial progress as organic herb and produce farmers to invite a crowd to celebrate with us. All our holiday guests seemed to enjoy Sol's appearance most of all during the fun activities and bounty of food that day. He wins the hearts of all who meet him. We bravely hosted a farm-to-table charity event up at the farm that next spring. At one point, ten popular (and very confident) chefs were happily gathered around for an audience with the irresistible little fellow.

He is a total professional and relishes every opportunity to put on a show. He tilts his spotted head to one side and squints one eye at his fans, almost winking. The fans squeal and heap "oohs" and "aahs" in his direction. We don't blame the cute little donkey. He's simply a star and knows it.

Here's our standard Thanksgiving menu for the farm's critters. The little red calf already has her head buried up under momma, so we know what she's having. Sol will get delicious bits of a couple of fat alfalfa cubes, broken off for him with one hand, while the other scratches his chin and ears.

Each horse will be having a sweet red apple, plus chin and ear scratches. Our gorgeous rectangular red Devonshire cows will be given tasty molasses feed. Not the new baby calf. We'll keep her on grass and hay for about nine months.

The sheep and the chickens, in addition to their usual organic grain fare, will get a delicious holiday bonus of precious alfalfa hay. The chickens delight in pulling this hay apart, sending hundreds of tiny green leaves flying all around them in the yard. Thanksgiving Day will provide some very tasty pecking for our poultry workers. There's a new crop of tiny grasshoppers about, so the guineas are enjoying those in celebration of the season.

Our cat who thinks he's a dog, Tommy Cat, insists on Pete's priciest feed store cat food, so he gets Thanksgiving meals every day. But Annie and Liz say he earns his keep with mouse-kills. I have to admit he's a reliable rodent assassin.

~

One recent evening, shortly after the farm's memorable moonlight hayride, Annie and I were reading ourselves to sleep. We sometimes take turns reading aloud favorite passages from favorite books. She usually chooses verses from *The Odyssey* or *The Iliad*, epics recited by the blind poet Homer to a standing Greek audience over four or five days. Often, a day's recitation ended with a king and queen retiring to bed for the night. Annie likes those verses, and the parts when Penelope and Odysseus discuss the bed he made for her out of an ancient olive tree, a secret known only to the lovers.

Annie sometimes asks, teasingly, when I'm going to carve her an olive tree bed. I explain that I've planted an olive tree out near the herb gardens and it should be ready for carving in just under two hundred years. At bedtime, I like to read aloud from Kenneth Grahame's *The Wind in the Willows*, or something from the letters and essays of E.B. White. I'm especially fond of his humorous essays written for *The New Yorker*, in particular his accounts of the Whites' own little chicken farm up in Maine. Katharine Sergeant Angell White, author of *Onward and Upward in the Garden*, edited by White, was the discerning and famed fiction editor for *The New Yorker* from 1925 to 1960.

It's not unusual for Annie to drift off into slumberland in mid-sentence, lulled to sleep by the sound of her own soft voice. I could tell she was nearing that state by the ever-slowing pace of her words. I broke in, with "I've been wanting to get your take on something."

"You bet." she replied, putting her book on the bedside table, and turning back to lean into me. "I'm all ears." she said, while laying her head on my chest. "Well, one ear anyway." I observed.

I recounted the surprising moment's glimpse I witnessed, or thought I witnessed, of Vern and Liz holding hands and cuddling at the back of the trailer during our moonlight hayride.

"Have I been missing something?"

"Everything, I think, regarding those two." Annie looked up at me with those big green eyes.

"I mean, Vern's like family. You know? Isn't it kind of weird?"

"Not to them. You love him like a son already. That seems like a plus to me."

"But their age difference...." I ventured. "Liz is what, three or four years older than the boy."

Annie raised her torso up on one elbow, leaning back a bit and looking at me very seriously.

"You're almost four years older than me." she said, one eyebrow slightly raised.

I ventured again, putting my arm around her raised shoulder. "Yes. But that's...."

She cut me off. "If you say, 'but that's different' you'll get no 'sleep tight' kiss from me tonight."

I didn't say it. After an eternity's pause, Annie put her head back onto my chest, sighing.

"You've seen them as big sister, little brother, somehow, over the years. But that's not how they've seen each other. Nor have any of the rest of us for that matter."

"Honestly?" I thought about it for a moment. "I must be blind."

"No, Sam. You just sort of wind up being 'Dad' to kids you care about. It's just the teacher in you. It's a good thing. But Liz, the little daughter you parented alone, is a grown, discerning woman. You raised her to think independently. Vern's her choice. He's not a son, but will be your son-in-law, no blood required."

"What? They're getting married?"

"Calm down, old man. Not yet. But it's coming. Look, Vern has adored Liz since he was in high school, even while she was away at college. She's just been waiting for him to grow up a bit. And he's been trying to get there as fast as he could."

It was too much information for me to absorb in one evening. I fell asleep wondering why life can't just make simple sense, flowing at the pace of a gentle river, like it does for Ratty, Mole, Badger, and Toad.

Blaze in the Pasture

FIVE

Bee Balm and Beatitudes

Annie loves Bee Balm. She loves the plant, its leaves full of minty aroma and flavor, the gloriously spikey red, pink, or purple flowers it produces, and its attraction for pollinators to the garden. She drank Bee Balm tea with her grandmother, a famous quilter, straight from a genuine red-clay ceramic Brown Betty teapot. Generations of grandmothers handed down the knowledge of Bee Balm's healing properties to their daughters and granddaughters, for everything from tea for upset tummies to relief from a bee sting or scrape, treated with a balm poultice application.

The Greek goddess Hecate gave her daughters, Circe and Medea, the gift of Lemon Balm, a sacred plant of healing and vitality. In medieval times it was linked to wisdom, virtue, and abundance, and used in devotional practices. In the garden, brushing against the Balms, ancient ambrosia fills the air and floods all your senses. "It is salve for the soul," Granny used to say.

Annie and Liz tend the Bee Balm and Lemon Balm in our gardens. I'm convinced they channel their female ancestors while doing so. Like mint, the Balms can take over a garden, so best to keep the plants within the borders of raised beds. Bee Balm is a favorite of beekeepers since Bronze Age Greece. Always quick to appropriate a good thing, the

Romans spread the art of beekeeping over their whole empire. The wooden hives they invented haven't changed much since.

We sell a bit of Bartlett Farm honey in twelve-ounce glass jars at seasonal farmers markets. But we're not interested in big production. The herb-rich honey really serves us best as goodwill birthday and holiday gifts for our chefs and most loyal customers.

Poets and artists have long appropriated nature's bountiful creations as props for their narratives. All Flemish painters filled their compositions with flowers, herbs, leaves, and trees that symbolized the best divine virtues, the Beatitudes. No plant is just a plant in any painting by Robert Campin, Jan van Eyck, or Hans Memling.

Jan Praet, a poet from Bruges in about 1400, wrote "Mirror of Wisdom," proclaiming that the daisy is the sign of mercy, columbine is humility, marigold is faithfulness, lily is purity, and the rose is love. Praet's writing served as a kind of lexicon of symbols for artists of the lowlands.

This year, our October garden sales were replete with ancient symbols, no doubt. Pumpkins, for pagan carvings, did very well. We harvested striped eggplant, pineapple sage with edible flowers, Malabar Spinach, Genovese basil, purple ruffle basil, Hill Hardy Rosemary, French tarragon, Rocket arugula, garlic chives, sweet marjoram, silver lemon thyme, Greek oregano, and Bee Balm.

Chefs were particularly happy with the abundant fall harvest of fresh herbs for soups and sauces. One of our favorite restaurant customers over in Abilene offers a fun "Healthy Herbal Marinara" on the menu. The sauce features fresh "Bartlett Farm Bee Balm" instead of dried oregano, served over angel hair pasta. Served last, in typical Italian custom, is a pretty fall salad of our wild arugula, sliced sugar pear, and Brown Turkey figs, sprinkled with pecans and gorgonzola.

In between the end of summer's rigorous farm schedule and the onslaught of fall's seasonal chores, the men of Irene and environs loaded their sons and nephews into the beds of their pickup trucks and hit the road for adventure. The one-hour road trip to Lake

Whitney seemed a much longer and exotic journey to the eager boys. For all our excitement, you'd have thought we were headed for the Rockies.

The boys would position themselves amongst the assorted duffel bags, backpacks, folded tents, and Army cots (WWII vintage), ice chests, and the like in the bed of the truck and discuss the coming adventure's specifics. We younger boys of course had little to say, except for the occasional question like "is there a diving board?" The older boys described exhilarating experiences like swinging far out over the edge of high cliffs on long ropes and letting go to free-fall hundreds of feet into ice-cold water. They told chilling stories about strange creatures that lurked around the lake at night, including a ghost-woman who wandered the shores and woods early every dark morning in her white nightgown. They said you could hear the folds of her gown fluttering in the wind.

Many of the fathers who arranged this annual adventure for us boys had helped build the impressive dam at Lake Whitney. For me, it counted as one of the wonders of the world (on my personal list). Near Hillsboro, the reservoir was started in 1946. The dam opened to the public in 1951. It's a beauty, still maintained by the Army Corps of Engineers, along with the surrounding parks of Kimball Bend, Lofers Bend, Soldiers Bluff, and McCown Valley.

In my child's mind, the dam was something out of Buck Rogers, a space-age favorite strip in the "funny papers," as we called the Sunday comics. A concrete panorama of modern engineering unfolded itself beneath your gaze from above. Like looking down from the top of an enormous playground slide, we could imagine hurtling forever on the long descending curve, our backs pressed hard against the smooth endless white surface into the pretty blue Brazos River below.

Annie and I often reminisce about wonderful family trips to state parks as children. Growing up in different parts of Texas and Oklahoma, we've enjoyed most of the parks in both states as kids, and as adults. Fall is the time to visit a state park in Texas, for sure. The weather is cooling, the crowds are diminished, and the nights seem clearer, probably due to less air conditioners in surrounding towns going full blast.

State parks in every corner of Texas celebrate and preserve the flora, fauna, and waters of this unique part of the country. Texas Parks and

Wildlife publishes a huge array of histories, maps, events calendars, and guides on their website. Fall activities range from the October "Butterfly Walk" at the World Birding Center in the Bentsen-Rio Grande Valley State Park to the October "Texas Camel Treks" at Monahans Sandhills State Park.

A couple of years ago, artist friends from England came to the farm for a visit. Part of their Texas trip included a West Texas jaunt to Amarillo. They were thrilled to learn that we could reserve a cabin for them in Palo Duro Canyon State Park and that they would be able to stay overnight at the canyon. They enjoyed seeing the striped cliffs display their famous, colorful "Spanish skirts" at sunrise and sunset. The vivid polychromatic qualities of Palo Duro's reflective surfaces have inspired many artists, including Georgia O'Keeffe, who lived in Canyon and taught art at West Texas State Normal College (now West Texas A&M University) between 1916 to 1918.

O'Keeffe painted over fifty watercolors while living in Canyon, just a few minutes' ride down into the splendors of Palo Duro in her Ford Model T. The artist said she liked to take her lunch break from painting beneath the shade a favorite mesquite tree. Of a morning, if she arrived a bit late to the canyon, that shady respite would already be occupied by a local Apache family who would rest there throughout the day's hot sunlight. O'Keeffe said that on those days she would crawl beneath the high clearance of her Model T to enjoy her lunch and a nap in the shade of her tall vehicle.

This past summer, we ventured far eastward, all the way to Telephone, Texas. Annie has a favorite cousin there, Billie, whose mother's family farmed near Muskogee, Oklahoma. Attending an Armistice celebration USO dance in Tulsa, Billie's mom met and fell in love with Corporal Earl Ewing, honorably discharged, on his way home to Honey Grove, Texas. Earl's train stopped for service and refueling over a few hours in Tulsa. After the dance, he and Billie looked at each other intently and talked all night on a bench outside the railroad station lobby.

Annie and I stayed a couple of fun days and nights with the Ewings in Telephone. They took us to nearby Bonham State Park for a leisurely picnic and restful day surrounded by lush Northeast Texas hardwood trees. Bonham's is a 261-acre park in Fannin County, with a lovely 65-acre lake, rolling prairies, and beautiful wooded shorelines with many peaceful nooks which include picnic tables in the shade and comfortable trails. This park will reduce your stress level. The CCC (Civilian Conservation Corps) constructed Bonham State Park in the early 1930s. We find it one of the most charming parks in the state. It was not built to be a mammoth reservoir. It does not produce energy for an adjoining power plant. The park produces its own energy in the form of recreational exercise and contemplative solace for Northeast Texas families to enjoy nature with amenities.

As a youngster, I thrived on the annual outing of fathers and sons to Lake Whitney. It was an important seasonal ritual for the boys and men alike from the county's farming towns. The rite signaled the end of summer and celebrated the sheer joy of simple play, if only for a couple of days a year. School would reopen soon. The hard work of farming was left behind for a while. The hard work of fishing and swimming all day led to well-earned sleep on cots beneath star-filled skies. The pleasure of awakening out of doors to the smell of bacon frying in black iron skillets over open fires remains fresh in my boyhood memory.

Daily demands of gardening and farming build an anthology of comparative experiences, a personal history with particular landscapes, terroir, and specific lessons learned from nature's plants and animals. Over time, this history becomes a kind of agrarian lexicon that travels with us, informing observations and decisions made in every experiential aspect of our lives. Ancient authors like Cato, Virgil, Juvenal, Horace, Terence, and Seneca all referenced Roman society's public discourse about the virtues of rural living versus the vices of urban residence.

Terence could have included our teen neighbor, Brad, in one of his comedies portraying a Roman kid plucked from urban noise and entertainment, just to be plopped down into the comparative quiet of the rural countryside. Brad's mother, Brenda, was the driving force behind moving from city to farm. Bradley senior commutes from office to farm when not traveling for work, which he enjoys. He keeps his cellphone in a snug scabbard attached to the dash, always on speakerphone, always on high volume. He's an annuity broker and has explained to me (without being asked) that he must be available at all times to best serve clients and make deals. Serving clients sounds good to me. But honestly, I dread seeing the guy.

He always greets me with an eager handshake, followed by the same inquiry every time: “Hey, neighbor, are you still satisfied with your retirement portfolio? I've got some great products to show you.” I assure him I'm happy. He concludes, “No worries. I'll keep checking.” I'll probably slip one day and blurt out what I'm silently thinking in response, “I really wish you wouldn't.”

Brad's adjusting well. Good grief, the kid has his own splendid Appaloosa as a pet. Granny would say, “That's high cotton.” Brenda confided to Annie that her boy no longer lies on the couch all day playing video games. He visits us regularly now, joining other horse lovers for training and exercise sessions in our big round pen at least once a month. Pete and Penny down at the feed store have taken quite a liking to the boy, and he makes spending money over there helping out a few afternoons after school per week.

Recently, Annie and I took Robin and Brad with us for a day trip over to Mineral Wells State Park on one of those balmy November days with sunshine we sometimes get in North Texas. The teens and I took our folding camp-chairs down into the ravine with us, scouting for the best angles on atmospheric perspective views of the steep, ragged cliff-face. We had the scene to ourselves that day, but on some visits, we've been treated to students learning to climb and rappelling up and down the naturally sculpted walls. The various arrays of ropes and carabiners make for linear compositions against the stone face, like Cy Twombly's colorful abstract drawings.

Annie stretched out under the shaded canopy of a tall, lacy ash tree in her folding lounger, napping off and on during her re-reading of Seamus Heaney's *Beowulf* translation, a favorite book companion of hers on trips. She sometimes falls asleep imagining herself in King Hrothgar's mead-hall, beneath a lofty thatched-roof, dreamily watching a waft of smoke drifting slowly upwards from the central open hearth.

Sometimes Grendel lurks outside the hall in her dreams, but she says she always wakes up before the hideous beast breaks in.

Soft compressed charcoal is the perfect choice to convey all the subtleties of nature's rough-hewn stonework across the irregular, jagged, surface of the cliff-face here. Depending on the angle of morning or afternoon light raking down into the ravine, individual formations become lighted or shaded, shaped anew like a morphing animation on the organic wall. Jean-Baptiste-Camille Corot's sketches of cliffs and rocks provide good lessons in tool-in-hand manipulation to simulate such surfaces. Pay attention to how Corot uses opposing planes of light and dark to suggest volume.

Robin has gotten quite proficient using the broad side of soft charcoal sticks to apply a variety of values simply by varying pressure on the tool. This technique is especially effective when blending a dominant tone across the paper surface. Brad, the teen cartoonist, is struggling with the concept that realism demands at least five values: light, medium light, medium, medium dark, and dark. He is convinced that three values, consisting of light, medium, and dark should be enough. I sympathize because I thought the same during my own teen cartoonist years. Good college drawing teachers taught me that "close enough" is not a valid defense during class critiques. Just like young Brad, it took me awhile to see that realism and comics have different requirements.

Comics usually require only a few values (lights and darks) and few strokes to convey volume. Suggestion of depth is almost always linear in comics. Realism, or more accurately described as *representational* drawing, requires five or six different values, and the artist must imply volume by marking in the surface direction of the form, as in blending the surface of a tree trunk in a "u" shaped direction to suggest the trunk's cylindrical nature. You can't shade a cylinder with horizontal marks, which would imply a state of flatness, not volume.

Brad's depiction of volume is improving, as is his understanding of changing the pressure on a bar of soft charcoal to suggest the shifting values apparent in the myriad array of striations and cracks of meandering stops and starts up and down the cliff walls before us in the ravine.

~

Speaking of seeing things more clearly, Homer, the formerly blind lamb, has been for several years the chief ram of our flock of Tunis sheep. Our old vet, John, took a great interest in Homer's sight issues from the get-go. Like me, I think he was touched by Homer's gentle behavior and the little ovine's completely trusting nature. After a bit of research, John began a regimen of medication for the lamb during his first year on the farm. John's son, Doc Russell, has continued the treatment, though with much less necessary frequency. Now only twice a year does Homer the ram get a B12 injection and a dose of cobalt at the same time.

Homer doesn't bump into things anymore. He is dependable and consistent at his job. Amazingly, the old boy has not passed on the blindness trait to any of his considerable offspring. Somehow, he has retained his gentle nature, possibly because I was imprinted as his parent or guardian on his baby brain so early. Homer still leans into me whenever close by. Like a goat, he will sometimes extend his nose into my barn coat pocket in search of a sweet carrot. He's often rewarded by discovering one, of course.

Homer, even as a young lamb, always aimed his head toward mine. Originally, he did that, I'm sure, just pointing his head toward the sound of my voice. I'm convinced now that he sees my face, and I often find him looking me right in the eye, just like the dogs and horses do, when I'm speaking directly at him. Sheep always have a docile, pleasing gaze, but sometimes Homer looks intently at me like an equine, as if waiting for instruction.

If only I could get Homer to train Sol so that he, too, would look at me for instruction. Sol's gaze at me is usually a look of skepticism, with one eyebrow cocked critically. Unlike my trusty ram, the word "obedience" is not in my little donkey's vocabulary. Sol is a leader, and he knows it. He also knows that sheep are followers, that they're supposed to follow him. Like Homer, Sol takes his job seriously too. Sol just doesn't take me seriously. In our relationship, Sol sees himself as Don Quixote, and I'm just the other guy.

Unlike Don Quixote, Sol is an effective problem-solver when he puts his little donkey-mind to it. Last winter, an overnight deep freeze caught everybody unaware, including the sheep. I had stayed up late in the studio working on a new sunset painting with fireflies. I paused after painting the small bright yellow circles that would serve as the opaque base coat for dozens of the little illuminated beetles. When dry, I'd begin painting the transparent layers of colors over this bright, reflective yellow. Such glazing of many layers of thin colors demands care and patience. It also demands using numerous test panels off to the side of the main canvas. Trial and error is best experienced on a less crucial, less permanent surface.

I was happy with the painting's progress but found myself yawning as I watched and waited for the paint to dry. The wind coming down over the Ouachita Mountains and across the Red River had increased speed and force. I could hear it blasting itself stronger against the studio windows. I unlatched the door of my cast-iron Ben Franklin stove and added a new log atop the existing embers. Closing the door, I peered through the small tempered-glass pane to make sure the split oak fuel was catching fire at the edges properly. I narrowed the damper a bit more, satisfied the old stove would supply enough heat for hours. I turned out the lights and fell fast asleep, reflections of flickering flames dancing in my sleepy periphery. At some point during the night, I dreamed that my dark studio was filled with fireflies, their little lamps lighting bits of my paintings now here, now there, flashing on and off like tiny moving spotlights.

I woke to see that dawn had raised her lovely head enough above the east horizon to pour some faint morning light into the studio. I got up and walked to the bathroom on the south end of my second-floor space. I washed my face to help me wake up and stood at the window, towel in hand, looking out over the sheep pasture below. I blinked my eyes several times to make sure I was seeing accurately. Winter had arrived with hammer blows.

The ground was frozen, covered in a thin layer of frost mixed with sleet.

The night before was brisk but certainly not freezing when I finally retired. Caesar the Great Pyrenees and Sol had spent the night outside with the sheep. Caesar has two natural coats, as do Tunis lambs, for warmth. Had I anticipated a hard freeze, Sol would have on his little blanket or I would have put him in his stall overnight. The flock had huddled into the round stone sheepfold, probably as the winds picked up and the temps fell during the dark hours. Caesar and Sol, my shepherd patrol, had probably stayed guard at the entry to the stone semicircle, nodding off as needed throughout the night, taking turns at watch duty.

Sol was rubbing his hairy chin side to side across a layer of ice covering the surface of the full but top-frozen water trough at the fence beside the gate into the sheep pasture. A couple of thirsty ewes, their red-furred lambs in tow, stood on either side of their donkey guardian. They knew Sol would figure out something but were getting anxious over the unexpected predicament. The oval-shaped water tub came up just to Sol's chest.

Suddenly the clever boy reared up on hind legs and struck down hard with both his narrow front hooves on the frozen crust top layer. Ice chips flew up. Anticipatory lambs licked lips. Sol completed the downward striking motion twice more, breaking the surface and quickly drawing front legs back and down onto terra firma; in this case, more terra permafrost. As one donkey head and numerous sheep heads plunged into the newly exposed thirst-quenching water, several of the larger ice-shards were forced out over the sides of the trough by the water's wake, shattering like small icebergs as they struck the hard ground below.

Even tall canine Caesar joined the ovine remuda to lap up gulps of the refreshing, chilled elixir with his spotted pink tongue. The remarkable event is an unforgettable film-reel on my memory. I swear, at one instant, Sol raised his long-lashed eyes up toward mine as I stared down upon the little miracle from my studio office window. Maybe he was just relishing a long, steeper swallow of cold water. But more likely he was registering, in that over-sized head of his, an account of likely points he had just accumulated during such an impressive display of equine problem solving. I'm confident that Ignatius of Loyola would back me up that I had just witnessed an authentic little miracle in real time.

~

We are delighted that daughter Liz is back home for a while. But I was looking for the cardamom the other day and it had disappeared. Annie wanted some for her coffee. She likes cardamom in her coffee in the winter. Liz has never been one to put spices—or kitchen utensils for that matter—back in their proper places. Knives reside in perfect contentment with spatulas and ladles alongside, as far as Liz is concerned. Maybe it's the result of her having lived in so many dorm rooms over the years.

To be helpful, I've applied labels to the fronts of cabinet shelves for spices and dried herbs to be located on the correctly corresponding lazy Susan, such as "Indian/Chinese/Mideastern," "Mexican/Italian," or "French/Cajun." Even one for "Baking Items" (allspice, cinnamon, nutmeg, Madagascar vanilla extract, poppy seed, et al). All to no avail, I might add. You're as likely to find the Chinese Five Heavenly Spices next to Ancho Chile Powder scooched closely up against a colorful jar of kid's birthday-cake sprinkles, as you are to finding it properly positioned beside ground ginger.

Years ago, Annie worked for room and board one summer at a Buddhist monastery high above Highway 101 in California. She worked in the kitchen helping prepare meals and in the gardens planting and harvesting fresh organic greens for paying guests. She said that for her short breaks during work shifts, she simply stood still outside, in awe of the endless Pacific that stretched "Ever westward, toward the East" (I love the way my sidekick uses words). When her summer's meditation came to an end, friends at the monastery gave her an elegant open-lattice, ceramic chopstick holder, with the Chinese "Double Happiness" symbol centered in the design for good luck.

The serenely glazed grass-green chopstick holder, with drain holes on the bottom, hangs quietly, efficiently, above our kitchen sink today. Yet somehow, the occasional errant chopstick still manages to find itself tossed in amongst paring knives or skewers or peelers in a utensil drawer. Annie and I have given up pointing out these kitchen improprieties to Liz. Her mind is simply too busy multi-tasking between items on her mental to-do list, such as Beech Tree Bark Blight, forestry residence grants, or instructors' grade entry deadlines. When considering such lofty issues, with a few rinsed chopsticks in hand, any drawer will do. I guess that's Zen, to Liz.

Our poet friend, Brian, has written a wonderful poem about growing up in a family of "kitchen anarchists" who threw caution to the winds at every turn when it came to compartmentalizing silverware or kitchen utensils. The poem suggests it became a family game, seen by everyone but young Brian as a harmless, hilarious past time to keep any sense of order far away from the kitchen drawers and cabinets. His siblings knew that their little brother would always put things right anyway.

As the poem unfolds, the teen target or butt of the joke (the poem's protagonist) never perceives the perpetual disorder as a personal attack against himself. Rather, the drawer and cabinet calamity in his family kitchen becomes a metaphor for how the boy in the poem came to see his parents and siblings in a broader context. That is, he noticed the same lackadaisical attitude carried out in his family's general behavior, their carefree lifestyle, and disheveled demeanor. They weren't all of that exactly, but it's how he began to see them in most aspects of their daily lives, how they functioned in a world society beyond the family kitchen. Their joke, largely missed by Brian, became a convenient lens through which their scapegoated brother could shape his views of them. His siblings, particularly, provided unsightly landmarks he would avoid completely, all his life's voyage. Unknowingly, they all helped form a hopeless perfectionist, successful at any task he took to hand, including delightful poetry full of irony.

~

Our cherry tomatoes are producing big time, well into November this year. We've had a couple of deep freeze nights, but Robin and I were able to get cold cloth secured over the plants during daylight hours both times. We were harvesting winter lettuce and greens in the gardens today, and both paused to admire the huge display of bright red heirloom cherries all around us. The chefs will be delighted with surprise bunches of the tiny, tasty tomatoes that we'll deliver along with the greens on Friday.

I noticed, with some apprehension, the bright red cardinal family lined up on a rusty garden gate nearby. Were they eyeballing our cherry tomatoes? That old gate seems to be a favorite daytime perch for the cardinals, season after season. But I'd seen no evidence of avian assaults to the garden's tomatoes so far this fall.

The looming presence of the red-feathered squadron prompted my recall of a humorous tomato battle I fought long, long ago, before I had discovered the great heritage and flavor of heirloom tomatoes. I once had a great scarecrow that loomed over my urban tomato garden. I could see it from just outside my studio window. Tomatoes growing just outside the studio were always good distractions from whatever drawing or painting problem I might be struggling with. I approved the scarecrow's menacing effect. As I lived in the city at the time, it was a patio garden with tomatoes occupying the perimeter. My neighbor, Hank, was a good gardener and had suggested a then-new tomato from A&M, the Merced. The plants were living up to rave reviews.

The only problem I was having with the Merceds was that enthusiastic birds were also giving rave reviews, voting with their bills. I was driven to create this monstrous apparition of a scarecrow because of the appetites of a couple of families of greedy cardinals that had decided to homestead my back yard that year. They acted as if my garden was some sort of commune, with me the major donor. However, philanthropy has its limits, tomato-wise. Indeed, the cardinals' brilliant colors were beautifully contrasted with the dark green plants, and the males were a match for the brightest of the red, plump fruit. The plants were bountiful. I didn't mind sharing, but I had not intended the whole harvest for the birds.

The scarecrow wore a thread-bare blue cotton denim shirt of mine, a favorite. It was lightweight because of age and so many washings. The long, thin sleeves could be lifted by the slightest breeze, so the shirt moved in a ghost-like dance. The head was an empty gallon milk jug, stuck upside down on a mop handle with an old straw hat on top. Its painted face glared sternly out at all winged visitors to the garden. The pants were a pair of my old Air Force fatigues I'd rummaged out of a box in the garage. I guess I thought a military element added to the design might demand some respect from the pesky thieves. I hoped my scarecrow projected an aggressive defense posture.

A colorful kid's pinwheel was stuck into the scarecrow's frayed straw hat. The pinwheel spun ferociously at times in heavy winds. A couple of tin coffee-can lids hung on string from one sleeve. They clanged together with any breeze. You would have thought the noisy din alone would drive the redbirds away; alas, no.

The day I gave up on the tomato war was the day I looked out the studio window to spy a number of cardinals on the ground beneath my tomato plants. They chirped and hopped happily all around the trunks of the plants and right below the ersatz terrifying scarecrow. Its sleeves were flapping, the tin lids were clanging, and the pinwheel whirred, all to no avail. The birds, including babies, totally ignored the menacing apparition, which flailed about pointlessly above their little heads.

I was about to rush out to do personal battle with the feathered fiends but stopped. On closer look, I realized it was a momma cardinal holding class for her numerous offspring. The eager students followed her every move and instruction, as the mother showed the children how to step under this and that fat red tomato and simply peck up into the juicy globe. Free dining on the fruits of my labor—pretty smart.

I was so taken with the will of that little red-and-brown-feathered mother bird, teaching her charges something very practical for their survival, I decided to let them have all the tomatoes they wanted. I probably would have lost the war anyway. I certainly couldn't watch the plants around the clock, and my labor-intensive scarecrow might have been keeping crows away but was clearly no match for the momma cardinal.

The other morning, seated at the kitchen table, I was enjoying a bowl of Wheaties and granola with sliced banana, strawberries, and a few freshly shelled pecan halves. A drizzle of our farm honey on top added the perfect mix of sweet and floral characteristics for the palate. I sipped my cup of rich, dark-roast Sulawesi coffee, made with beans a former student recently brought us from her trip to that exotic island. Ever the adventurer, art historian Jenn connected with some colleagues in Australia who invited her to join them exploring newly discovered prehistoric cave drawings on Sulawesi. Quite a trajectory, I'd say, for a farm girl from Meeker, Oklahoma.

Jenn's grandmother lives in Elysia, so that's how the young brainiac showed up in my art classes at Barnes County College some years ago. She showed us her photos, all unpublished, of amazing prehistoric cave drawings. Even in her amateur photos of the dimly lit paintings, the animals depicted on the natural irregular wall contours retain their original magical character. Time will tell, but Jenn suggests the cave art on Sulawesi may date from 50,000 BC. If accurate, that would be the oldest yet. Annie, Liz and I sat in silent awe of our young art historian friend's touch with the prehistoric art world.

I poured myself another cup of the exotic brew from an exotic island I will likely never see. Through the kitchen window, I observed the angle of the morning's first horizontal rays of light falling across the back patio. I still had a few minutes to let my mind wander amongst varied topics such as Thanksgiving soon to come, cold cloth removal from the winter lettuce crop before the day gets too warm, Annie on the road for a writer's seminar she's giving down in Austin, the suspicious-looking feral hog wallow down near the cemetery, the painting I'm avoiding, and reminiscence of childhood mornings with the relatives who had raised me in Hill County.

On the back of the cereal box before me was the entire life history of some racecar driver. It was not compelling information, but the illustrated narrative prompted a wave of memories for me. My favorite cereal as a kid was Cheerios, but Nabisco Shredded Wheat had the best promotional inserts. I asked my mother to buy the cereal for me because of a series of 4-by-7-inch cards that were inserted between the layers of shredded wheat biscuits.

The comic illustrated on these cards was "Straight Arrow," featuring the story of a Comanche hero who righted societal wrongs, as any good comic-strip super-hero should do. As my mother explained, the idea was to read the cards as I finished each layer of biscuits. Sure.

The minute Momma left the kitchen, I'd carefully remove each of the biscuits and place them on the table so as not to break any. Crumbs were okay and easily removed. When finished reading the precious document, each card and layer of biscuits was replaced in reverse order, as if untouched. As a child, I was always convinced I would have made a great secret agent. Subterfuge was clearly my specialty.

Straight Arrow was not only about a Comanche hero's exciting adventures and rescues but also gave excellent descriptions of Indian costumes and customs, with detailed illustrations of bow-making, campfire building, arrowhead types, and the like. I laid out the 4-by-7-inch Straight Arrow illustrated cards before me, in sequence, while I ate one biscuit, dry like a cracker.

I'm sure my joy over these cards, as early discovered art treasures, was no less than when, as an adult, I first saw the glorious illustrations of the priceless Lindisfarne Gospels manuscript in the British Museum. Like my student Jenn, who made her pilgrimage to illustrated caves in Sulawesi, I made mine to Holy Island. Also called Lindisfarne Island, it is the site of the monastery that created the magnificently illustrated *Lindisfarne Manuscript* or *Gospels* of about AD 715. The illustrated narrative of early illuminated manuscripts unfolds not unlike modern comic strips.

It's interesting to me now that both types of artworks, comic strip cards or illuminated vellum, were illustrated allegory, lessons on how to properly live one's life with meaningful purpose.

~

As a boy, I often enjoyed long stays at the farmhouse of my Aunt Lorene and Uncle Bill in Hill County. Breakfast at their table was a huge affair, necessary for a good start to the workday. Everybody, including myself, the youngest, had a full day's chores ahead. The family sat around a large circular table while my aunt fried up bacon and eggs, baked biscuits, and poured glasses of farm-fresh milk for us kids.

After saying grace, the early morning feast began. In the middle of the table were assorted boxes of cereal, to be eaten almost as a dessert, after the hot food. My cousins usually ate corn flakes. I recall the large rooster illustrated on the box cover. I'm sure I thought it was on the box because of the farm, somehow. Aunt Lorene always kindly included a box of Cheerios for me. Those were wonderful family breakfasts on the farm, with warm laughter shared around the table midst four cousins and my uncle and aunt.

Artists have always celebrated the family meal in genre paintings of domestic interiors. One of my favorites was painted by the eighteenth-century French master, Chardin, and another by America's popular illustrator, Norman Rockwell.

Jean-Baptiste Chardin's 1740 masterpiece, "Grace Before a Meal," features a mother setting the dinner table with two daughters seated before her. It is typical of Chardin's unfailing ability to capture an intimate domestic moment in paint. The mother silently observes the older daughter's earnest instruction of her younger sister on how to say a proper grace before the meal.

The little daughter sits upright in her child's chair, hands dutifully pressed together before her, reciting the prayer. We viewers observe the touching scene, perhaps through the eyes of the unseen but appreciative father.

Also, in response to a famous 1941 speech by President Franklin Roosevelt, Norman Rockwell completed his 1942 painted expressions of Roosevelt's "Four Essential Human Freedoms," including the artist's iconic "Freedom from Want." Better known as Rockwell's "Thanksgiving Dinner" picture, a family holiday meal is in progress. Posed against a large dining room window, the grandmother places turkey and platter upon the table, her aproned silhouette overlapping the grandfather's dark suit.

He, prepared to do the carving, completes the top of the triangular composition. Around the perimeter of the frame are nine smiling faces, eagerly anticipating the meal set before them, including the traditional celery, pickle and cranberry trays. In the lower right corner, one face in the family is turned toward the viewer, as if we are invited, but unseen, guests at the table.

~

Thanksgiving is my favorite holiday, since childhood. Yes, Halloween is a great lead-in for a kid to Thanksgiving and then Christmas and then New Year noise. But my earliest memories of Thanksgiving just felt more fulfilling, less dramatic, less hectic. The weather usually allowed time outdoors to play with my favorite cousins, tossing footballs and horseshoes or riding bikes on mostly empty rural county roads. Thanksgiving was simple, wholesome, and all our mothers were master bakers.

I think it's a bit of a surprise, shocking even, for some Americans traveling abroad to discover that Thanksgiving is not a global holiday. Not that societal gratitude is not expressed in another form abroad, just that Americans expect our tradition of the holiday to occur every November, kind of everywhere. Our neighbors up in Canada have a national holiday of Thanksgiving every October. When I taught in the UK, I learned that some of my Derby colleagues celebrated "Harvest Home" in September or October, a kind of fall festival but without turkey and dressing.

I was a young widower the year of my teacher exchange to the UK, and it was the first Thanksgiving for little Liz to be without her mom. She was in a good primary school right around the corner from our place, a narrow two-story abode, one of a row of connected brick homes built in the late nineteenth century for British Rail employees. A narrow, pedestrian *snicket* ran efficiently between cozy, closely trimmed backyards on either side. It was a year of discoveries for both of us, healthy diversions during our shared grief.

Liz was quickly learning local dialog from her school friends. One day, while I was upset and grumbling over trying to figure out how to get the small, wall-mounted tankless water heater restarted, Liz shocked me. Leaning in the kitchen door jamb, little arms crossed as her mother would have done, my child was observing my growing frustration. She calmly advised me, "Dad, don't have a *MENTAL*." And her, not nearly yet a teen! "Rough sailing ahead," I thought, considering the years to come too soon.

My kind mother-in-law, Linda, joined her favorite granddaughter and me for that week in November while folks back home celebrated the holiday. In one of her suitcases, she'd tucked away two big plastic storage bags of pecans from San Saba. Linda was determined that Liz and I would not be without her famous pecan pie that Thanksgiving. It was a loving gesture. We three had lost a daughter, a wife, and a mother, all in one person's passing. We grieved together.

On Thanksgiving Day, the house comforted us, full of the holiday's memorable aromas of ginger, cinnamon, nutmeg, savory dressing, butter-basted turkey, and two pecan pies in our small oven. It had taken us all a while, but with help from Liz, we soon figured out that 350 degrees Fahrenheit is 177 degrees Celsius in the UK. All was right with the world.

Liz and I sat on the floor of our little parlor, just off the kitchen, drawing colorful live turkeys, English pilgrims, and Wampanoag Native Americans with lush soft pastels on pure cotton paper. (Britain has a long history of superb drawing materials). Linda was in the adjoining room setting the dining table with seasonal-colored flowers, napkins, and candles. We'd planned to eat our holiday meal much later that afternoon, sharing with a couple of neighbors we'd invited.

At about 1:30, thc friendly hand-twist chime in the middle of our sturdy front door cheerfully rang out "r-r-r-ing, r-r-r-ing" twice.

"Good grief!" Linda exclaimed, as she escaped to the kitchen. "Your guests are too early!" Liz kept drawing. She's always been good at staying on task.

I walked down the narrow hallway and opened the front door. Standing on the stoop was a serious-looking man wearing a suit and tie.

"Hello," I said. He looked down at a list of names on a clipboard he held and asked "Mister Bartlett? Samuel Bartlett?"

I wondered to myself "Gospel Lighthouse? Latter Day Saints? United Way?"

The man in the suit held out his hand and spoke.

"Mr. Bartlett, I am Detective Tom Mann, of the local Derbyshire Constabulary. I'm with the alien registry division."

As he paused, I could hear Linda huff just behind me and storm back to the kitchen. She had followed me to the door and probably didn't like the sound of the word "alien." I shook the detective's hand and invited him in.

"Just a few questions" he assured me, as we stepped into the dining room.

"Would you like a cup of coffee?" I asked, knowing a pot was still warm on the hob, as my Brit neighbors would call the stovetop.

"That's very kind of you. Lovely, thanks." As I excused myself to the kitchen, he sat down while placing his papers on the table before him.

Linda helped me prepare a tray. Through a tightly clenched jaw, she managed to complain in an angry whisper to my ear, "YOU are no alien!" I held the tray, while considering her heated opinion.

"Well, actually I AM an alien. Legal, but still alien." My protective Texas mother-in-law pursed her lips with silent rebuke aimed in my direction.

I returned with a tray that held two mugs of coffee and a matching sugar bowl and creamer set that Liz had chosen at a rummage sale we attended in Bakewell. The pattern was a single violet crocus bloom on white. Liz had sneaked into the dining room to get a look at our unexpected guest while I was busy in the kitchen. She ignored the scowl I sent in her direction.

Already seated at the table beside him, Liz was proudly showing the detective her Thanksgiving drawings. I allowed her a couple of minutes to run down the list of items soon to be enjoyed for our holiday dinner, as Tom Mann seemed happy with their little chat.

Suddenly, little Liz sat back in her chair, arms crossed in bewilderment, and asked of the man in the suit, "Really? You've really never had *pecan pie*?!" Looking at me with a disapproving glare I'd seen before on her grandmother's face, the one in the kitchen, my daughter huffed an audible rebuke, "Daddy!" To her, it seemed somehow, I was responsible for this major pie injustice, an international tragedy.

I said, "Okay, honey, that's enough. Mr. Mann and I have business to discuss. Go help your grandmother in the kitchen."

"Happy Thanksgiving, Mr. Mann," she said sincerely, almost with tears in her eyes, and left us without looking my way. It's a blessing and a curse that your own child thinks you orchestrate all of life's comings and goings.

Detective Mann explained that during the first several months of a legal alien's arrival, the county constabulary must have an official agent visit the recorded residence of said alien and verify that all is legit. That seemed reasonable enough to me. I answered his list of questions. The whole interview took only about forty minutes. He told me that his son was doing a culinary course of study at my college. Tom Mann had grown up in a family of sheep farmers out in the Peaks District, near Tissington, so we each had farm stories to share.

After Linda realized I wasn't going to be hauled off to Alien Prison after all, she insisted that Tom should have a piece of her famous pecan pie. Liz applauded the idea with glee and helped her grandmother with the preparations. We all talked and laughed over coffee and pecan pie, served up with a rich dollop of clotted cream on top. Thus, our new friend, the Derbyshire detective, experienced a little slice of a Texas Thanksgiving.

Jackrabbit Grooming

SIX

Wild Things and a Farm Table

Mornings of late have been very chilly up at the farm. The day begins by moving horses from stalls to paddocks and pasture, their big lungs and nostrils exhaling great blasts of warm steam into the cold air. Next, the Tunis sheep are turned out of the sheepfold, their round, sturdy drywall stone windbreak, into pasture. The ewes and lambs are greeted by their guardians, Sol the little donkey and giant Augustus Caesar, the full name of our Great Pyrenees/Akbash canine cross.

Most mornings, Solomon spends a few minutes herding the flock this way and that just to reaffirm who's in charge. Caesar yawns and stretches his long curving back in a "downward dog" yoga pose, resembling a snow-covered ski ramp. With the sheep being put through their paces by the little equine, the tall dog takes the opportunity to scan the horizon for signs of wild undesirables, like feral hogs or coyotes. In the spring, during lambing season, the big guy watches the sky too, just in case a soaring owl or hawk gets a hankering for tiny and tasty still-red-colored Tunis lamb infants.

Recently, just at dawn, I was outside gathering kindling for the studio wood-burning stove, while a pot of coffee brewed inside on the iron stove's top flat plate. It was one of those unexpected moments when nature thumps your senses with a pleasant surprise. I was at the edge of the pasture, picking up fallen tree stuff along the woods that skirt Hackberry Creek. I looked up from my search directly into the eyes of a stunningly beautiful red fox staring back at me, as if to ask, "What are YOU doing here?"

A field mouse hung limp in the delicately pointed mouth of the pretty fox. A mouse morsel for her kits, no doubt. Apparently, we were both hunting in a prime area for our desired prey, field mice for the fox, kindling sticks for me. Our cold morning encounter was brief, as my ever-vigilant canine companions spotted the wild creature and immediately gave chase. Nike, the Bluetick Coonhound, and her elder running mate, Blackie the mutt, normally spend most of their time during such morning walks racing ahead of me to get to the best sticks. The canines immediately shifted gears from their "tease the farmer" game to "let's chase the fox" game, a major distraction that instantly ripped their attention away from suddenly unimportant fallen tree branches. An unexpected adventure like this must be pursued with all the vigor that eight paws can expend. Later that afternoon, the hound and mutt duo would elaborate and inflate the fox-find event into epic proportions and significance for sharing with big Caesar and Tommy Cat.

The last I saw of the magical wild creature was the white flag at the end of her fluffy red tail, flying off into the creek bottom. Needless to say, the wily vixen was into the thick underbrush in an instant, eluding the well-fed pair of domestic critters now in vain pursuit, their canine paws moving laboriously in deep snow along the creek bed banks.

Wild creatures amaze us, especially when we trespass on their home turf. We are in awe, really, because wildness seems so beautifully harmonized in situ, compared to discovering a wild creature rightfully fearful or defensive on civilized, "developed" property. One minute, the animal in nature is invisible to us. In the next, the thing appears, confronting us with our own domestication, our tameness in uncivilized environs. Seen before me is a creature I don't feed, one that does not identify me with food, compared to, say, the farm's gentrified bluegill and small-mouthed bass that leap at the surface to gulp down game food pellets I spread across the lake's surface for them. When the weather is warmer, with them swimming close to the top, they'll gather just at the sight of my profile at the water's edge, fish-food bucket in hand. Like all sentient beings, fish have strong recall of reliable food sources. Ours at the farm just don't have to work very hard to get regular meals, unlike wild trout in a mountain stream.

From my second-story painting studio, I catch glimpses of wild things throughout the day and night, especially winged ones. From my elevated aerie windows, I look out over the front horse pasture toward the pecan grove off to one side and Hackberry Creek on the other.

This fall, at about 4:30 every afternoon, I've been treated with the sight of a Great Blue Heron that glides down over the front pasture like some prehistoric bird, his broad shadow disappearing into the sumac and Water Oaks along the creek. There he strolls amongst tall marsh grass and cattails, moving stealthily, carefully, like an acrobat on stilts, selecting choice items along nature's own buffet of raw fresh-water sushi.

On rare but spectacular occasions, from the second story studio I spot a huge two-foot-tall Ferruginous Hawk perched on top of a nearby powerline pole. He stands erect, surveying his wide domain, a grand bird's-eye view of his own buffet of small field mammals scurrying here and there across the pasture below. His broad white chest and exquisite white tail feathers make him look like a bedecked king. He should be a king. That one pole, his tall throne, cost me over a thousand dollars when the power coop installed it.

It's worth every penny just to watch this regal flying hunter swoop down over the front pasture. From my own studio-nest high up in the air, I get to see all the colors and movements of those active articulated hawk feathers of wings, back, and tail, from above his royal personage.

There is a unique, standoffish kind of beauty to wild things, an austerity about them. They stand apart as we human "developers" further shape and define their wild world into forms we consider more habitable for ourselves. The wild things, apparently unlike us, cannot live on concrete. They have no need for tailgate parties and don't mind getting their bare feet dirty.

The nineteenth-century French Realist painter Gustave Courbet captured the rawness of the world of wild things in a graphic painting that is included in the collection of the Dallas Museum of Art.

Courbet's "Fox in the Snow," c. 1860, is a very animated picture of a fox dispatching his rodent catch on a cold winter's day. The setting for the drama is a wild wood covered in a thick blanket of snow.

Typical of Courbet, the painting is denied mythical majesty for the cause of realism. There's no romance in the style. There's no neoclassical allegory at work here, no anthropomorphizing of the wild creature. The snow and the fur and the rocks are tactile. The fox is hungry. The fox eats.

Blood spatters from the rodent-prey stand out starkly against the pristine crispness of the white snow-covered ground. The fox is not at his leisure, as we *gourmands* might dine. Ancient Romans would have been even more casually hedonistic at mealtime than we are. In proper Latin prescription, their august physicians advised the public that eating in a prone position, lying down, was best for delicate human tummies. In the compelling painting, Courbet's wild subject's *canidae* spine is in a pronounced reverse arch, his crouched body ready to spring away in an instant at the sight of another wild interloper that might challenge him for the catch. Or is he scanning his surroundings for a two-legged hunter?

~

A Farm Fable

Jack lived on the far western edge of Bartlett Farm, out on the broad semi-arid plains. His small homestead was landscaped by nature with mainly desert grass and sagebrush, plus the occasional wind-stunted mesquite that provided the tallest foliage above the mostly flat expanse. He had napped long and late, so arose to a spectacular sunset that was well on its way.

Stretching his long frame across the full length of his safe sleeping space, Jack paused to clean his ears and proceeded to give them a vigorous shaking. Behind the vertical cover of a small mesquite tree, he sat up straight, extending his long ears up into space like weather antennae. Chill was still in the air. He sensed a bit of foreboding frost as well, so instinctively contracted the thousands of blood vessels in his giant ears to smaller diameters, preserving body heat for the cold night's foraging that lay ahead.

Jack surveyed his surroundings in all directions. With an eye on either side of his head, he could achieve this task while his body remained still as a stone. He recognized other members of his tribe, the *drove*, scattered here and there, each performing similar in-place reconnoiters, getting the lay of the land. While scanning the horizon for signs of danger, he simultaneously made a head count. To the human eye, the jackrabbit array would have appeared motionless, just so many figurative sculptural figures, like silent garden gnomes.

But the assembly was a serious hunting party made up of albeit herbaceous hunters and foragers. Foraging with family provided extensive surveillance for safer dining for all. Their defensive skills were notable, especially including the ability to be stone-still, while blending into the sparse high mountain desert landscape. If caught, by, say a bobcat or coyote, Jack's long hind legs will go into action immediately as formidable weapons, with the punch of a donkey's kick delivered repeatedly. Along with this painful foot assault, the jackrabbit simultaneously projects from his larynx a deafening shriek, frightening in its volume and pitch to all within range. Sometimes the piercing, demonic scream alone is enough to prompt an escape for Jack's kind. The underside of Jack's black tail is white. This bright flag is flashed when needed to warn other jackrabbits, if the bearer is lucky enough to escape a wannabe predator. A jackrabbit can leap twenty feet in one bound, run 40 miles per hour, and turn on a dime, zig-zagging its way to freedom.

While counting drove members, Jack instinctively cocked his right rear foot into the air, beside his head. He stretched his four toes apart for deep cleaning. Extending his long tongue like a flexible vacuum cleaner hose, he located and removed a deep-seated desert sticker bur that had irritated his sleep with bad dreams. He discharged the stubborn burr into a furrow of his protective mesquite tree's rough bark.

Jack's ears, flipping back and forth independently, picked up a faint but disturbing sound. It was human talk coming toward the drove. Though nature provided the family members with effective camouflage coats, they were a large drove, scattered over a wide area of sparse cover. Out of his left eye he caught sight of two boy-humans coming up over a low, sandy rise, their contours outlined against the open sky. One of the teens carried his dad's bolt-action .22 rifle loosely over his shoulder, like a jaunty soldier. He hadn't loaded it yet, waiting till they would get closer to their destination, a small stand of Hackberries with a couple of post oaks thrown in, that the boy hoped would be full of squirrels. The other teen rested his small .410 side-by-side, double-barreled shotgun, hung open like a hinge over his elbow. He was hunting for birds.

The human talk grew louder as the boys approached the drove. Jack instantly sounded the alarm, notes of such a high pitch the human forms' tiny, inferior ears couldn't detect them. Some members of the drove froze in place, their contours and fur-tones blended into the same-colored striations of mesquite tree trunks. Others lay prone, stretched out on their bellies, making the line of their backs as horizontal, as flat as possible against the gray and brown earth. Some lay on their backs, limbs stretched out flat, so to be able to rotate their eyes in all directions, scanning the air around them for any sight of the teen hunters, come to kill. With only the occasional tuft of desert grass or weed to hide their lanky bodies, the drove was vulnerable. At Jack's first command, the drove would scramble, zigzag, in all directions. Though they made formidable moving targets, some would likely die, especially amongst the young and the old.

Unbeknownst to the frozen-in-place drove, the walking boys were engaged in serious discussion about the veracity of performance specifications of this pickup truck or that one. The boys called them "specs." Neither was old enough yet to drive off the farm, but like all hopeful rural Texas kids they envisioned themselves one day hitting the road for exotic destinations on their own set of wheels. The boy-humans walked and talked right past the motionless drove without ever looking in their direction, their adolescent brains focused on future pickups and nearby squirrels and birds just ahead.

Moments passed, then half an hour, since anyone's keen ears in the drove had caught even the slightest hint of human talk. Then came the occasional sound of a rifle and a shotgun being fired. Though muted by distance, the pops and booms were alarming. The boy hunters had arrived at the wood grove, far off from the wary drove of hares, who resumed foraging cautiously, as before. Night was coming, so the boy-humans would retire to their own families soon, hopefully leaving the drove undiscovered.

Jack, along with a couple of other middle-aged hares, munched on a tasty and colorful purple prickly pear supper. Seeing only the colors green and blue (dichromatic color vision), everything else is perceived in extensive variations of gray by jackrabbits. Seeing a limitless range of values (lights and darks) and having a keen sense of depth perception is everything to the survival of drove members against predators. Green and blue identify sources of food and water. Millions of monochromatic grays identify sizes and shapes of predators and the distance between hare and hunter. The bright yellow flowers of the prickly pear stood out to Jack's big eyes, but only as an intense lighter value than the purple flat cactus pads. In the hottest time of summer, cacti become the major source of water for Jack and his family. Jackrabbit families are devoted to each other largely because survival depends on it.

Jack's small foraging trio neared the elder doe, Healer. In her aged, noble presence, all the hares paid honor. Jack placed a tasty piece of prickly pear at her feet. She smiled through squinting, aged eyes. Smelling his unique scent told her it was Jack, the drove's adult buck leader. Her ancient eyes had developed a kind of fog, inhibiting her vision. She had known Jack since his first day of inhaled breath, taking nature's world into his young kit's nostrils. He had grown up under her watchful eye, earning her respect at every turn. She admired his wit and his cunning way with would-be predators, especially how he kept the drove one step ahead of human forms and their unnatural motives. The drove watched out for her, regarding Healer as the ancestral mother of them all. Several hares always stayed close by so she could keep her navigational bearings through their presence and should have easy access to food and water. In hot summers, the water was often brought to Healer in the form of heavy cacti pads, incisor-chiseled into respectfully appropriate-sized portions for her.

Having foraged undisturbed for an hour or so, some of the drove's members paused in awe of the last rim of sunlight, a thin band of yellow fire clinging to the horizon like a single fallen blade of Arizona Cottontop grass. Several lucky hares came upon a treasure trove of winter-growing wild arugula. They feasted and murmured mutual appreciation between full-cheek chews of the piquant leafy green, their long whiskers now redolent with a horseradish-like aroma.

Jack's ears shot toward the sound of human talk, not far off. In the fading evening light, his keen eyes detected the form of two approaching boy-hunters silhouetted against the sunset. Considering options, Jack decided that confusion and carnage might result if the boys find a large array of hares all at once. In near nightfall, the young humans might even wound or kill each other during a melee. Healer would not approve of such a disaster.

The young hunters were too near the drove's closest perimeter. Jack radioed clear instructions to his corporals in ultra high-pitched frequency. The boys heard nothing unusual, but the hares all listened intently, preparing themselves. They were to remain still until Jack offered himself as a distracting target for the boys, and then quietly disperse into the dark in a broader formation away from the distinctly possible fracas. High-pitched murmurs were whispered amongst themselves, unheard by other species.

"Wait for the signal," one of the young bucks said. Some younger kits quivered with fear but stayed in place.

"Don't jump the gun," advised one of the elders.

"Shhh. FOCUS," an ancient doe admonished.

Jack calculated the distance between the two boy-humans' walking bodies. He studied the angle of flight he must take to turn their attention farthest away from the drove's location. To maximize opportunity for the drove's escape into the darkness, Jack would aim for the last remaining glow of sunset on the horizon, far away. At just the right moment, while the boys were laughing and snorting at each other in that silly human way, Jack leapt twenty feet ahead, his trajectory propelling him in the air on a line exactly halfway between the hunters' bodies.

Startled and a bit frightened by Jack's preemptive mid-air maneuver, the boys did their best to keep eyes on the speedy target, while struggling to get their guns reloaded quickly. The bird-hunter was fastest, dropping two shells in place, snapping the little shotgun closed, and aiming in the direction of the elusive prey. Jack was racing here and there, zigging and zagging, while the drove stealthily disappeared into the dark night. The boy knew how to lead a bird or dove, firing only when sure the dove would fly into the pellet pattern just ahead of it. He had turned first left, then right, then back again, when he decided to fire, deciding that the big buck would either turn into the pattern or away. He had a 50-50 chance.

The resultant bang sent a murder of crows scattering loudly out of the hackberry trees in all directions, thus further distracting the boys. Jack had veered correctly but was hit in a hip by a couple of pellets on the outer edge of the boy's shot-pattern. The big hare went to ground immediately, trying to gauge the extent of the wound before attempting to bound twenty feet into the air again. He lay perfectly still, hoping to sense reasonable blood flow and flexibility of the injured leg. Flat on his belly beneath a short, wind-whipped sage bush, he feared his heart was pounding loudly enough to give him away.

In the distance, Jack heard one of the boy-humans moaning and cursing. He was also lying down, having tripped on a large clump of desert grass and fallen forward, rifle and shells flying into the dark air ahead of him. The bird-hunter would search for a dead jackrabbit (he hoped) shortly but decided to help his friend stand up again. He tried to help dust off the fallen boy, who let out a high-pitched yelp of pain in the process.

"Get off me, ya' damn fool! Ya' shot me instead of the buck!"

Indeed, the poor novice hunter had moved forward quickly in the dark and at an angle that put his own hip just at the other extreme edge of the shot-pattern of pellets. So, the boy and Jack were clipped with a few pellets each from the same shot, most of the serious pellets having fallen harmlessly between hunter and hare in the dead space between them.

Jack stayed prone till his long ears convinced him the young trophy hunters had given up for the night. One boy walked, the other limped. His mother would later weep at the sight of two pellets slightly imbedded in her careless son's upper buttock. She would patch up the humiliated boy's wound while wiping away tears of joy that he hadn't been killed.

Two elders joined Jack as he, too, limped back toward the drove. They brought him to Healer, who carefully smelt and felt around his wound with her long muzzle and whiskers. He was at such a distance that the several pellets that reached him when fired had already fallen away from the slight indentions made in his padded hip. Healer advised he lie on his side, wounded hip down, directly upon the recently discovered bed of aromatic arugula. "The herbal oils will reduce the swelling," Healer explained. Jack followed her instructions that he should lie still for a few hours that night. She said he also needed time for his heart rate to return to normal. The little engine that pumped his blood was pounding, still. He closed his long-lashed eyes, comforted by the care of his family.

The drove resumed its normal night-foraging. Low conversations in the dark could be heard as the hares talked admiringly and with gratitude for Jack's bravery and leadership skills. Stories were shared of other near-disasters averted due to his cunning and agility. Weariness brought sleep upon the resting buck as others discussed the likelihood that Jack would become a legend someday.

~

A sharp cold wind howled outside, rushing around the corners of the barn. The interior walls groaned a bit in response. Rafters creaked now and then overhead. There's a sometimes-annoying rhythmic whistle below the metal roof's southeast eave on windy nights. I kept hoping it would stay tame, as I was enjoying a bit of a reverie downstairs amongst my four-legged critters. Along the barn's deep expanse, a horse head would occasionally stretch over a stall's top-rail out into the wide hallway. Excess oat crumbs fell out the sides of Samson's big mouth, extended as it was several feet into the hallway space. His head was turned slightly in my direction, curious perhaps as to why his master was seated downstairs with the animals instead of upstairs painting a picture.

Mind you, Samson's never been upstairs, but he has a good imagination. The dogs and a cat are frequent studio visitors, of course. But they've never bought a painting. Now that I think of it, one of my four-legged livestock critters did pay a visit. Young blind Homer, when just a little red ram-to-be, once climbed the steep stairs to the second floor.

Following closely behind me, as he always did in those early days on the farm, he ascended those steps with the agility of a mountain goat.

Mammals, like Homer, are capable of amazing adjustments of attention amongst their numerous senses. That is, when one sense is diminished through injury or age, mammals adjust to compensate. In little Homer's case, he followed me around the farm like a dog, relying on his acute sense of smell and sound. And up and down the studio stairs he could confidently go on sensitive tiny legs related to distant cousins like bighorn sheep.

It would not seem unusual to my barn residents for me to be up in the studio late at night painting or drawing on a new commission, quite likely with a looming deadline. But Samson, my giant equine intellectual, is observant enough to notice I'm lingering longer downstairs tonight than usual. I'm reflecting on recent days, recent evenings just past. I'm stretched back against the closed feed room door, sitting on a short stack of empty burlap feedstore bags, boots resting ahead of me in the midst of assorted tired canines and one cat. The cat is curled up in my lap, of course, purring away. On one hip is bony-headed hound Nike, her long, pretty snout raised up on top of my pants pocket, her black nose occasionally caressed with cat fur. The pretty hound doesn't mind. She and Tommy Cat are simpatico creatures. They share a love of frequent naps in close proximity.

Blackie, our elder canine, has her arthritic back pressed firmly against my left thigh. I'm wearing some well-worn, heavy wide-wale corduroy pants that Annie and Liz found for me at a thrift store in Wichita Falls last winter. The warm fabric must be a comfort for the loyal mutt's old spine. Augustus Caesar, ever independent, is just across the hall, fast asleep in front of the stall I've put Sol into for the night. These two shepherds brought all the lambs and ewes up under the barn's east side covered shelter earlier in the chilly evening. So, the ovine gang is cuddled together soundly, out of the wind and free from possibly heavy snowfall tonight.

Sol is audibly, contentedly, crunching the last bits of oats and alfalfa cube flakes in the bottom of his feed bucket. Though too short to be seen, once he's tucked inside his stall, every now and then I detect his big, dark donkey's eyes peering out through the wooden rail's horizontal gaps. Occasionally, the little ass looks over at me so intensely that he chuffs emphatically. Like his big friend, Samson, Sol probably also is wondering what I'm up to, leisurely sitting on the floor. But mostly while chewing away, he glances down at his canine pal's fluffy white back just below him, asleep on the hallway floor. At some angles, our resident Pyrenees looks much like a polar bear.

Tonight is a kind of a winter reverie for me during this annual lull between Thanksgiving and Christmas. It is certainly a unique holiday season this year, the weeks and months ahead promising big changes at Bartlett Farms. I've come to learn that later in the new year, a boy who grew up as one of our part-time hired teen farmhands will become our full-time son-in-law. Still can't get my head completely around it, but Annie and Liz are already busy at planning a rural wedding party next year to rival their recently successful hullabaloo, the moonlight hayride. Typically, I was the last to learn of this momentous turn of events.

~

Vern had been home from UTA for a couple of days, just before the recent cold snap and my mid-winter reverie, a holiday bonding time with all my four-legged pals in the barn. His schedule on the cusp of final exam week to come, Vern's mom probably washed and ironed shirts for him all weekend. Like Annie, the boy likes a little starch in his shirts. After helping his dad all day Saturday at the Elysia Volunteer Fire Department, he'd come over to have supper with us. At the station, the father-and-son team were installing new modular shelving and reorganizing the fire department's large supply room based on Vern's assessment and new space-saving design. Garland must be tickled pink that his son is already able to put that soon-to-be-completed engineering degree of his to good use.

It was a crisp evening, but dry, so it was pleasantly comfortable sweater weather. Vern and I sat caddy-corner to each other in the old Adirondack chairs. A warm red winter sun was lingering over the herb gardens up on the distant hill. The girls had shushed us out of the warm kitchen where we'd been trying to have a standing discussion about tractor horsepower. They wearied of our pretense at providing help, us moving from position to position across the room to avoid collisions.

Annie finally said, “Okay. Stop.” We all stood still, awaiting instructions.

“I'm tired of this kitchen floor dance. It's unpleasant and unproductive. Men need to leave. Go out back. Solve the world's problems out there. Now, please.”

Liz and Annie's arms all stayed crossed over chests till Vern and I made hasty retreats out the back door. We descended the short flight of steps down to the flagstone patio, our wine glasses hastily in tow.

We settled back, pausing in mid-thoughts, in the secure arms of the old wooden chairs. Our still half-full glasses of a great Nebbiolo rested comfortably on those wide level arms. Often this time of the year, a family of owls takes up residence in the trees surrounding the patio. Their low-toned but audible murmurs to each other inspire human silence.

We did not take up our erstwhile horsepower conversation that had begun in the kitchen. Those data-driven thoughts and comments faded into oblivion, drifting away into the calming sunset.

“Sam.” Vern broke the silence, saying my name aloud, with a serious period on the end. I was halfway through a sip of the rich red nectar from Italy. I swallowed quickly.

“Yes?”

“I want to ask you something. It's important.” Okay, not about tractors then, I thought. Then a second thought struck me, one full of portent, “Here it comes, Sammy.”

I took another short sip, swallowed, and said, as reassuringly as I could sound, “Shoot, Vern. What is it?”

I knew what it was. In a few seconds, all the years of visual memories of my little Liz growing up reeled before my mind's eyes. Paralleled beside those images was a less distinct but equally valid mental video of Vern's own maturing life. During a sometimes-daily presence here at the farm, I've watched him grow from teen to man. Vern is a good man of few words. He's never been one for much small talk.

He took a sip of wine. Leaving his glass on the arm of the chair, he leaned forward, elbows on thighs, clasping his hands before him.

Looking me in the eye as directly as possible in the dimming light, Vern spoke.

"I want to ask you for Liz's hand in marriage. For your blessing, Sam."

More momentous words have never been spoken to me. I wanted to let them sink in longer, but I didn't want Vern to think I was hesitant to answer.

"Yes, to that, Vern. And yes, to my blessing for you both."

"Thank you, Sam. Thank you," Vern repeated as we stood and happily hugged each other. Returning side by side up to the porch steps, we saw the back-lit silhouettes of Liz and Annie. They were standing arm in arm, having been watching us the whole time from just inside the porch screen door.

Lost Caboose

SEVEN

Epiphany on the Veranda and a Firefly Landscape

June has greeted us with an explosion of color all around the farmhouse. Annie designed long curved beds for flowering plants at the front. The beds parallel the curved contour of the county road as it gently arcs toward the farm's main entry to the east. Our own crushed rock road broadly curves by the barn, around the front horse pasture and pecan grove, then up the hill to the herb gardens. At a "Y" in the road, a branch leads off northwest to the house.

Getting around to the house takes a few moments. But I figure by the time visitors arrive and get parked near the back patio, mentally they've been able to leave much of the noise of society behind them.

The curved beds out front have plenty of sun exposure right up till one or two in the early afternoon. Then the giant old Bur Oak on one side and our gorgeous Red Oak on the other, along with the tall hip-roofed two-story house itself, all cast a wide skein of cooling shade on the flower beds. So, the soil and the inhabitants of those curved beds are kept in the dark, so to speak, relatively unaware of the blistering sunlight hours of a Barnes County afternoon. From the porch, even on the hottest of afternoons, the front yard is a spectacular mosaic of dappled light and shade shapes, the kind of natural composition that Monet and Renoir captured in paint.

The beds are diversely arranged so that different flowering species rub elbows with each other. Throughout the mostly warm months that we have here, there's and ebb and flow of blooms that are vibrant for a time, then fade and fall to make room for some other family to show off. Robustly blooming now are the dwarf Rose of Sharon, yellow and orange lantana, orange and coral coneflowers, black and blue salvia, and Wandering Jew, with dark green variegated leaves and perky purple blossoms on top.

For all of May, the tall red yucca stalks, bountiful in evenly spaced pink and yellow skinny bell-like flowers, hosted countless hummingbirds in the daytime and countless moths at night. The prickly pear cacti's fat yellow flowers fed an army of butterflies for many weeks. If you listen closely, you will hear big bumblebees tumbling and bouncing about inside the many ball-shaped prickly pear blooms, drunk within each yellow labyrinth of sweet nectar walls. Those translucent walls seduce bumblebees with vivid ultraviolet light that humans cannot see. Nature's gifts are highly selective, fine-tuned for each species. Humans get certain gifts. Bumblebees get others.

Annie chose to include dwarf Rose of Sharon just for me. She knows how much I love those large white flowers with deep red centers. It's the very same flower that blooms on hibiscus, okra, and cotton, as well. They're all members of the mallow family. Rose of Sharon takes a bit of frequent watering at first to get the roots established. But once it's off and running, it's drought resistant, too, with infrequent deep watering. They last about thirty years, so there's a good chance these will outlive me.

Several flagstone paths meander between the flower beds, leading from the front porch steps. Our veranda wraps around the front and east side of the house. I painted the beadboard ceiling the same pale blue color my grandparents used on their porches. Every farmhouse did the same back in those days to keep birds and wasps from building nests above human heads. Granny said that winged creatures like yellowjackets and starlings are smart enough to know they can't build nests in mid-air, so "Make them think the porch ceiling is made of sky." I believed her.

On some mornings, Annie and I have our coffee on the front porch to breathe in the rarefied air of a spectacular sunrise. We sit together in the wide porch swing, holding hands like we did in college long ago. We are struck speechless, awed by nature's symphony of color; a symphony painted by the "rosy-tipped fingers of Dawn," as Homer might say.

The house we live in came to me by way of a serendipitous meeting with Margaret Hawley, who was an institution in Elysia and environs back in the day. Freud likely would challenge me for emphasizing the element that chance or good fortune played in my retelling of how Margaret and I became great friends. That's okay. I've learned a lot about myself by reading Freud. I'm human. Humans look for meaning, for significance of purpose as we consider events that changed our lives, especially the coincidental ones. Homer was a human.

As I said, Margaret Hawley was an institution in Elysia and environs. Her husband, Reuben, as owner of the First National Bank, had loaned money for land, vehicles, surgeries, et al. to generations of Barnes County families. I met Margaret in her much later life, years after she was widowed. Margaret loved art, so we met, by chance, at a Fort Worth gallery opening that a younger mutual friend had brought her to see. My work was included in the group show. She liked one of my small colorful abstracts in particular and asked if Helen Frankenthaler's work had influenced me. She'd asked a discerning question. With a kindred grin, I replied, "It will take a few days of your time for me to tell you about her influence on my work." She bought the painting on the spot.

Over the following years, she attended a few of my public lectures and attended my art openings when she could get a ride. She often had lunch in the campus cafeteria, dining enthusiastically with me and my students. Margaret even took a couple of my art history classes at Barnes County College before health issues restricted her ambulatory ambitions. By the last days of her life, we had become devoted friends.

In early 1939, Reuben surprised her and their children with the announcement of his plans to build a more-or-less grand house in a style that Margaret loved, Greek Revival—in particular, Doric Revival, the columns of which rose to simple, stoic capitals. She disapproved of the fussiness of Corinthian style that soon became the rage. Reuben also announced to the family that he'd purchased thirty acres of farmland not far from Elysia city limits.

Margaret nearly fainted for joy. She would have plenty of room for a big vegetable garden, flower gardens, a fruit orchard, and the kids could get a horse. They had a good life on a single lot in town in a medium-sized but distinguished brick cottage. Their house near the square in Elysia even had an indoor bathroom, which most domiciles in the county didn't achieve before 1930. But the lot was too small for a functional garden. Margaret loved Reuben, but she'd grown up on a big sheep farm. He was a city boy, but she missed open spaces.

Reuben could be pompous on occasion, but he adored Margaret, and through their entire courtship and marriage he always kept an eye out for opportunities in his mind to make her life more enjoyable. He loved surprising her. The biggest piece of furniture in their house was a robust Baldwin upright piano that dominated one end of the dining room. Reuben had ordered a genuine Stickley expandable table that could be easily downsized. When he could persuade her to, his talented wife would play Chopin, Debussy, or Satie, her favorites, on the piano for guests.

He ordered the Greek Revival bungalow from Sears, Roebuck and Co. in Chicago. The whole house arrived by Union Pacific train, stacked in pieces on nine long flat cars. The stacks were so high that kids lined up to see if they would (hopefully) be too tall to clear the elevated footbridge that spanned over the tracks downtown. Kids love deconstruction. Reuben's old Army friend, Shorty, was in charge of construction. Shorty could build anything and had been a member of the Carpenters' Union since 1908. He was obligated to take a brief break from carpentry to work as a doughboy for three years, fighting a war in Europe.

Shorty had read up on prefab materials and methods before the war, so was excited to have a chance at building a home from a kit. He knew this to be the future, and the present, of modern domestic home building. He wanted in on the ground floor.

The home-kit featured a wide covered veranda that wrapped around the north and west sides, including five wooden Doric columns. An appropriately unadorned lintel stretched the whole length of both sides. "A dignified beam," Margaret called it. The roof featured two distinctive pyramid-shaped hips at the front and back of the house, connected by gabled sections. A handsome hip lantern rose high above the second floor and provided interior daylight for the tall attic.

Generous Margaret made sure that her two grown children understood that her artist friend Sam Bartlett would have right of first refusal for purchase of the house and farm when the time came. She included that proviso in her holographic will just in case I ever needed it. Margaret, with me in tow, gathered her children by conference call one day in the mayor's office downtown. She felt that being in the mayor's office added official gravitas to the moment.

Witnessed by her old family lawyer and her Methodist minister, she made her instructions crystal clear. As her children were raising their own families in other states, in other homes, she explained her plan for sale of the homestead. The kids affectionately admired Margaret's ever-vigilant pragmatism. We all laughed and cried over the communal speakerphone. Her son commented about their mom still "...taking charge, even into the beyond." They were content that if their mother's artist-friend Sam wanted the property, she would be honored in memory by me being on the place.

That's how Margaret's majestic farmhouse, that we live in, came to me.

Our resident mechanical engineer, José Cantú, took charge of restoring the Greek Revival edifice, along with help from me, several teens, and frequent days-long assistance from George Clay and Bill Goodman. We replaced some of the exterior with new shiplap pine. But much of the wood at the front of the house had been protected by the deep covered wraparound porch, and Margaret had done a good job of upkeep on the structure. The original front doors with vertical side windows were still in place as was the amazing dormer window above, complete with the hardware to open and close the dormer for ventilation through the hallway.

During one day's stripping and sanding of old lead-based paint, José gleefully called my attention to a particular front porch window. Clear as a bell, on one freshly stripped board, were pencil notations made about structural dimensions. Included were a couple of small, precise drawings, diagramming installation instructions for the wooden window frames. It took a few moments for it to register that we were admiring the hand drawn notes of Shorty the carpenter, who had built the house almost seven decades before.

Several such unexpected gifts have come to me over the years of occupation in this house, from Day One. The day I closed, after having signed and initialed the endless reams of papers related to title, deed, mortgage, and insurance, and transfer of the existing ag exemption, I headed out to my new homestead in the country, daughter in tow.

There was still a narrow driveway leading to the house back then. Cars were narrower in those days, and gravel drives rarely needed to accommodate more than one auto. Liz came home from college for a couple of days to celebrate with me. She always liked the proximity of her dorm rooms to classes, but she was excited to see the big open space that would be the new home. She also knew it would be a good escape from cabin fever when she needed one. Liz had met my friend Margaret at a couple of gallery openings but had not visited the farm before.

It was fall when I closed on the house and picked up the keys. Liz and I paused at the immense grandeur of the old Red Oak towering over much of the front yard. Every one of its millions of leaves was ablaze with fiery hue. A sudden breeze created a loud rustle across those ancient leaf-filled limbs, causing a diagonal cascade of the crisp autumn leaves to fall across us and the brick paved path to the front porch. They made percussive clicking sounds as they tumbled amongst and against their kin, on us, and finally floated like falling red kites to Earth.

Stepping up onto the airy veranda, Liz was drawn instantly to the old bench swing. It hung lopsided, with only one arm clinging to a rusty chain. It was a damaged diagonal swing. One end rested on the porch floor, with a few rusty links of chain curled like a snake alongside. It was a pitiful site. Liz touched the elevated arm gently, like Florence Nightingale might have done with a wounded patient. She gave me that reproachful look she's always sent my way when I haven't lived up to her expectations.

"Dad." Liz said the word as if it had a dozen slowly pronounced a's in it. The word hung in the air like a whole sentence.

"Okay," I relented. "We'll fix it."

"Today?" Liz wanted confirmation. "We'll fix it today, right?"

I sighed, audibly. "Yes, Marshall Dillon. Today."

"Marshall who?" she teased and took my arm as I unlocked the door.

We stepped into the long hallway that led to all the rooms of the big house, with a solid wood staircase to one side. The newel post finial mimicked the Doric columns of the porch, Margaret's favorite classical style. Turning to the right, we entered the light-filled parlor, through a handsome wide portal. I had enjoyed good conversations about art and music in this room with my old friend. Once she surprised me by playing Satie's three *Gymnopedies* with only silent, contemplative spaces between the pieces. The grand room resonated with the vibrations of each melancholic melody. Margaret rested her aged but confident hands in her lap and waited blissfully as those vibrations from her beloved Baldwin upright were peacefully absorbed into the parlor walls.

The room was empty, but in my mind it was full. No piano, no furniture, no coffee table books on art museum collections or classical architecture. The wallpaper was flawlessly intact. The rich but delicate pattern always made me think of the lively floral background in Botticelli's *La Primavera*. The Uffizi Galleries was a favorite for both of us, as Florence was mutually a favorite town. Margaret was a rather quiet person in public. I think she just found it difficult to tolerate small talk for very long. In private, she loved to pronounce precisely the proper Italian name, "Firenze," having fun rolling the "r" and emphasizing the middle syllable. Margaret could laugh at herself.

I was somewhat lost in my own nostalgia about the parlor that now was mine. My eyes focused on the wallpaper, up close and personal. The spell was broken by a single word, spoken across the room from behind me.

"Dad."

I turned to see my beautiful daughter smiling at me from the other side of the room, her back against the wall. Liz turned her face to the left. Next to her, at eye-level, was a small abstract painting suspended midst a sea of floral-patterned wallpaper. It sported a pinewood floating frame, stained only with a few applications of tung oil by my own hand. The little painting did its best to pay tribute to Helen Frankenthaler. It was the very painting that Margaret had bought the evening we met many years ago. The parlor was not empty after all.

~

For my art appreciation classes, I always compared looking at abstract painting to hearing a classical orchestral composition. Though Helen Frankenthaler made familiar seaside sketches, her abstract color field paintings are about composition and using liquid color as pure phenomena. You don't listen to Satie insisting that each chord change or tempo change must represent a herd of cattle crossing a stream, or a chirping bird, or a laughing child. You are caught in the arrangement of the notes, the blending of tones moving in and out of each other. The composition is what you hear, not mimicry of literal sounds. The music, or the abstract painting, may cause emotional or tactile responses from us, a softness now, breathless expanse then, equivalence now, asymmetry then. But neither is an illustration or depiction of some specific thing outside itself.

~

For most of my professional career, I've painted large abstracts that featured fluid, poured layers of organic forms partnered with defined contours on opaque shapes. The two main influences on these abstract compositions were Helen Frankenthaler and Morris Louis. Their so-called "color field" style showed me the lush visual possibilities when allowing paint to emphasize the natural tendency of it to flow, like rivers or streams of liquid color. The sheer beauty of the paint itself attended each creative decision, initiated by its own phenomenal presence as natural as a sunset or rainbow.

But I started drawing as a little kid influenced by cartoonists and illustrators. And now, in the later years of my career, I've returned to illustration. I render representational shapes and settings, the content of which often use color field technique and process. Like a cloud that looks liquid because it's poured, not brushed. It's a kind of combo of selected effects, visual favorites that my older artist brain desires to see together within the same shared frame.

For most of those mature years of painting abstracts, I was simultaneously teaching college students how to draw objects, still life, nudes, landscapes, and narrative. And then how to paint those subjects. But I've only recently discovered an observable pattern of behavior demonstrated by years of pages in my sketchbooks.

Unconsciously, I used the sketchbooks not just for practice and regimen, but also as a foil, as a way for me to maintain two streams of thought at once. That is, the sketchbooks show me that during years I was painting large abstracts, I was sketching common objects, people, pets, or recognizable interiors and landscapes. In periods when I was painting large representational narratives or scenes, my sketchbooks are full of abstract forms and compositions. My brain needs both considerations, I guess.

All this review of lifelong intent and purpose in artmaking brings me to the subject of a disturbing dilemma I found myself in a couple of years ago. I experienced a kind of unexpected "intervention" at the hands of a few longtime art friends. Their intrusive criticism of my return to illustration, to representational scenes and images, was hurtful, to say the least. These close friends confronted me all at once, seeing my apparent departure from abstraction as a kind of betrayal to modernism.

One said I was crazy to abandon abstraction for realism—"for nostalgia and romanticism" were his exact words. I suspect the popularity of these large "nostalgic" landscapes, commissioned for public spaces, made them fair game for discussion due to their wide exposure. I tried to be objective in response. Perhaps my friend was concerned that after years of commitment to abstraction in exhibits, and my work having finally achieved a following, I was turning my back on supporters. He got very close, in one heated exchange, to accusing me of "selling out" for profit. I knew better. The muse has never steered me in the direction of profit over poetry.

These few very concerned old friends seemed unaware or perhaps just inattentive of my parallel love of representation, of illustration, though it's been there all along, alongside of my abstract investigations. Good grief, I taught scores and scores of art students *how* to draw and *how* to see reality, the real world, for days and days and years and years. But somehow this group of friends, having finally come on board my abstract color field train, decided that I'd turned onto the wrong track. Representational art was not the niche they wanted to see me in.

~

As luck would have it, my neighbor across the street in Derby (pronounced Darby), became a valued friend during my UK teacher exchange year. John Nickel was neighbor and colleague, a fellow "lecturer," as profs were called there. John taught sculpture at the same college just a couple of miles east of the old Victorian iron-and-glass-covered market downtown. I taught drawing and painting in a building on one side of a manicured green quad. Sculpture was on the other side, in a separate, more noisy building. A number of John's 3-D students were in my required drawing classes. John and I, of like minds, have had an ongoing conversation about composition and context for decades, mostly by post, but more recently by lengthy emails.

My next-door neighbor was named Madge. A long-widowed and long-retired native of Derby, Madge was called "the Village Newspaper." Madge knew everything about our street and had all the news about city comings and goings. She was a great friend to me and little Liz. If the water department had a shut-off planned for the next day, for example, Madge would give the chime on our front door a couple of spins and announce the hours of inconvenience ahead for our neighborhood to expect. She became like a second grandmother to Liz and had us over for evening "tea" several times. That meant supper, in old English.

Madge often played baby-sitter to Liz when needed. Liz found her to be great fun. They laughed at each other's different pronunciation of the same words. Liz loved to hear Madge say "caff" instead of "cafe." Liz thought Madge was saying "calf," which the child found hilarious. Madge's own kids lived in Australia, so she only got to see her grandchildren for extended stays a couple of times a year. So, Liz got spoiled by her kindly elder neighbor, who would read aloud the same paragraphs over and over from my little girl's favorite book, *The Wind in The Willows*. Liz liked shy Mole the best.

With help from Madge that year in Derby, I was able to take useful day trips by train to superb exhibits around the UK. Derby is really the center of Brit Rail, the hub for all directions on the big island. My guide for these art treks was knowledgeable and witty artist neighbor, John Nickel. John was also a gardener who had an "allotment" only a few blocks away from our street. Liz and I would occasionally help with planting or pruning or harvesting in John's little corner of a big neighborhood garden.

John, now also retired, came to visit us at the farm in autumn last year. He stayed a couple of weeks with us. During that time, he got a good taste of daily rhythms at the farm. He was thrilled at the size of the gardens and the variety of heirloom herbs and produce we were harvesting. John loves what he calls Tex-Mex food. José Cantú's wife, Mary, sent a variety of her homemade tamales as a gift to our foreign guest. John pronounces the word 'taco' as 'tack-o,"' by the way.

John's had little experience riding animals, so of course we made him do a trail ride with us. Teen Brad saddled up Firewheel and arrived before breakfast on the selected day, anxious to meet our visiting British artist. Brad was a bit disappointed at first to discover that John is not an illustrator but warmed up as the Brit sculptor was able to give the boy a solid art survey course on equestrian statuary.

I rode tall Samson, who's always up for any mounted campaign with the farm troops. He nodded his long head in approval as I secured the cinch to his equine undercarriage. Riding Samson in the lead provides a high sight line for what lies ahead, which is an advantage in West Texas. However, he is not the best ride for maneuvering through low-hanging limbs, as in the Piney Woods of East Texas, for example. We put John on Douglas, our noble swayback, who's probably the most level-headed animal on the farm. Douglas greets every day with enthusiasm, so grateful to have finally found his tribe. Robin followed atop orange Blaze, who was taking a break from the rodeo circuit and boarding with us for a while. Brad brought up the rear, happy to be in earshot range of Robin enough to chat a bit on the trail.

Sol was already at the lease-pasture next door, with big Caesar, the Pyrenees, guarding sheep for the day. His feelings would be hurt if he saw us all heading off on a family adventure without him. I made a mental note to take the little fellow next time, maybe with just me and

Samson. Less critters to distract him into mischief that way. He'll need to focus on his job as sure-footed packhorse, not the class clown.

We rode past the cemetery, crossing the county road at a safe spot, and started the climb up a well-worn trail toward a neighbor's small but historic ranch house that sits on top of a wide mesa. Lena is the descendant of ranchers who first raised cattle here, not long after Barnes County became such around 1860. Her elevated promontory provides a splendid view of the broad valley beyond to the west, including an ancient creek on one side and a wide ever-flowing tributary off the legendary Brazos on the other.

Lena is an amateur anthropologist with a deep sense of stewardship for her "little piece of heaven," as she calls it. We climbed up through the dense shade of a very old stand of tall red oaks and pecans. The morning sun was behind us, still trying to cling to the eastern horizon. There's a soothing, almost hypnotic rhythm to the moves and sounds of a trail ride. Added to the pleasant creaking of saddle leather or the occasional huffing of a horse is the gentle side-to-side rocking motion for each rider. More than one novice has fallen asleep in the saddle and fallen off as a result. This outcome was not likely for Brad, who was giving his full attention to the rhythmic back and forth sway of Robin's own blond ponytail just up ahead.

Coming out of the wood, the trail abutted a steep rock wall that rose beside us. We were all excited to see an elegant Golden Eagle circling overhead. Her big nest was quite visible, just above our mounted troop, scaffolded tightly against the cliff with assorted natural lumber supports. As we climbed ever higher above sea level, the temperature cooled noticeably in a sequence sometimes accompanied by ears popping.

We arrived at Lena's about 10:30. She suggested we dismount and rest the horses and ourselves for a short while before we all descend the western side of the mesa. We deposited our bedrolls and backpacks on a long table at one end of a metal-roofed open pavilion Lena provides for overnight hikers. Along with the crystal clear air at the top of the mesa, our hostess invigorated each of us with a cup of coffee and a palm-sized fried peach pie. We were pretty much stunned into silence with such rich refreshment in our hands and our eyes full of grand views of high mountain desert terrain stretching all the way to the western horizon.

We individually strolled about, quietly absorbing the experience and giving our lowland lungs a chance to adjust to the altitude. Admiring the view and soaking up the experience, John turned to me, and we clinked our coffee cups in a toast to the morning. Through a broad grin and sunburned cheeks, my old friend from Derby said, "Thanks, mate."

Saddled up and ready to ride with us, Lena soon announced, "Okay, you farmers, time to mount up before you all fall asleep on me." Descending a steep course on horseback is a whole other matter than climbing. It can be a bit of a topsy-turvy feeling to notice that those riders ahead of you are no longer above your horizon line but well below it. It's one reason you don't see a lot of drawings and paintings of objects high up in the air. The artist's neck soon tires of the novel view. Looking down is not the same as looking up. It's why Lena took lead, maintaining a steady pace gained from experience of the surrounding canyons and ravines since her youngest days.

The day's tour took us to Indigenous sites of burned floor middens, clamshell middens, and a stone burial cairn. Over the years, Lena has found a number of lovely small natural pearls inside some clamshells. We paused for a late lunch in the shade of a timeless cottonwood. A lush broad meadow stretched northward along a bend in the creek. Lena said research done at the level site suggests it was a large community at one time with ring marks spaced to indicate as many as a hundred tepees.

Brad, the young illustrator, was lost in thought, imagining the sights and sounds of this village a hundred and fifty years ago. Lena liked the boy right away. She was moved by his awestruck silence, by his respectful fascination for the place. He blushed a bit when the rancher said to him, "Son, your fine spotted pony fits right in here. The Comanches would probably have wanted to make a trade with you."

The highlight of the mounted sojourn was late afternoon as we climbed up a less well-traveled path that eventually led us onto the main vehicle cutback road that led up to Lena's homestead on top. The path out of the meadow took us past amazing outcroppings of formations, the edges of thick shelves of layered limestone and dolomite. We dismounted, tying the horses to hitching posts Lena's grandfather had installed long ago. We walked back and forth, as if in an obstacle course, avoiding the tall and lethal lotebush plants that defy any weed whacker.

Whenever possible, we stood on larger flat-topped rocks for good balance as we peered up into an astounding array of Indigenous pictographs. Unfolded before our eyes in painted stone was the graphic illustration of the history and beliefs of consecutive farming cultures back to Neolithic times.

These symbols and stories were painted on the relatively smooth, front-facing surfaces of the geological shelves. Linear contiguous drawings on accommodating stone-canvas stretched beyond our viewing periphery. Some of the images related to each other sequentially, not unlike classical continuous narrative bands of information. Lena explained that generations of natives and visitors had repainted the same sacred symbols atop each other numerous times. Occasional bits of more contemporary graffiti were included, added first by Spanish soldiers on expeditions, then U.S. cavalry, bivouacked nearby in later centuries.

Native animals were well represented in the pictographs, with sometimes attentive details and animated gesture. My favorites were the long-eared and long-legged jackrabbits. A successful stick figure hunter, with bow and arrow in hand, was encircled by symbols of sustenance; a big turtle, a long-whiskered catfish, and a leaping jackrabbit. All the prey were depicted within an arm's reach of this wiry West Texas Stone Age human hunter.

That evening, back up top, our mounts were secured in Lena's nearby paddock, an old but sturdy structure with thick cedar posts, rails, and slats. A generous large circular clearing, a kind of roundabout, held a fire pit in the center. It was to be a clear night, so we'd sleep in our bedrolls beneath the stars that night. Lena kindly served us steaming bowls of homemade posole and more flakey peach pies for dessert. We sipped our coffee, admiring the polychrome western evening horizon.

From behind us, on the dark eastern rim of the world, the leading edge of the Milky Way curtain was already starting its rise.

The sunset outdid even master British landscape painter J.M.W. Turner's verbose efforts. The orange, pink, red, and yellow streaks of the original were reflected in the waters of the creek on one side of the valley, and the impressive Brazos River offshoot on the other. Both rippling lines of reflection converged in the distance, as if reaching into the actual horizon. Nature's all-encompassing resonance nudged my thoughts toward the seventeenth-century Japanese poet, Basho. Had he joined us on the narrow path up to this remarkable view of three simultaneous sunsets, he would have composed a haiku on the spot.

~

Days after our mounted troop's successful westward campaign, John and I sat on the veranda one evening sipping rye whiskey after supper. My friend had served single-malt whiskey to me during my stay in Derby. So, it was only fitting that I introduce him to good old American rye. We watched the last rays of sunset to the west spill over the top of the house, now falling in fading pastel patches onto the yard, the trees, the road to the east.

Faint light from the dining room gently fell through the old front door's beveled glass onto the welcome mat below. We sat in two porch chairs covered in poultry-patterned prints. John would be going home soon. I figured it was now or never, even if John might think the issue a bit trivial. I had to share something of the "intervention" dilemma I had experienced at the hands of a few friends_art friends, who had admonished me for turning from abstraction to representational painting.

I explained the complex situation as best I could. I especially wanted to convey my frustration over not being able to clarify for the naysayers the clear need that I had to "follow my gut." I wouldn't have explained it exactly the same to the interventionists, but John accepted my reasoning with an understanding nod.

"As I've always done," I continued, "I responded to a Muse-inspired directive. I felt I needed to get some air! To see the landscape and the sky. To feel that expansive space reaching beyond my periphery. I guess I just needed to paint a view; to depict a story."

John sat his drink down on the porch railing beside him. He leaned back, crossing his arms, and spoke with a compassionate voice.

"Sam, I know exactly why you turned to narrative. I watched you do it. From afar."

I put my drink down and was all ears.

"I watched you do it. This embrace of narrative, your drive to return to the country. Your purchase of this farm, repair of this old house, painting the porch ceiling blue. All of it was your response to 9/11."

My mouth went dry. Artists sometimes take years to see why certain forms, certain compositions were necessary to be painted years after painting them. Sometimes the compulsion to paint a picture or write a poem overrides our intellectual understanding of motive at the time of the execution of the thing. Only in reflection, years later, can the artist remember, or get in touch with their mental state, with historical events or attitudes, of understanding *why* a certain thing needed to be painted at that certain time. It took an Englishman, a foreigner, to clarify my reasoning, to explain the shift from abstract to representational. It was 9/11.

"You retreated to a place of comfort, of reassurance, of safety. You went to the security of certain aspects of your childhood that nourished you, made you happy, reassured you that the world had not always been off its axis. You went to a place of memory that reminded you of civility, of kindness, between people who lived and worked in nature." John understood.

A retreat to familiar landmarks, he'd said. That was true. Like Odysseus looking for home, Poseidon persecuting him all the way. Poseidon doing every mischief he could think of to discourage Odysseus, to break his spirit, to crush all remnants of hope. Monumental disasters penetrate our deepest empathetic selves with very personal, very painful grief.

John's acute observations gave meaning to my need to see expanse around me, both in the canvas landscapes I began painting and the natural landscape I began planting. No tall urban buildings. No wide windowless buildings. More sky. Less ground covered in concrete. Less unnatural noise, like the loud and incessantly beeping timers at fast food establishments, alerting mindful teen employees that the fries are done, or an order's ready, or the milkshake machine is out of order again. Such frequent, high-pitched alarms distract one from problem solving, discourage mindfulness, interrupt contemplation, and emphatically prohibit even a few moments of creative daydreaming.

My teen farmhands are not subjected to the tension-inciting background noise of buzzes and beeps of digital commercial spaces. Ambient noise at the barn might be a purring cat nearby, or a horse nickering appreciatively to the human hand that slowly guides a grooming brush along the full length of its elegantly curving back. Ambient animals chewing oats, shaking flies off their ears, or yawning effusively, encourage calm thoughts and feelings in humans, not tension. In the garden, the sound of a bumblebee bouncing and buzzing around inside a big white okra blossom is nothing like the spinning whir of a ventilating fan on high all day. The sound of cornstalk leaves suddenly lifted and rustled against each other by an unexpected breeze does not give one alarm.

~

Annie and I sat on the veranda this morning, coffee cups in hand, watching dawn awaken Barnes County residents, domestic and wild. A soft rain fell across our view, which was still quite dark at 5 a.m. A light breeze flowed around the corner of the porch. We sat together in the sturdy rattan loveseat left to us by Margaret Hawley. We both admired, even in the early morning darkness, how vividly bright were the hundreds of Rose of Sharon white flowers making themselves known to us.

Annie had Margaret's loveseat cushions recovered at Higgenbotham's Upholstery down between Buffalo Gap and Abilene, an establishment still in the same family for four generations. Annie's old writing pal, Bonnie, recommended the place. So, they made a trip together, long-serving tattered cushions in tow. Higgenbotham is well known for its wide assortment of colorful, very busy, very Victorian print fabrics.

In a humorous mood, Annie had already decided she wanted to have a chicken theme. The idea came to her when a trailer load of white leghorn pullets overturned and escaped out front on the curve in the county road. Chickens scattered everywhere. Neighbors helped the poor driver gather up as many pullets as they could catch, but loose homeless chickens are tricky escape artists. The morning after the trailer mishap, at dawn, Annie found seven roosting leghorns on the front porch. Four were nestled in the porch swing, rocked comfortingly by a gentle breeze. The other three huddled closely on the old ratty rattan cushions. All were content, still half-asleep, making that soothing purring sound that only restful chickens can.

Annie and Bonnie found a stylish, exquisitely turn-of-the-nineteenth-century print at Higginbotham's. Our front porch rattan loveseat cushions now sport a colorful array of mostly hens and a handful of roosters on a dark forest green background. The poultry print could have been drawn by William Morris, famous chicken artist of the Arts and Crafts movement in England. Almost an example of *horror-vacui*, or *kenophobia* (both terms refer to fear of empty spaces), every inch of room between the birds of this poultry pattern is filled with vibrant flowers, large and small.

Whenever Annie sits on the veranda with visitors, she loves to recount the story of the day she rescued seven chickens roosting on our loveseat and swing. "Runaways from the butcher's" is how she describes the winged orphan pullets to guests who are themselves seated on the very loveseat and porch swing in her story.

~

My canine staff and I communicate well. They run the farm's dog department with a sense of dedication and duty. They are loyal, which provides constant comfort and reassurance for their caretakers. Anyone who thinks their dog can't talk just isn't listening. Dogs don't require huge vocabularies to get the job done, however. This means that they achieve assigned tasks with brief, to-the-point memos. No long review sessions or seminars needed. Repetition helps them prioritize tasks.

Dogs are most articulate when fun is afoot. They lose their sense of boundaries, of decorum. For example, if I've encouraged play while in the house, the dog deserves some grace if a lamp or vase gets broken.

Dogs love bedtime stories. A favorite tale my dogs like to hear is the one Homer, the Greek poet, gave us. It's about Argos, the most loyal dog in history. Argos waits twenty years for Odysseus to return home to the farm in Ithaca. The old boy greets his master with wagging tail, then finally allows himself to die, to rest forever, his aged canine mind finally at peace.

I tell my dogs about their predecessors. I tell them about Jackson, the giant bloodhound with ears the size of saddlebags. In my youngest schoolboy days, Jackson joined us for all fishing and hunting excursions into the bayous and swamps of the near-prehistoric environs that flow back and forth between Deep East Texas and Louisiana. I guess the waterways down there, too many to count, must have had trouble deciding which way to travel, east to the Mississippi or west to the Neches. In the end it didn't matter, really. Either river carried you down to the Gulf of Mexico.

Young Nike, our slinky Bluetick Coonhound, while resting beside me, her long head in my lap, loves to hear stories about my old boon companion, her predecessor Bluetick, Murph. She listens reverently as I tell her once again how Murph came into my life, wet, shivering, with pellets in his backside from impatient owners. I tell her about his famous nose, which she never tires of hearing. Murph could smell a raccoon or possum across a wide ravine, or at the bottom of a deep hill, or in a tree on the other side of the pasture. And, oh, the wail he could project to announce his find to the world. The decibels that boy could emit echoed the volume of Joshua's trumpets at Jericho. At this point in the tales of Murph, Nike sometimes rolls her big eyes up to mine, as if to acknowledge her admiration. She never met the fine fellow, but Blackie and Caesar remember him fondly. Occasionally, during my tales of Murph, they will join in with a hearty "Amen" or "That was Murph, for sure." Blackie, Caesar, Solomon, and Samson all attended Murph's burial with heavy canine and equine hearts. Murph was legend, a hound who could fly above the Earth in his dreams.

~

Along the upper ridge of our neighbor Hank's little farm, almost right up against the farthest fence, stands an abandoned yellow caboose at the end of the line. Perhaps the railroad ran out of track or just decided its cheerful rear car no longer served a purpose, so it truly got left behind.

Recently, Annie and Liz packed the necessary fixings to prepare a hot supper for Hank. We all delivered the planned meal, both to bring some healthy nourishment and some good company for our old friend. Teen farmhands Robin and Brad joined us. The dogs and cat stayed home.

We arrived late in the afternoon, parking in the drive behind the same old car that was there when young Vern and I carried Hank to the hospital through surrounding prairie fire smoke. Seems like every time I visit the place, a different tire has gone flat. The teens and I changed out the flat for the spare, while Annie and Liz took supper into the kitchen at the back. They worked quietly so as not to interrupt his afternoon nap. The loud snoring coming from the bedroom adjacent to the kitchen alerted Annie, so she pressed her forefinger to her lips and made eye-contact with Liz. With both arms full of groceries, she nodded her understanding and used her heel to let the screen door close quietly behind her.

Annie paused for a peek through the open doorway, checking on our old napping neighbor. He was on his side, curled up like a child atop a faded bowtie quilt. Decorative ivy vines curled above his bald head for the full width of his old-fashioned wrought iron bedstead. It was the same sturdy frame that had supported Hank and his beloved, now departed, wife for many decades. Annie closed the door with a gentle hand.

Over the next couple of hours, the girls would prepare a feast of Hank's favorites. The kitchen was becoming an aromatic masterpiece. First to go into the oven was a brined and rinsed roast chicken, seasoned with fresh silver lemon thyme and hill hardy rosemary. On the stove top, collard greens simmered gently in pot liquor melding the hearty flavors of finely chopped onion, pancetta, a tablespoon of apple cider vinegar, some raw cane sugar, and a dash of red Louisiana hot sauce. Yukon gold potatoes slow boiled alongside to become what Grandma called "creamed" potatoes. Hank liked his mashed potatoes with lots of butter, so Annie got ahead of the game by starting with very yellow potatoes in the first place. Warm cloverleaf rolls were the icing on the cake. At supper, Hank would gleefully separate each yeasty "leaf" carefully, joyfully, like a child.

Tire change efficiently achieved, Robin, Brad, and I headed up toward the ridge, our arms full of folding canvas field chairs and drawing boards. We followed a path we kept mowed with pretty much every visit over to Hank's place. We still had a good two hours of light before full sunset. My two landscape students were proficient enough now, both with compressed charcoal and with the principles of atmospheric perspective, to achieve a reasonable eighteen-by-twenty-four-inch drawing in an hour and a half and a bit.

We sat near enough to occasionally glance at each other's progress in a cozy clearing hewn amidst a sea of softly waving big bluestem and switchgrass. I directed the seating so that we were positioned facing the southwest corner of the yellow caboose. The front door and handrail of the forlorn caboose faced the angled shafts of sunlight, as vivid as Rubens' dramatic stage lighting. The long side of the abandoned car sported two square windows with glass busted out long ago by kids' target practice or an errant quail ignorant of the properties of clear glass. I thought of what an interesting tableau we all must appear: silhouettes of three artists and a caboose, arranged atop a small West Texas mesa at sunset.

Drawing until less than a half hour of light remained, we all paused suddenly, stunned in unison at nature's power to quell our noble task of artmaking. Grinning with children's open faces, we watched the grassy sea around us swim with flickering fireflies. The magical creatures flew up from the ground into the sky, into the open windows of the little caboose, now cheerful once more. Many of the lightning bugs alit for brief instants upon our clothing, our drawing boards, our hands and fingers, and then floated effortlessly into the dark evening sky around us.

A deep, scratchy voice spoke behind us: "Wow." The word seemed stretched into many drawn out, yet connected, syllables. We three turned in the direction of the momentous and appropriate one-word affirmation. Standing in the path, with fireflies dancing like sparkling stars around their bodies, were Annie, Hank, and Liz. Soaking in all the evening's magic, Hank leaned forward on his old hickory cane, supported on each arm by a neighbor woman who cared about him.

~

The dark sky turned boisterous this morning. At five o'clock, the pot of coffee I'd started a few minutes ago was ready. I poured a cup. The house was dark with only a single recessed light turned on just above the coffee maker and fixings. The assembled kitchen items, as if spotlighted on a stage, looked like the kinds of "common object" still life drawing assignments I'd given hundreds of Drawing One students over the years. Beginning drawing students do best when drawing objects they're familiar with: a coffee maker, toaster, blender, flashlight, running shoe, headset and the like. I start them off with one "common object," and after a couple of weeks, those single objects get arranged to assemble a still life composition. It's quite a thing to see what happens in the progression of drawings of beginning art majors in the first two months or so of their undergraduate journey.

Leaning my aching back against the kitchen counter, I raised the mug for my first taste of freshly ground Sulawesi beans. Before reaching my lips with the rich-smelling brew, the outside world lit up like daylight, just for an instant. As learned from childhood, I counted the seconds to the sound of the booming thunder. I stood in the kitchen doorway, looking out across the screened-in back porch, the mud room. Waiting for it, the boom that came rattled the dishes in the cupboard and shook the door jamb.

Suddenly, the patio, the backyard, the car shed, the road leading up to the herb gardens, everything lit up with the all-surrounding universal and surreal light of an Hieronymus Bosch allegorical landscape. The flash of light that illuminated the whole farm lasted half a minute, no more. Then complete darkness and another Earth-shaking boom. That strike was close. I looked back into the kitchen to see if the recessed light over the coffee maker was still on. It was, thank heavens. No power outage yet.

I heard shuffling women's slippers at the top of the stairs. Sleepily, simultaneously, the women of the house, from above, asked "Dad? Sam?"

I could imagine the two of them rubbing their eyes, each holding onto a Doric newel stair post as they awakened to the reality of a grand storm upon us.

"I'm down here," I called up.

As Annie and Liz descended Margaret Hawley's grand staircase, side by side, the daughter asked, "Is the internet out?" I smiled to myself in the kitchen doorway, figuring that Liz had not finished recording grades for her students last night. She had partied too late with colleagues after a departmental soiree off campus. Been there. Done that. For years. She'll remember it fondly.

"Coffee's on."

The instant I said the two words, all of Barnes County must have been exposed to satellites around the world as if it were suddenly daytime on this arc of the big ball, but during nighttime hours. So bright and all-encompassing was the long flash that we three wondered, for just an instant, if there was darkness anywhere in the world at that moment.

We three stepped onto the screened-in back porch to watch further developments. The girls settled into cushioned easy chairs, feet curled up beneath them.

I started to take a sip of coffee but thought I should offer some for my two favorite women first.

"Coffee?"

"Yes, please." In unison, like a classical Greek chorus, was the response.

The heat of July was just upon us, so I wouldn't be adding cardamom or cinnamon to world traveler Annie's cup. That's her fall and winter preferred blend. A bit of raw Texas cane sugar for her summer brew.

Liz likes stevia and half-and-half. I prepared and delivered their steaming mugs of coffee out to the silent, dark porch. In unison, their two audible "thank you's" soothed any mental concerns I might be building about the looming storm. I even allowed myself a pause long enough to anticipate the sound of rain falling on the porch's metal roof.

I walked back into the kitchen, forgetting where I'd put my own coffee. I perused the perimeter, searching. At last, I spotted it pressed up against the kitchen breadbox—the same breadbox that Sol had discovered so long ago when his deceptively quiet little donkey hooves had followed me into Margaret Hawley's house. I think Margaret would have secretly enjoyed Sol's invasion very much.

I raised the cup to my lips, taking the first sip of the morning. Despite it being July outside, my coffee was cold as winter. I rolled my eyes, took a breath, and marched my cup over to the microwave. I punched the "beverage" button and stepped away from the digital contraption out of precautionary habit. I could hear the girls laughing softly about something while sipping their hot coffee.

The microwave screeched rudely that my coffee was reheated. Projected into the dark kitchen, at least three or four LED lights illuminated numbers and words in glaring red and blue colors. Little light darts vying for my attention. I reminded myself I'd thought of making a painting about a dark domestic interior full of tiny bits of color from dozens of digital devices across the room. But I was too distracted and irritated at the moment to pursue such a painting anytime soon.

I lifted my cup from the microwave just as another loud thunder-bomb shook the house again, causing me to spill the hot brew over my thumb and fingers. The open microwave door lighted the counter below, and the not-quite closed utensil drawer underneath. I could see clearly the several rivulets of spilled coffee seeking gravity, flowing over the counter and down into the utensils below, in whatever disorder other hands may have left them.

I placed my sticky cup off to the side and grabbed a washcloth draped over the sink. I proceeded to clean and dry all the drawer's coffee-soaked utensils, deriving some relief from the fact I was able to replace the tools in their proper order. I refilled my coffee cup and marched the pot out to offer more to the women on the back porch who watching the early morning light show.

"Refills, ladies?"

"Mine's perfect," Annie replied, in her soothing morning voice.

"Yes, please," said Liz, holding her mug aloft. A gift from one of her students, it sported the image of a broad live oak with the instruction "Hug a Tree" printed below. I could see the cup in her outreached hand clearly, as the whole farm lit up once again from night to day just at the instant I'd started to pour. Liz, Annie, the porch furniture, the stream of steaming coffee, my bare feet below, all of it illuminated at once as if by a giant outdoor arena strobe flash. We three were like a Diane Arbus figurative tableau, frozen for an instant in a big black-and-white photo.

The world went dark once more. I could sense the girls smiling. We all were counting seconds, but not for long. The boom that came shook the hinges on the screen door, metal tapping on wood. I'd made a mental note to re-tighten those screws after sunrise. If sunrise was coming.

Down the hill from inside the barn, we could hear Nike howling and imagine her lovely and long spotted muzzle raised high in the air. I'd left her in the barn to sleep and dream with the rest of the canine gang last night. The equines were secure in their stalls, waiting for Robin to arrive and serve up their breakfast of oats and hay. I knew the sheep would be huddled in the round stone sheepfold, comforted by the presence of their diligent Pyrenees guardian, Caesar. Dawn would be here soon, and she would light their way out to pasture. If the rain got heavy, the lot, including Caesar, would position themselves on a high rise, scattered with old mesquite trees like living umbrellas.

I saw the faint light of my cellphone emitting from the kitchen counter. I stepped back inside, to retrieve the phone and replace the pot on the coffee maker hotplate. It was a text from Robin.

"I'm here," she typed. "Hope the storm isn't scaring my girls."

She meant the chickens, probably still huddled in their darkened palaces up on the western hill near the herb gardens. Robin would tend to her feathered flock after serving the horses their breakfasts.

It's summer, so Robin is working full days at the farm, saving up extra cash for her first college semester in the fall. Next week, she's hosting a "Produce and Poultry" event at the farm for the just-graduated Elysia High 4-H seniors. Ag teacher Angus and I will assist on the day of the event. Depending on the longevity of the looming storm, Annie, Robin, and I were to lay out the order of instruction regarding herbs and produce for her presentation. Ambitious Robin originally wanted to call the event a "Produce and Poultry Colloquium," but Annie suggested the title sounded more pompous than fun. Robin's ego was deflated a bit but recovered quickly as my discerning sidekick assured her that the "Colloquium" term could more appropriately be revived for grad school... in four years.

I took a sip of ice-cold coffee, retracing my steps across the kitchen. I stuck the brew back into the microwave and hit "Beverage." I went upstairs, put on work clothes, and returned to the mudroom/porch to pull on my wellies. I expected a real gully-washer would be produced from this noisy storm. Instead of walking down to the barn under a sky full of lightning, I drove the trusty, rusty old Rodeo. Might be some skittish critters in the barn due to the grouchy heavens above, so Robin would appreciate the help and the company on such an unsettling, still dark, dawn.

As often happens in early July in West Texas, the huge electric storm floated away, *en masse*, off to the east. No rain for Barnes County this morning. No doubt, the moisture-filled front followed the Red River all the way to the Piney Woods before finally deciding to dump a bunch of water three hundred miles away on the other side of Texas. Poseidon must be in charge of water distribution these days, still angry with Odysseus and his fans.

~

The day cleared off nicely, leaving us with decent temps and a bright blue sky with occasional cloud puffs, not unlike gauzy cotton-candy servings at the county fair. Peter Max would have made the sky a dense lapis blue with rounded clouds of powder pink.

The horses and one short donkey were happy to get out of the barn and into the front pasture to kick up their heels. The Tunis ewes and lambs were already grazing, having left the confines of their sheepfold now that the morning's psychedelic light show was over. Their moms resembled creamy cloud-puffs, while the April-born babes were still cinnamon-red from head to toe. The rectangular Devonshire sisters had their curly heads pressed into a huge and tasty cylindrical haybale turned on its side. The dog gang and one cat had scattered to the four corners of the Bartlett Farm's section of Earth.

While I finished closing stalls and feed room doors and opening the big sliding doors on either end of the barn, Robin made her way up the hill to the chicken palaces. Annie was already there to assist with watering, feeding, and gathering eggs. She'd agreed to be part of the planning session this afternoon to help Robin organize the upcoming "Produce and "Poultry" show here at the farm. Gathering eggs was Annie's least-favorite part of helping the farm's teen poultry authority. She understood that the occasional black Texas rat snake is not a venomous threat, but they sure look like serious business when one is found coiled up in a hen's laying box. She bravely confronts the possibility of encountering one of the five-foot-long reptiles anyway, but always with trepidation and a rehearsed plan of defense.

Liz was teaching a summer course at the college, so was already on the road. Her fiancé, Vern, was finishing up a post-grad engineering project he'd agreed to assist his favorite advisor with at the Arlington campus. So, he wouldn't be home to Elysia for full-time summer residence for another week or so. It's still awkward for me to introduce Vern to folks as "Liz's fiancé," him being like our adopted son for so many years anyway. It will be easier to identify him simply as my "son-in-law." A word like fiancé sounds unnecessarily formal, or kind of pretentious, at least in old Vern's case. Liz is always amused that I have a bit of trouble just pronouncing the word.

Mid-day chores accomplished early, we three adjourned to the house for our working lunch.

I sat at the kitchen table while Robin and Annie prepared our plates. While retrieving silverware I'd washed earlier in the morning due to my coffee spill into the utensil drawer, I was reminded that I'd not had my coffee today. At eye-level, I spotted my cup inside the microwave. I pushed "Beverage" again.

Standing beside me, holding the pitcher of iced tea in her hands, Annie asked, "Aren't you having iced tea?" Her big, beautiful green eyes always nail me to the wall.

I answered, with an audible sigh, "Yep. I'm having coffee *and* iced tea today."

I'm sure my response came off fussy sounding, as her big green eyes rolled. Annie drew out the word "Oh-h-h-h-kay." I just retreated silently and proceeded to arrange placemats.

Annie came over and kissed me on the cheek like she might a petulant child.

"You want me to make you a fresh cup?" I hugged her close.

"No, thank you. Drinking that cup is a goal I've wanted to achieve all morning, followed by a glass of iced tea."

"Understood," my college sweetheart answered.

We sat down to a delightful meal together. Our repast included a vivid red, white, and green stacked caprese salad of huge Purple Cherokee tomato slices, interspersed with Genovese and lime basil leaves from the garden, and buttery Buffalo mozzarella discs kindly provided by one of our restaurant customers. Annie demonstrated for Robin how to pour a single stream of virgin olive oil over the salad stack, followed by a drizzle of fig-infused, aged balsamic vinegar.

The salad was followed with a heaping bowl of Annie's own chilled gazpacho with toasted croutons made from the Ronning Bakery's left-over sourdough bread. Annie includes pureed Scarlet Nantes carrot in the recipe, which adds not only sweetness, but also gives the cold soup a lovely red-orange hue. A sprinkle of finely diced dark green serrano pepper across the top and I'm close to nirvana.

After lunch, Robin and I cleared the table and washed the dishes. Annie brought her laptop and a couple of legal pads to the kitchen forum. Robin was confident of the upcoming event's afternoon "Poultry" presentation she would be giving, so our task was primarily just to help her organize the morning's "Produce" portion of the event, which would include a display of fresh herbs for sampling, and a brief discussion of their uses.

Sweet Bell Peppers

EIGHT

"Teen Team-Teaching"

Robin is an inexhaustible young woman. Annie and I had allotted a whole hour and a half to assist her in planning the morning "Produce" half of the "Produce and Poultry" fieldtrip she's organizing for fellow 4-H graduating seniors. As we approached hour three at the kitchen table, my legs felt like stone, and I was concerned that my L5 was now permanently hammered into my sacrum, never to flex again in any direction.

Annie is very patient with Robin and identifies with her youthful, creative energy. Like Liz, she's convinced that Robin has a brilliant artist inside, and the two of them are determined to help the girl achieve her potential and manifest that dream. I'm just praying that we make it through the summer and that Robin gets the heck out of Elysia and off to college before a confrontation occurs between three strong-willed women, two of which are not the girl's mother.

Robin's mom has come to accept that her smart, successful daughter is capable of excellence in any field of undertaking she desires. But like the senior high school counselor, does not think that art is as important as math and science. She sees art as a benign past-time or hobby. "Like golf," I've heard her say.

For the first twenty minutes of our meeting, tireless Robin

proceeded to lay out how she planned to discuss and demonstrate uses for all thirty organic, heirloom herbs, all thirty examples of organic, heirloom produce, and all thirty organic edible flowers, just in the morning session. So, Annie and I spent the first hour and a half whittling down the number of selected topics. Robin respects us, but reflexive gestures couldn't hide her frequent frustration with most of our editing suggestions. I'm sure she regarded those suggestions as slash-and-burn demands, a term she would appropriately associate with agriculture.

Robin's "tell," a term used in detective novels to describe a suspect's physical facial giveaway of intent or emotion, is always impossible for her to disguise. Even with engagingly direct eye contact of her big brown eyes, suggesting openness and acceptance, her mouth cannot deceive. When unhappily confronted with issues or events she can't control or change, Robin presses her upper and bottom lip together so hard that her mouth disappears into a single thin slit just beneath her nose. You can almost hear her teeth cracking. But I guess it's still better than literally biting your tongue.

She's assured me that she's got the afternoon poultry session "in the bag," which I suspect she thinks must be an old farmers market term. Annie and I first agreed we'd trust her to organize the heritage breed chicken discussion and demo all by herself, what with her passion and knowledge about the subject. But while trying to help Robin focus on just a few produce examples, I kept imagining her in the afternoon session doing her darnedest to introduce each of her beloved hens (100 of them) to each of the assembled 4-H seniors (twelve of them).

Robin seems sometimes to be one of those rare individuals, an anomaly, who is precisely one half emotional and one half rational. That dilemma becomes most evident when she must make a decision between which is best, sharing her passion or sharing her knowledge. It's the eternal conundrum for good teachers. If you read the class wrong early in the semester, you look either too "feely" or too "aloof." It's like using a recipe that calls for a merging of savory and sweet in precisely measured amounts.

Finally, Robin accepted defeat and agreed to prune her presentation. I suspect she was relieved that she wouldn't have to eat the whole elephant at once in the time allotted. Her shoulders relaxed first. Then her jaw. With a sigh, she nodded her head, ponytail swishing up and down, while saying simply, "thank you." Annie reached over to squeeze the girl's hand and said, "Okay. Let's have some fun." We clinked our iced tea glasses together and put our heads together toward an effective agenda for Robin's presentation. I was delighted at the idea that this top-of-her-class graduating senior's capstone event was to be delivered outdoors, surrounded by the sights, sounds and smells of earth, plants, and poultry. Farms are ancient institutions of learning.

Annie explained how each of the garden items to be discussed during Robin's talk will be included in the lunch menu for the gathering. Robin liked the idea that even the meal would be an integral part of the day's instructive program. We convinced the recent graduate to discuss and demonstrate three herbs and three examples of produce: fennel, basil, and nasturtium, and tomatoes, carrots, and cantaloupe.

Fennel serves as an example of both herb and vegetable, so will be the transitional hinge-item for the morning's herb and produce platform. Herb Fennel displays immense feathery foliage and seeds for flavoring, while Florence Fennel is cultivated for its bulb-like vegetable. Herb Fennel is the rich base-note of Italian sausage. Florence Fennel bulb is spectacular when brushed with olive oil and grilled and becomes the unique center-note of a fresh salad of thinly sliced fennel, red-onion, and orange circles.

Robin and I heartily endorsed Annie's menu for the senior 4-H lunch. Annie will print the menu in a fancy font. Robin thinks her classmates will appreciate the souvenir and that most will tuck it inside their yearbooks. Annie asked our young artist/farmer to provide her with small ink drawings of a tomato and a chicken, one for each side of the menu's heading. Here's Annie's handwritten rough for the menu. At the kitchen table, Robin read it to me out loud. She gushed that it sounded "really elegant." Annie was happy the teen approved.

Elysia Highschool 4-H Senior Summer Lunch at Bartlett Farm

Grilled Italian sausages, fennel bulb, and red onion slices, whole Nantes carrots (veggies all brushed in olive oil and balsamic vinegar before grilling)
Grilled Pecos cantaloupe wedges, with Nasturtium blossom garnish
Caprese salad: sliced Purple Cherokee Tomatoes, basil, and buffalo mozzarella cheese
Annie's Chocolate Mint Brownies

The day arrived for Robin's talk in the blink of an eye. The mid-June mid-morning sky that served as backdrop for her "Produce and Poultry" presentation could have been painted by Thomas Moran. Huge cumulus clouds bumped into each other like cantaloupes on a conveyer belt. The distinctive contours of the giant billows of water vapor, layers of white and gray folds, stood out starkly against a vivid cyan blue sky that seamlessly stretched from the Red River all the way to Waco. It appeared anything but normal. The sky looked like a vintage poster advertising Yellowstone National Park.

Robin was brilliant. After each bit of descriptive instruction, she paused for her 4-H friends to gather thoughts into questions or comments. They could tell she had worked hard on this and wanted to be supportive. And they learned some things they didn't know. Most were aware of nasturtiums, for example, and that some people ate them, but they had not really considered the colorful plant an herb. Robin elaborated that Annie would be garnishing the grilled cantaloupe wedges with nasturtium flowers and that the pretty blossoms would add a nice peppery contrast to the concentrated sweetness of the caramelized melon.

Her fieldtrip audience was fascinated with the two types of fennel and their uses both as an herb and a vegetable. Robin encouraged the class to brush their bare hands through the fan-like fennel fronds, thereby releasing the rich fragrance into the air around them. "It smells like pizza!" one girl exclaimed. Robin smiled and gave her a "thumbs up."

The rainbow-colored carrots got everybody's attention. Questions flew left and right. Ag teacher Angus stepped in to give Robin some assistance, reminding students that red carrots contain lycopene, as do tomatoes, and that the purple carrots get their color from anthocyanins. Some of the teens breathed a sigh of relief that the topic of carrot colors had not been on the final ag exam.

Several of the students took note of our neighbor, young Brad, as he loped handsome Firewheel near the herb gardens and down the road to release the rump-spotted creature into the front horse pasture. He was thrilled to see Robin acknowledge him by waving from the garden as he rode past bareback, of course. The young horseman unclipped the lead rope from Firewheel's halter and let his dark Appaloosa join equine pals Samson and Sol for a good lunch of fresh ryegrass.

Brad walked back up the hill to help me and Angus at the grill station. It was time for humans to lunch, as well. Like a Pony Express veteran, Brad transported lunch items to and from the kitchen flawlessly, without a misstep. After Annie's hearty lunch and lots of teen laughter, it was nearing siesta time. A few seniors took charge of clearing the long-extended dining table, efficiently rinsing items in the big double sink and loading others into the dishwasher. The long table and eighteen chairs are easily accommodated, due to Margaret Hawley's insistence that Reuben provide her with a dining room big enough for large cultural dinners.

Several seniors stayed at the dining room table, talking about their futures. One long and lanky boy was wisely stretched out on the living room sofa, already napping. He had asked Annie for permission before, which pleased her. Another had fallen asleep in one of the easy chairs, his shoeless legs draped over a worn leather ottoman, arms clutched across a frilly square pillow on his chest. The floral print on the cushion echoed the density of the room's wallpaper pattern, itself inspired by Botticelli's "Primavera."

A few gathered around the kitchen table to admire Brad's new comic strip featuring Greek-mounted "Soldiers Without Saddles" (his title). The boy illustrator was in his element and relished every minute. His fellow farmhand, Robin, sat beside him, playing the role of assistant. She helped him locate various drawings and sketches, holding them up vertically for all to see. They've discussed each other's artworks often enough that she could anticipate which image he'd likely need next to match his commentary.

One of the senior girls, Janet, was an accomplished barrel racer. Robin says she has a different award buckle to wear for every day of the week. At our 4-H senior summer lunch, the champion teen cowgirl wore a starched white cotton Western shirt with stitched yokes front and back and mother-of-pearl snaps on pockets and cuffs. She had a sincere, if somewhat severe, demeanor that I think was just a natural extension of her intellectual curiosity. Concentration dominated her expressions. But she had a lovely smile that often surprised people because it broke out suddenly, unexpectedly, as did Annie's, back when we were in college.

With that sudden smile, Janet reveled her admiration for an 11-by-14-inch watercolor of a Greek horse and rider descending a steep, craggy hillside. Brad told me he painted it as a possible cover for his first complete illustrated story on the theme. He's been copying watercolors and oils of horses descending diagonally, rendered by Frederick Remington and Charlie Russell. Brad's depiction of the imagined scene was impressive to everyone at the table.

Cowgirl Janet was thinking how she herself might handle such a daring mounted descent, so her lovely smile vanished, turned to concentration. With her squinting eyes still firmly planted on the compelling image, she asked a question in Brad's direction.

"So, the Greek horsemen rode bareback just like the American Indian?" Somewhere in the back of her mind she recalled having seen photos of carved horses and riders on some ancient temple in Athens.

Brad straightened his back, not bristling, exactly, but certainly to give his response a sense of gravity. It was a favorite topic of his.

"Well," the younger teen bravely began, aware that the seniors gathered around the table had every advantage over him, like maturity, experience, graduation, and such. But he could draw. That was his advantage over everyone in the house, save Robin and me. And he knew that his place in our little farm art club was well secured.

"It does seem that Greek horsemen rejected the idea of saddles, even though they must have seen saddles on horses from the east. The oldest known saddle is actually Chinese."

Janet lifted her eyes up to Brad's, waiting till his gaze matched hers. Then she spoke.

"I noticed you rode over from your place bareback. Do you prefer to ride Indian style?"

"Well," Brad started over. "Native American tribes all had saddles. Hollywood promoted the myth that they only rode bareback." He paused, concerned he was talking too much.

Then he added "Firewheel's just really so easy to ride. He just likes coming over here, honestly."

Janet encouraged him by adding a supportive comment with a smile of affirmation.

"Yeah. I've wondered about that. I mean, Spanish cavalry brought the horse to America, so the Indigenous tribes saw saddles on horses from day one, right?"

I was quietly delighted that the pretty barrel racer thought enough of young Brad to assure him that she knew academic nomenclature on this topic.

Brad beamed. "Exactly!" he effused.

Attentive Robin noticed her young friend's enthusiasm and obligingly searched briefly through a separate folder of sketches, finding a sheet of line drawings copied from photos of Comanche saddles. She handed the sheet to Brad, grinning knowingly at me across the table as she did so. We were mutually happy for the youngest member of our small art club to have his moment in the sun.

Brad proceeded to explain the basic construction of early Indigenous saddles made of rawhide stretched over a wood frame, first modeled on Spanish saddles with tall horns front and back. He delighted in showing Janet his drawing from a photo of a tribal woman's saddle, replete with long strands of decorative leather fringes hanging from both horns.

The boy artist was on a roll now. He was unstoppable.

"Comanche cavalry (Brad's term), were called 'The Lord of the Plains' due to their mastery of hunting or warring while riding. Like good soldiers, they studied the equipment of their enemies and began making saddles based on U.S. Army examples seen during battles and parleys. They added leather strap stirrups with a single loop at the end, hung over the sides of their rawhide pads."

Brad took a breath. I figured he'd never consciously delivered a talk with so many words in all his young life.

Janet, a senior, was impressed, and Brad, not yet a sophomore—for three months more!

~

Siesta drew to a close. Robin had scheduled her poultry demonstration and talk to begin at 2:30 p.m. Brad would assist her. The heritage breed chickens were in good hands. Angus and the 4-H students headed up the hill to the chicken houses. We'd set up our largest market tent for her presentation so the seniors and the featured hens would be in the shade. Robin would be showing three of her favorite hens—a Cuckoo Maran, a Speckled Sussex. and an Araucana.

The Cuckoo Maran has markings that can be mistaken for a Barred Rock, but the Maran's feathers are much darker. Robin likes them because of their demonstrable maternal skills and disposition. They're not only broody, but also will nest whenever the opportunity arises, and not always where you want them to. Their feathers are big and soft, making for a very fluffy bird, kind of like hugging a large, soft stuffed animal, except alive. The Cuckoo Maran's eggs are dark chocolate brown and are my favorite.

Speckled Sussex are beautiful birds. The painter in Robin is attracted to the contrast of colors in Sussex feathers: dark mahogany, with random green and white splashes. Our Sussex chickens look like Jackson Pollock paintings. They lay pale beige eggs usually but often produce lovely pink shells as well.

Our non-tufted Araucana chickens have elegant plumage in colors to rival any Tintoretto or Titian palette. Burnt umbers, dark ultramarine, forest greens, and crimsons abound, with tail feathers, wingtips and manes of pure gold. The eggs are blue or green, with occasional surprises of pure pink.

Robin had rehearsed her poultry lecture and demo with me, Liz, and Annie a couple of times the day before, all the way through. By concentrating her focus on three breeds only, her audience would stay fully engaged and Robin could stay on track.

Annie took my arm, adding a little tug.

"Robin will do fine. Let's take some time for ourselves. Let's go down to the studio so I can see how the new painting's coming along." Annie said all this while texting Robin to proceed with her talk without us.

I knew Annie had writing to do, so it was a gift for her to suggest some private time for us.

"Good idea," I said, adding a kiss on the top of her head.

The sunlight was still muted by giant cumulus clouds filling up the sky, so we cavalierly walked bareheaded down the road to the barn and upstairs studio. Sol spotted us as we walked along the edge of the horse pasture. He trotted over to say hello. In the background, Samson, Firewheel, and Dolly continued grazing, but mainly just idly shifted horse weight from one set of legs to the other. They were enjoying their own slow-moving equine version of a siesta, shaded by tall clouds with surprisingly cooler temperatures for early July.

Annie showered the little scamp with soothing "sweet nothings." He raised his long head in appreciation and to give her a better vantage point to scratch his hairy chin. She obliged and cooed some more. Sol batted those absurdly long eyelashes of his in her direction. He's a charmer. But we've been associates long enough for me to know to scan the horizon for signs of donkey mischief, especially during affectionate displays like this. He trumpeted a bray of gratitude to Annie before trotting off to join the other taller equines. At a distance, he glanced back over his shoulder at us, probably to evaluate whether he had managed to distract us from whatever wreckage he's been up to.

In the few moments it took us to arrive at the barn, we'd acquired a pack of curious canines. Always on the lookout for a good time, Blackie, Nike, Caesar, and Tommy Cat danced animated circles around us, tails wagging hard enough to create a cyclone. Even the cat joined in, as best he could, stirring the air with his long, snake-like tail.

Satisfied with a dog biscuit each and some kibble for one, the gang plopped down in the wide hallway to an audible chorus of canine crunching. We took advantage of the lull and headed upstairs to the studio. From a few steps above me, Annie turned, smiling.

"Close the door behind you, Sammy." she said. I obliged, securing the stairwell from four-legged or two-legged visitors.

~

Robin was in the process of wrapping up her poultry talk at about 4:30. As we approached, she was in mid-sentence answer to a fellow senior's question about the fluffy Cuckoo Maran resting in Robin's arms. The beautiful bird laid her head against Robin's chest and purred contentedly. Justin, a boy who helped Pete at the feed-store on weekends, had just finished asking her to explain why the Marans lay those dark chocolate-colored eggs.

I suspected that Justin was one of the students relieved that the natural process involved in the resulting color of a carrot was not on the final exam. So, finals over, he'd boldly asked his question about the Marans' eggs uniquely dark brown hue. I noticed that ag teacher Angus kept silent, his arms crossed to remind him to give Robin time to reply first. Annie and I had no doubts that our resident teen poultry professor would nail it.

Robin looked at us, smiling, just before she spoke.

"It's a brown pigment called *protoporphyrin IX*. It's applied as the egg passes through the shell gland pouch of her reproductive tract."

Angus gave her a thumbs up signal from one of his folded arms. Justin, thinking about the natural mechanics involved in Robin's answer, replied, "Kind of like spray-painting an Easter egg, huh?" Robin was happy that her classmate was imagining the inner workings of the gentle hen held in her arms. She grinned widely at Justin.

"Yeah. Kind of like that," she said. The fluffy hen was fast asleep.

The teen audience gave Robin an enthusiastic round of applause. Angus thanked her for a full day of excellent farm lecture and demonstration and thanked Annie for the special farm to table lunch she prepared. The students echoed their thanks to us for a fun day at the farm, probably the last official fieldtrip they'll ever take together.

We learned that Janet, the champion barrel racer, was Elysia's 4-H Club president. Behind her hung the local 4-H Club banner. Its four-leaf clover symbol includes an "H" in each leaf, signifying "Head, Heart, Hands, and Health." She approached us with a wrapped gift box about the size of a kitchen cutting board. The wrapping sported a print of dozens of cute yellow chicks, so we had no trouble discerning who must have chosen the paper. Janet thanked us for hosting the event, handing me the gift box and Annie a huge bouquet of roses, tulips, and daisies. I held the bouquet for Annie a moment while she unwrapped the gift box. Inside were two handsome, appropriately sized, white Western-yoke shirts, embroidered with words in two lines, above and below: "Bartlett Farm, Elysia, TX." The letters were sewn in cursive in grass-green thread.

After hugs all round, the graduates strolled down the road to cars parked near the barn. Brad walked with them to retrieve Firewheel for his brief ride home. Robin exhaled a sigh mixed of joy, relief, and sorrow, all at once. This was a huge day for her, a crowning achievement she'd remember fondly, tempered with the awareness that life at Elysia High was no more. She felt a sense of hesitation about the future.

"It's just a lot, you know?" she said, more than asked, of Annie. She wiped away a tear, trying to laugh about it. Annie hugged her again.

"We're not too old to remember, Robin, all those feelings hitting at once."

Robin smiled, nodding her head.

"Sam and I will always need a good chicken expert for advice, you know. We'll put you on speakerphone and have poultry conference calls together."

Brad rode by atop his fine, dark Appaloosa. As he passed, he held his thumb and pinkie up to his ear, a signal for Robin to call him sometime.

"I will, Brad." she affirmed, while waving back. "Thanks for helping today!"

Mourning Dove

NINE

Nesting Couples

Liz's and Vern's afternoon wedding went off without a hitch. Well, except for the important one. They opted for a small service in the little side chapel at the Methodist church in Elysia. It was built about the same time as the county courthouse, in the same understated Romanesque style. The humble chapel, with two short but stout windows, looked particularly English to me on the day of the wedding. Vigorous Virginia Creeper covers much of the chapel's red brick exterior, but is religiously, acutely, kept hewn out of those round arched window frames. The stained glass of one window features lilies, the other depicts roses, symbols of purity and love in medieval churches. Both windows are in the delicate Pre-Raphaelite foliate style.

Liz's grandmother, Linda, was able to attend. Her presence prompted my memories of the year I taught in Derbyshire. She thoughtfully made a November visit to Britain then to see how little Liz and her recently widowed dad were coping. She made pecan pies for us, with traditional "Western Schley" pecans, probably descendent nuts from West Texas' original San Saba Mother Pecan. Her visit provided reassuring comfort for all three of us. Liz and Linda have remained close through every year of her granddaughter's life. Liz stayed with her for whole summers twice while I was on art projects abroad.

Sidekick Annie and mother-in-law Linda enjoy each other's company. Both are thoughtful, generous women, but also very independent self-starters. (They don't wait for permission.) Together they arranged the colorful display for the wedding altar with cut flowers from the farm, of course. Coneflowers, lantana, Rose of Sharon and sunflowers all rubbed elbows and vied for attention like a big box of kids' crayons. Annie was sensitive to the fact that Linda must be having a range of deep emotions, especially that the bride's own mother died much too young to be able to celebrate Liz's and Vern's big day. Ironically, Annie and Linda find a kind of solace in each other, one without her mother, the other without her daughter.

Linda approves of Vern, thank heavens. Though a good-hearted person, she's never been shy about sharing her evaluation of the character of others, especially slackers. During a visit to the farm a few years back, she met young Vern doing afternoon chores at the barn. After observing him for a while, she commented to me, "Well, there's a young man who's not afraid of work." I nodded in agreement, though neither of us foresaw then that my hired hand would one day take the hand of my daughter in marriage.

I did my duty at the altar, kissed my precious Liz on the cheek, and gave my son-in-law Vern a sincere hug as well. Then I took my seat, joining the little congregation. I was welcomed with a kiss on the cheek for myself from Annie and a big tearful smile from Liz' s grandmother. Just across the aisle from Vern's parents, Annie, Linda, and I sat in the opposite front pew, all in our best Sunday togs. We all grinned proudly at each other, pouring familial love and hope upon the couple standing before us.

Colored sunlight from the chapel's stained-glass windows danced a kind of kaleidoscopic pattern across the sleeveless white eyelet dress that Liz wore. Her grandmother had worn the same lovely cotton dress to her senior prom, held despite the Korean War booming overseas. I can only imagine the layers of vivid memories over decades that seeing beautiful Liz in her own 1950s soft Sea Island Cotton dress must have prompted for Linda. I thought the tiny eyelet fabric of the pretty dress itself echoed the pretty freckles on my daughter's joyful face.

Annie and I held hands. Sometimes when we do that, I can't help thinking that Annie's mother is turning over in her grave. She did not approve of me even after many years of time passing before Annie and I reunited. Even though I had achieved a respectable full-time teacher's job, she could just never forgive me for being an artist and for having been a "gangster, a union man," working my way through that first two years of college by loading trucks. I thanked the Lord that I was sitting beside two women who cared for me very much, watching the girl I'd raised get married. Vern and Liz held hands, loving each other with a shared gaze.

As we left the chapel, the pastor wished us all safe travels, even though we were almost all locals. His blessing may have implied he was thinking of a broader life's journey for us, or he was just being cautionary about Elysia's busier roads these days. He shook my hand enthusiastically while squinting at me under furrowed brows. I think he was trying hard to remember who I was due only to my lackluster attendance record, not to any personal doubt about his own state of cognizance.

Preparations were well under way for the evening's dinner party upon our arrival back at the farm. The entertainment committee was hard at it but paused to greet us with cheers and hugs. Robin, Annie's pal Bonnie, and my old art colleague Suzie supervised set-up and decoration of the patio and backyard, all surrounded by a vibrant hedge of red and green Turk's Cap.

If you want butterflies, hummingbirds, and bumblebees all summer into fall, plant Turk's Cap, a flawless perennial. The fez-shaped flowers and the lush leaves are edible. Young Turk's Cap leaves can be steamed like spinach. The bright red flowers are appealing to sight and deliciously sweet to taste.

Brad, the former brat, Bill Goodman the goatherd, and artist George Clay followed directions well. They'd already set up and arranged tables and chairs, strung lights, and positioned a couple of industrial-size fans for convenient access if needed for a cooling breeze or to discourage table flies. Eager to help, I watched for a moment as the men moved from here to there, awaiting more instructions, as the women's decoration team began arranging flower and candle centerpieces.

With the party's set-up mostly accomplished, the teens headed off to other chores—Brad to prepare supper for the horses, and Robin to gather eggs and feed chickens...and maybe chase snakes.

The teamsters being of no more use, I suggested Bill and George follow me and Vern's dad, G.T., out to the grilling station just beyond the patio. All the men loosened ties and unbuttoned collars. We carried a cooler of beer and sodas between us. I didn't really expect there'd be much for us to do, but I couldn't stand watching Bill and George shuffle around like shy boys anymore, wanting to help but also wanting to stay out of the women's way. They eagerly retreated from the entertainment area and followed us in the direction of smoked ambrosia filling the air.

I'd previously recruited Angus the ag teacher, and G.T. had enlisted a couple of well-seasoned Volunteer Fire Department grill masters to take charge of all such grill and smoker duties. These veteran omnivores would ensure perfectly grilled chicken, sausages, and vegetables, all carefully turned precisely on time. The protein crew had also dry-rubbed and prepared ribs and brisket for arranging on tiered racks in a big mobile wood smoker before dawn that morning.

Beneath a 12-by-12-foot pop-up tent, two men were seated chatting quietly while another napped on a folding camp-cot. The men had been tending the smoker's meat and heat contents since the wee dark hours, alternating nap times on the cot. None of these men could be talked into staying for the party. They needed to get home to their families. Nor would they take any payment.

Annie and I put on an annual fundraiser fish fry for the Elysia Volunteer Fire Department here at the farm, and Angus knows to use our place as an ag education annex for his students anytime. It's what friends do. We help each other. Annie and I take great comfort from the fact that all these men are happy for Liz and Vern having gotten hitched. They've watched the two of them grow up and know our two families as neighbors.

G.T. and I were delighted to see our respective grown children, the newlyweds, arriving at the grilling station right behind us, arm in arm. They'd walked over together to thank their friends, the Elysia Volunteer Firemen, for staying up all night on their behalf. Joys and hugs passed all around, along with cold beers, the grill masters toasted the happy couple and went on their way.

Bill, George, G.T., and I transported roasting pans and platters of smoked meats and grilled vegetables over to serving tables near the patio. The farmhouse buffet of fresh garden salads, protein, and produce would have made Augustus Caesar proud. Cato would have written about it.

Having secured the equine residents in stalls, with buckets of oat rations and probably an extra alfalfa cube for each, teen artist Brad turned to the dogs' and one cat's meal preps. He made sure that all their bowls were filled before opening the barn doors to the boisterous canine gang that had gathered outside, hungry for their supper. He closed the barn doors on the dog diners and went upstairs to shower and change in the studio before heading up to the house to join the wedding dinner party.

As he neared the patio, I noticed Brad had dressed up for the wedding party. He was wearing a white shirt, pressed jeans, and clean boots. I'm sure he wanted to impress Robin. I was standing beside Brad's mom, Brenda, who also noticed her son's choice of attire for the evening's celebration. She paused mid-sentence, proud of the young man her boy was becoming. We smiled at each other as her teen approached closer, walking into the light spilling over from the patio.

"You've raised a great kid," I said quietly to her.

"Thank you, Sam, for caring about my boy."

"Easy to do. He's a good kid and a good artist."

Brad finally stood before us, grinning like the cat that ate the canary. He sported a handsome bolo-tie that looked vintage.

"Awesome bolo," I observed.

"Thanks!" Brad said, adding proudly, with a nod to his mom, "It belonged to my grandfather." And like a shot, he was off to find Robin.

~

Late the other evening near dark, we were relaxing, enjoying the peaceful patio all to our own two selves. The sun had set below long diagonal swaths of fire-orange, lemon-yellow, and lush pastel-pink bands of color that looked hand-painted in layers by someone like Rothko. Fireflies ringed the patio, flickering their ever-changing, ever-kinetic patterned lightshow. Nike lay beside me, flat out, having given her whole pretty bag of bones to Earth's insistent gravity.

My own arm, having loosed itself from the armrest, was gravity-drawn straight down too. My thumb and fingers simultaneously caressed the inside and outside of Nike's large hound ear. Its texture always has the feel of the softest fine velvet. Her slow, deep breathing told me she was in a state of *ataraxia*, the ancient Greek term for bliss.

Annie got up, deciding that the potted hibiscus plants, cousins of okra in the garden, and The Rose of Sharon out front, looked a bit droopy and dry. They're dwarf hibiscus trees. Being essentially tropical, we move them inside the greenhouse before first frost every year. Annie, of the green thumb variety, cuts the little trees back almost to the trunk every winter. They don't seem to mind and are once again prolific in the spring.

I once was in the presence of a 15-foot-tall hibiscus hedge that spread for thirty feet across an ancient stone wall in Chania (pronounced '"Ha-nyah") on the northwest corner of the island of Crete. The giant floral array covered the wall on the north side of the courtyard that led into the then-named Chania Maritime Museum. The museum is located at the entrance of the thirteenth-century venetian harbor of Chania. I was there on a mid-August cloudless day. The sky above and the sea below blended as one seamless skein of Aegean turquoise blue, with no discernable horizon. Ancient Greek mariners must have wondered at times if they were sailing in sea or sky. The majestic hibiscus hedge was aglow with fat white blossoms that lit up like hundreds of warm incandescent light bulbs, blazing even at midday.

Our own Bartlett Farm potted hibiscus flowers glowed a bit, even in the dark of early night ime Barnes County skies. Annie, having risen from repose with determination to do some watering, reached down to lift the nearby patio garden hose. Instead, she pulled up a 5-and-a-half-foot-long gray Texas rat snake. It took her a second to realize the garden hose was already moving in her hand before she turned the spigot. She dropped the startled snake that instantly stretched itself as straight and flat as possible along one side of a raised bed of nasturtiums.

As I rose from my patio chair, I watched her race up the steps to the back screen door. She reached inside the porch, grabbing a flashlight we kept there on a hook. She whirled around, not moving from the porch steps, and held the flashlight out in mid-air toward me. I dutifully took the device in hand, and shortly I found the horizontal snake playing dead, pressed against the raised 2-by-6-inch cedar board. I quickly noted the tail and head of the beast, confirming in the dim light of the weak-battery torch (as the Brits call it) that it was not a rattlesnake or copperhead. I thought a moment, deciding the creature was far from the henhouse and thus not an immediate threat to any of our pricey heritage breed chicken eggs. I turned off the torch and watched the nonvenomous snake slither out across the moonlit patio. It now looked not so much like a serpent as simply one of the organic, meandering lines implied between the edges of the fragmented flagstone slabs. It moved quickly zigging and zagging, making good its escape off into the cover of assorted bushes on the perimeter.

Throughout the exciting backyard brouhaha, Nike the hound remained in a state of undisturbed *ataraxia*. Annie blamed me for charming the canine to sleep so deeply that she was oblivious to the serpentine danger we were all exposed to that evening. Annie's still a bit snake-wary on the patio at night, so she drags chairs and loungers to make loud scraping noises on the flagstones before taking a seat.

~

We are enjoying either the sweet hooting of two pairs of Great Horned Owls and their two offspring fledglings each, or one lucky couple whose five eggs all hatched fledglings. Our owl count is in flux. For almost three weeks this fall, we've been serenaded by these soothing owl and owlet family conversations in the trees surrounding the patio. Great Horned Owls are territorial, so they too are Bartlett Farm year-round residents.

The big owls sometimes build new nests, but most often make use of a neighboring Red Hawk's abandoned nest. That tends to indicate our West Texas owls choose mesquite or cottonwood trees, preferred for their thick, sturdy branches. We have enough of both in Barnes County, particularly toward the western climes of the county. But I don't think they're that picky as long as the repurposed nest is big enough and high enough. You won't find Great Horned Owls giving a second glance at the cozy little nest of a Tufted Titmouse.

Experts tell us that the owls recognize individual humans. I'm certain our owls know my face well as the farmer who provided tasty free-range heritage breed chickens his first year at the farm. I'm not a fast learner, but I am a frugal learner, so this farmer abruptly ended the popular "live hen buffet" the second year. The owls must have gotten over any resentment they felt as they've hung around and multiplied, albeit with an ample array of alternate protein choices—mice, voles, snakes, and lizards that we do provide here for free.

The proud couple (or two) and their owlet offspring are in familial conversation every night, surrounding us with the most pleasant chorus of gentle, happy "hoo-hoos" with an occasional awkward screech sound. The screech is probably expressed by some disgruntled teen fledgling, or a "tween" fledging whose voice is changing. As in human families, owlet kids hang around for a long time.

As I listen to the evening's owl chorale, I can't help thinking about Doc Russell's rescued Great Horned specimen, old Methuselah, by all appearances a contented fellow, yet one who must occasionally feel the call of the wild. Sadly, like other disabled old folks, Methuselah just can't feed himself very well. I've made a note to pay him a visit. I'll shred some deboned fresh chicken to bring him soon, an ironic gesture on my part, to say the least.

Epilogue

Annie, over the last couple of years, has helped me adjust to the realistic idea of "down-sizing" our organic herb and produce business. We sell to just a few chefs these days. They are old friends and reliable customers. The money generated from these sales allows us to provide Elysia's food pantry with fresh produce and to continue our supportive associations with the local 4-H club, the high school ag program with Angus, and college field trips to the farm for Suzie's landscape drawing classes.

Annie's publisher has convinced her that it's time for a memoir about her life of research and writing about the history of food sources, producers, and regional dishes. She's writing it all at home, using her desktop for the manuscript and her laptop for research. We look back with appreciation for our respective lives of "travel with a purpose." That is, we each traveled broadly for research or collaborative projects, not tourism, and the costs were largely funded through grants. We are somewhat bemused with ourselves because travel now is unusually serendipitous. It's a new kind of experience for us, doing all our traveling together. We rove without agenda, without publication or lecture objectives. Today, we explore Barnes County and West Texas with the eyes of tourists.

My paintings have downsized as well. I finished probably the last panoramic evening landscape commission many months ago. That painting may be my final poetic tribute to fireflies. I'm satisfied with the illusions of the magical creatures I've been able to capture. Unexpectedly, I find myself intrigued with the recalled faces of relatives who raised me. I mean, my mind's eye is painting their physical presence, the unique personae they still command in my memory.

It seems a bit odd to me now that I've sketched and painted portraits of the animals in my life much more than the people. I sketched Liz's childhood life, of course, and Annie is still my favorite human subject. The reality is that she's pretty much a sitting target most of the time. But the visages of my aunts and uncles, and especially my grandparents, are vividly available to me now more than ever. Perhaps the absence of their actual physicality charges my recall of their individual faces, posture, clothing; this smile, that furrowed brow, a tilted head, red cheeks, an Adam's apple, or dimpled chin. In any event, that's my current subject, portraits of the farmers, the men and women who raised me. Lots of deeply sunburned faces and hands of uncles in weathered hats and frayed, faded denim long-sleeved shirts. Aunts with sympathetic eyes, tender smiles, and hugs that smelled of rose water and baking flour.

Whenever I scold myself for being a slow learner, I remember Odysseus. And, in those moments of doubt about my own learning slowness, I think of a contemporary, the novelist Thomas Pynchon. He published *Slow Learner* in 1984 with an astonishing degree of candid reflection on his early writing interests, motives, and methods, including an example of his own act of near word theft. I gave copies of *Slow Learner* to my best student writers to keep them on their toes and remind them to stay honest and accurate about sources. Pynchon's new novel, *Against the Day*, should be out soon and I can't wait.

I've seen a 3,000-year-old olive tree in Chania, Crete. I've watched lambs and ewes grazing amongst the prehistoric Avebury henge and stone circles in Wiltshire, UK. I am comforted knowing that Homer's Odysseus was a farmer. I think fondly of the heritage breed Tunis sheep I've raised, first imported from Tunisia to America by Thomas Jefferson.

But I've pretty much neglected to think of the ancient, even Neolithic, farming families that occupied Barnes County before me. The evidence of their past lives here is compelling, even on our little farm. At a bend in Hackberry Creek, recent flooding has exposed a significant Indigenous clam-shell midden. A couple of younger anthropologist friends, including a former student, Eugene, came out to investigate. They will be back, convinced that we may find other signs of a community, likely to be Comanche or Lipan Apache. Though following in the footsteps of 1930s and '40s serious Texas researchers, our friends include material gleaned through interviews with living descendants, the Elders. Eugene says it's vital to document Indigenous oral history, passed down through generations, about the contextual nature of extant stone burial cairns, communal middens, and allegorical pictographs in West Texas.

Homer relied on the same cumulative process for his lengthy oral recitations.

~

Our daughter and son-in-law are in the Netherlands on a sort of informal internship with my Dutch engineer friend, Gerard Jansen. Vern is learning about mechanical levees, like the amazing Maeslant Barrier. Liz is studying the historic *polders*, land traditionally recovered from the sea via dike embankments, repurposed into farmland or forest. The kids have helped me and Annie to embrace a broader, more connective consideration for the physical portion of Earth that our little farm occupies. Maybe they see the macro relationship of places on the globe better than we do. They see the whole, perhaps partly because they've grown up with satellite photos of the big blue marble that floats in space. Annie and I still orient ourselves to the world via memorized maps, the globe flattened for our convenience.

Geographical similarities abound on opposite sides of post-Ice Age Earth. The Concho River, the Red River, the Colorado, and the Trinity all ultimately flow down to the Gulf of Mexico, just as the Tigris and the Euphrates flow south to the Persian Gulf.

The Nile is the oddball. It flows north to the Mediterranean Sea.

Likewise, the Red River of the North, flowing between North Dakota and Minnesota, flows "up" into Lake Winnipeg, Manitoba. Both rivers have similarly rich silt, deposited annually, over millennia, creating fertile valleys on opposite sides of the world.

It's taken awhile, but this slow learner is beginning to appreciate that Barnes County farmland is as old as The Fertile Crescent in Iraq.

~

We received a long, detailed email from Robin recently, all the way from Nacogdoches. She attached photos of ink and graphite sketches of Nacogdoches and environs. Lots of trees. Her letter hinted that she may suggest to her mom that she change her major to art next year. God help her. She threw in a teasing note for Brad, telling him that if things don't work out for her in East Texas, she expects to be able to get her old job back at Bartlett Farm.

Brad is our teen farmhand foreman now. In the future, he plans to spend two years at Barnes County College and then seek scholarship funds at a good art school for his BFA. My colleague, Suzie, will be his main advisor at Barnes County. She and I will help him put together a convincing transfer portfolio. His ability to see and render volume in drawn figures has grown leaps and bounds. These days, he's surrounded with admiring 4-H friends. Like Robin before him, he's a famous artist at Elysia High.

Every afternoon, the handsome Appaloosa Firewheel extends his elegant neck over the top rail of the entry-road fence, waiting eagerly for the site of his kindly human owner. He looks forward to the daily chat he will have with Brad on his back, riding over to our place. Riders share secrets and stories with their horses that rarely get told to other humans.

Reminding me of son-in-law Vern in his high school farmhand days, Brad also has conversations with Sol, Samson, Homer, Nike, Caesar, Tommy Cat, and all the critters he takes care of. They nod their heads or lean against him in response to some point he's making while pouring oats in buckets or brushing manes and tails.

At day's end, Annie and I take turns telling each other the same bedtime story. Sometimes we alternate telling sequential parts of the same story, now in her voice, then mine. On occasion, our voices are in unison. It's soothing that we are both comforted by the same narrative, time and again. Most often, one of us soon dozes off during the retelling. Sometimes both of us fall fast asleep and can't remember the next evening who narrated last. No matter. We know the tale by heart.

Odysseus gets safely home to Penelope. End of story.

Acknowledgments

My heartfelt thanks to publisher Loren Steffy, who first put the notion in my head that readers would want a sequel. Editor Kathryn Jones accurately navigated the sometimes-roiling rapids of my ebullient art and ag associations. Leslie Barrett and Danielle Acee deserve merit badges for the personal interest they take in promoting each Stoney Creek author's work.

Loren took a chance on *The Art of Farming: Sketches of a Life in the Country*, a first novel with a lot of moving parts. His risk proved worthy, and I am grateful to the many readers who've embraced my anthropomorphic characters, domestic and wild, at the farm and on the fringes. Special thanks goes to Kelley Robbins and Kyle Littlefield at A&M Press, whose wit and encouragement make every book-signing event delightfully memorable.

Indefatigable archivist friends Jon Frembling, Scott Davis, Maddie Hayko and Allee Austin keep the wheels of academia turning at The Amon Carter Museum of American Art Research Library. They consistently mined treasures for this book, and provided me with quiet, scriptorium-like space for reading manuscripts and writing notes.

Lastly, my thanks for several rewarding days spent with Leah Brosig at her ranch near Paint Rock. Abilene Christian University Professor Jeremy Elliott introduced me to Leah, and has been a font of knowledge for me, regarding Indigenous sites in Central and West Texas. My boots on the ground visits with Leah to stone cairns, burn-floor and clam-shell middens, and amazing cliff-face pictographs were invaluable. That tactile experience informed richer description of farmer Sam Bartlett's growing understanding of the agricultural history of fictional Barnes County.

Recommended Reading

Hold Autumn in Your Hand, George Sessions Perry, (1941), 1950, Whittlesey House, McGraw Hill Co. Inc, New York

The Cotton-Pickers, B. Traven, (1926), 1995, Elephant Paperback, Ivan R. Dee Inc., Chicago

Corduroy, by Adrien Bell, (1930), 1986, Oxford University Press, USA

Farther Off from Heaven, William Humphrey, 1976, Alfred A. Knopf, Inc., New York

Train to Estelline, Jane Roberts Wood, (1987), 2000, Univ. of North Texas Press

Like Water for Chocolate, Laura Esquirel, (1989), 1992, Doubleday Dell Publ., New York

Tender at the Bone, Ruth Reichl, 1999, Broadway Books, Random House, Inc., New York

A Wood of One's Own, Ruth Pavey, 2019, Duckworth/Prelude Books Co., UK

Selected Poems, 1965-1975, Seamus Heaney, 1980, Faber & Faber Ltd, London, UK

On Farming (De Agri Cultura), Cato the Elder, (160 BC), 1998, Translation by Andrew Dalby,
Prospect Books Co., UK

The Great Plains, Walter Prescott Webb, (1931), 1981, Bison Book, University of Nebraska Press

The Mind of the South, W.J. Cash, (1941), 1962, Alfred A. Knopf, Inc., New York

The Points of My Compass, E.B. White, (1954), 1979, Perennial Ed, Harper & Row, New York

Wood Eternal: Osage Orange/Bois d' Arc, Fred Tarpley, 2010, Tarpley Books, Campbell,
Texas

Seeds, Sex and Civilization, Peter Thompson & Stephen Harris, 2010, Thames & Hudson, UK

Catching Fire: How Cooking Made Us Human, Richard Wrangham, 2009, Basic Books,
New York

An Edible History of Humanity, Tom Standage, 2009, Walker Publishing Co., Inc., New York

The Sacred & The Profane: The Nature of Religion, Mircea Eliade, 1959, Harcourt Brace Jovanovich, New York

The Odyssey, Homer, Translated by Emily Watson, 2018, W.W. Norton & Co. Inc., New York

Beowulf, A New Verse Translation by Seamus Heaney, 2000, Farrar, Straus and Giroux, New York

About the Author

T.D. Motley is a Texas painter and academic. Born in Beaumont, he's been drawing since age three. His family has farmed in Texas from the mid 19th century. He and artist wife Rebecca live in Fort Worth. The couple marketed their organic, heirloom herbs and produce to North Texas chefs and farmers' market customers for years.

Motley has lectured about and published articles on organic, no-till farming and gardening, heirloom herbs and produce, and soil sustainability. He has written agrarian essays for *EatGreenDFW* and *Edible Dallas & Fort Worth.*

T. D. Motley is Professor Emeritus of Art and Art History at Dallas College. His drawings and paintings have been selected for national exhibits and are included in public and private U.S. collections. Motley's artworks are available at J. Peeler Howell Fine Art Gallery, Fort Worth.

Motley has lectured at the Dallas Museum of Art, the Umlauf Sculpture Garden and Museum, Austin, Texas, the SMU Meadows

Museum in Dallas, and the Amon Carter Museum of American Art in Fort Worth. He has published essays for museum catalogs, art periodical critiques and reviews, and National Endowment for Humanities research papers on art and literature of the Greeks and Romans. He is a contributing author for *Eutopia* and *ArtSpiel* and has written about mid-century modern Texas artists for *DB16/Dallas Biennial*, and the Grace Museum, Abilene. Motley has received Fulbright Grants to Belgium, the Netherlands, and the UK.

Motley is past Board President of Artist Boat Coastal Heritage Preserve, a Galveston non-profit, teaching students about coastal nature through art and science, and protecting hundreds of acres of contiguous coastal habitats. He was Chair of the North Texas Fulbright Teacher Exchange Peer Review Committee for many years. Motley was a printer in the U.S. Air Force, an illustrator for Ling Temco Vought Corp, and a cartoonist for the infamous Dallas Notes from the Underground. His first novel, *The Art of Farming: Sketches of a Life in the Country*, is published by Stoney Creek Publishing, and was released by A&M Press in August 2024.

www.ingramcontent.com/pod-product-compliance
Lightning Source LLC
LaVergne TN
LVHW041406260626
841735LV00001B/1

* 9 7 8 1 9 6 5 7 6 6 8 9 7 *